STARGATE
ATL

DI

"THIS isn't good," Sheppard growled. "Oh, this is really not good..."

The HUD ran with strange figures. The Jumper lurched sideways, scraping along the edge of the wormhole limits. McKay was thrown roughly against Ronon as the Jumper listed crazily.

"What is happening?" Teyla yelled.

"Ask McKay!" Sheppard snapped, battling for control of the Jumper.

"What? This isn't my fault!" McKay protested, heart thumping with alarm. "This didn't happen to the MALP!"

Unbuckling himself with fumbling fingers, McKay stumbled over to a control panel in the rear of the Jumper — and was nearly hurled straight into it by a fresh yaw sideways. "Keep this thing on the road, will you?"

"You wanna fly?" Sheppard looked like he was struggling to maintain control.

"We've got massive power loss," shouted McKay, desperately flicking a series of controls. "We'll need to use the Jumper's own supply to get us out."

Teyla gave him a sharp look. "Can you do it?"

"If I can't, we're beyond screwed!"

STARGATE
ATLANTIS™

DEAD END

CHRIS WRAIGHT

FANDEMONIUM BOOKS

An original publication of Fandemonium Ltd, produced under license from MGM Consumer Products.

Fandemonium Books
PO Box 795A
Surbiton
Surrey KT5 8YB
United Kingdom
Visit our website: www.stargatenovels.com

S T A R G A T E
A T L A N T I S.

METRO-GOLDWYN-MAYER Presents
STARGATE ATLANTIS.
JOE FLANIGAN   TORRI HIGGINSON   RACHEL LUTTRELL   JASON MOMOA
with PAUL McGILLION as Dr. Carson Beckett and DAVID HEWLETT as Dr. McKay
Executive Producers BRAD WRIGHT & ROBERT C. COOPER
Created by BRAD WRIGHT & ROBERT C. COOPER

WWW.MGM.COM

ISBN: 978-1-905586-22-6
Printed in the United States of America

With many thanks to the Fandemonium team,
especially Sally Malcolm, for superlative editing,
guidance and criticism.

Author's Note

This story takes place during the early episodes of series three, before the discovery of the Asurans or the construction of the McKay/Carter Intergalactic Gate Bridge.

CHAPTER ONE

"OK, REMIND me again why I agreed to come down here with you?"

Lt Col Sheppard was not in a good mood. Introducing Ronon to poker last night had been a good idea; introducing him to bourbon had not. The Satedan could put away a phenomenal amount of the stuff without even blinking. Sheppard's aching head, on the other hand, was witness that its effects on human physiology were the same as they had always been. The last thing he needed now was a morning with McKay at his most irascible.

"Because your devotion to duty knows no bounds, and I need your impeccable scientific credentials," said McKay. "That, or Zelenka's laid-up sick and you're the next best thing. And you never know when that ATA gene will come in handy."

Sheppard scowled and ran his fingers over his throbbing forehead. There were times when, despite all the provocation, he actually liked McKay. This was not one of them. He looked back at the four-strong team of marines stationed a few yards away in the corridor. They looked faintly sympathetic.

"It'd better be important," Sheppard growled, turning his attention back to the scientist. He was working away at the dismantled Ancient computer panel. "If you don't get this open in ten minutes, I'm outta here."

McKay turned around to face him, irritation written all over his face. "Oh, like what?" he snapped. "What's more important than finally getting to the bottom of this place? I mean, you might be happy spending your time in a city where we only understand half of what anything does, where the power ratios fluctuate every time Ronon sneezes, and where the machinery we *do* know about could fry the lot of us in a nanosecond if we happen to flick the wrong switch. Forgive me, but I'm not."

Sheppard gave him a warning look. McKay might technically be out of his chain of command, but there was a limit to how much crap he'd put up with.

"And your time is, of course, most appreciated," said McKay, taking the hint. "I'm almost done. Just a few more moments."

Sheppard gave a curt nod. The movement hurt his head. "Make it quick."

The two men were deep in the bowels of the Ancient city. After their last prolonged battle against the Wraith, a rare window of opportunity had opened. For once, scientific research had taken priority over survival and the civilian staff were making the most of it. Not that Sheppard minded that. It felt like they'd been high-tailing it from one crisis to another ever since arriving in the Pegasus galaxy. If the price of a little peace was making McKay even more insufferable than usual, it was probably still worth paying. In any case, they all knew the lull was only temporary.

Rodney turned back to his work. There were Ancient devices all over the polished floor, some retrieved from other parts of the city, some taken from the hole in the wall McKay was investigating. The gadgets, all of which were more or less meaningless to Sheppard, were mixed up with McKay's own equipment: oscilloscopes, signal processors, metal detectors, and Venusian death-rays. OK, so the last one was probably made up. But knowing McKay, only probably.

"This place has been out of action for a long time," came McKay's muffled voice from halfway inside the wall cavity. "I don't think it's been shielded for any particular reason.

It's just that the systems have malfunctioned and the access doors have locked down."

"Reassuring," said Sheppard, watching McKay fiddle with electronics behind the open panel. Wires and transparent circuit boards poked from the gap like entrails. "Like these places have never been wired before."

Bitter experience had taught the team to be very careful with unexplored parts of the city. Hence the marines. From the looks on their faces, it was clear they didn't relish being down here any more than he did.

"Ha!" cried McKay. "That's it. The field harmonics have distorted due to the burnt-out intake manifold. I thought it must be something like that."

"Yeah, me too. Suppose you tell me what that means?"

To his right, there was suddenly a low hiss. The marines perked up, and raised their weapons. With a click and a sigh, an entire section of wall slid smoothly back and upwards. What had been a blank, unremarkable section of corridor now revealed a second chamber. McKay pulled himself out of the mess of cables and circuitry, looking smug.

"It means, Colonel, that I've got us in," he said. "Whatever delights have been hidden in here for 10,000 years are about to be revealed."

"Not so fast," said Sheppard, hefting his P90 and gesturing to the marines to back him up. "We'll take this nice and slow."

With the marines behind him, Sheppard inched towards the open doorway. The room beyond was about ten meters in diameter and octagonal in shape. The usual geometric Ancient patterning stretched across all of the eight walls. A low light filtered upwards from wells near the floor, bathing the space in a dim orange. Like most of the rooms in the city, there was a minimum of clutter. The Ancients had never been ones for fussy interior decor. The only item of note was a raised column in the very center, perhaps three feet tall. It was also octagonal, and a selection of symbols glowed gently on its smooth top. It looked like a control panel.

Sheppard could hear McKay itching to come in, but the Colonel was in no hurry. His headache was still bad, and the scientist would have to wait. With a flick of his fingers, he motioned for the marines to fan out and check for anything untoward. With a cool efficiency, they began to sweep the walls. Sheppard walked over to the far wall, scouring the patterned surface for clues to the room's function.

"Oh, come on!" cried McKay impatiently from the corridor outside. "It's a minor control chamber of some sort. You don't need to—"

There was a muffled explosion. The orange light flickered and a warning klaxon began to wail. Slowly, the central column started to sink into the floor.

"Get out!" yelled Sheppard, darting back towards the door. The marines tore across the chamber. He just had time to see the last of his men slip through the gap before the wall section slammed shut in front of him. He was trapped inside. The klaxon continued to blare. Within the enclosed space, the noise echoed alarmingly. The central column carried on sinking into the ground.

"Rodney!" he shouted. "Wanna tell me what's going on?"

From the far side of the wall, McKay's voice sounded faint and indistinct. "I don't know!" he yelled. "One of your men must have set something off!"

Sheppard slammed his fist against the doors in frustration, then took a breath. Whatever was happening in the chamber was happening quickly; the column was now barely a foot above ground level and he ran over to it. There were Ancient symbols on the surface, still glowing, and the thing looked a lot like a DHD. But if there was a DHD, where was the gate? He looked up at the ceiling. Nothing. The column continued to descend, the klaxon continued to blare.

"Rodney, get this thing the hell open!"

"Trying, Colonel!" came the muffled response. "It seems to have gone into some kind of shutdown sequence! I'm working on it!"

That was not reassuring. Sheppard stepped back from the column, now nearly flush with the floor, and looked around. That's when he noticed the ceiling was sinking.

"Oh, great," he breathed, watching the rapidly descending arches.

He raised his P90, but the gesture was pointless. For once, it couldn't save him.

"Losing headroom in here, Rodney…"

He thought he heard a curse coming from the far side of the door. Sheppard dropped to his knees next to the sunken column. Nothing happened to the klaxon, nor to the slowly descending roof. The control panel surface was now level with the floor, and the glow had disappeared. The six Ancient symbols were still visible. Frantically, Sheppard pressed them in turn. Nothing. He tried in reverse order. Still nothing. He glanced up — the ceiling was now just a few centimeters from his head — and sank to his belly, letting his weapon clatter to the floor.

"Rodney!" he yelled. "You're gonna have to work this out quick, or I won't be needing those slimming classes!"

"I'm on it!"

The ceiling crept down further. Sheppard tried the sequence again. Clockwise. Anti-clockwise. Random. His fingers were slick with sweat, his breath short and sharp, as the ceiling drew relentlessly closer. What a way for a pilot to go.

He slammed his fist against the symbols. Something sprang free from a slot in between them. It bounced back down as it hit the ceiling. Sheppard grasped it frantically, desperate for anything. It was a shard of translucent matter, some kind of Ancient computer component. Not very helpful.

Then, with a shudder, the doors slid open. Booted feet filled the narrow gap and two marines threw themselves to the floor, arms extended into the chamber.

"John!" cried McKay. "Over here!"

Sheppard scrabbled round in the tight space and squirmed towards the exit. As he went, the irregular surface of the ceiling scraped against his body armor. Something snagged, but he thrust himself forward. Hands grabbed his arms. He was yanked out through the doorway. As his feet were pulled free, there was a dull slam behind him.

Shakily, he looked back. Through the open doorway, there was nothing but solid metal. The device had been well and truly shut down.

He took a deep breath and gingerly hauled himself up. That had been too close.

"You okay?" McKay's face creased with concern. He had that rare guilty look he wore when he knew something had gone wrong and it was probably his fault.

"What do you think?" asked Sheppard, recovering his poise. "You want to tell me what just went on in there?"

"I may have, er, crossed a few wires," he said, flustered. "These things are complicated. But that shouldn't have happened!"

"No kidding."

McKay scowled. "Anyway, we're not going back in. Whatever was in that room is lost for good."

Sheppard brushed his uniform down, his heartbeat returning to normal. "We might get something out of it," he said. "There was a gate address in there. And this."

He held up the shard he'd retrieved. McKay snatched at

it eagerly, his air of embarrassment quickly lost.

"An address?" McKay's eyes lit up. "And what looks like some kind of data panel. Or what's left of it. Interesting. Perhaps it's some kind of—"

Sheppard held his hand up.

"Enough already," he said. "I'm getting this place locked down and off-limits. Then I'm gonna brief Weir on the fun and games. You might want to consider joining me."

McKay gave a dramatic sigh and folded his arms in irritation. Sheppard ignored him, signaling the marines to regroup and follow him. As he made to leave, he paused and threw McKay a dry smile.

"Cheer up, Rodney. At least you cured my hangover."

Weir leaned forward in her chair and fixed McKay with a steely look.

"You did *what*?"

McKay shifted uncomfortably in his seat. "Look, how was I to know they'd go all Indiana Jones on us? It doesn't make any *sense*. I mean, it's pretty clear the Ancients were a kooky bunch, but even so..."

Weir's eyes flicked across to Teyla, but the Athosian remained unperturbed. Her respect for the Ancestors may have been dented in recent months, but she still had the potential to balk at Rodney's casual references to them.

"Alright," Weir said, running her hands through her hair. "Let's try and get something useful out of this. Give me your best shot — what was in that room?"

Weir sat at the head of the table in the conference room. A few hours had passed since the incident. Despite the seriousness of what had happened, the interruption to an already overloaded schedule was unwelcome. It wasn't as if they didn't have enough problems coming from *outside* the city. Sheppard, McKay, Zelenka, Teyla and Ronon also sat around the table — John looking a little paler than usual, but otherwise unharmed. He seemed to have a knack for getting out of these situations unscathed. It was a good quality to have in a military commander.

McKay leant forward and clasped his hands together on the table.

"Here's my hypothesis," he said. "I've had a quick look at the failsafe mechanism — the pile of metal that nearly flattened the Colonel. It's designed to withstand massive force. We can surmise that the walls and floor are similarly constructed. Clearly, the chamber was built to contain huge amounts of energy."

Weir listened carefully. McKay could be a pompous windbag when he thought he was on to something, but his hunches had a way of proving correct.

"Combine that with what Colonel Sheppard told us about a DHD-like machine in there," McKay continued, "and I think what we're looking at is a prototype transport mechanism. Either something to do with the city's Stargate, or perhaps even a replacement for it entirely."

Weir could see Zelenka's skeptical expression.

"Why would the Ancients build such a thing?" he said. "They had the gates. Sounds implausible."

McKay turned on him. "Have you looked at it?" he snapped. "No, you were in bed wiping your nose. Before you start questioning my judgment, you should do your own research."

Zelenka was about to retort, but McKay plowed on.

"I'm not just stabbing in the dark here. The Colonel managed to retrieve something from the control mechanism. He didn't use as much finesse as I'd have liked, so it's in pretty bad shape."

"I was kinda engaged with other stuff," sighed Sheppard. "Like staying alive."

"And we're all very glad you did. Thankfully, it's still usable, and I've seen stuff like it before." As he spoke, McKay flipped up the lid of his laptop and punched something into its keyboard. The translucent panel Sheppard had retrieved was jutting out from one of the custom ports in the machine. "Take a look at the screen."

All swung round to look at the screen in the corner of the room. The display turned into a mess of green zigzags.

"Nice pattern," said Sheppard. "Like what you've done with that."

"Thanks to some rough handling, we've lost most of the visual," McKay said. "Audio's intact, though. Keep listening."

On the screen, the zigzags began to break up. It looked like there was a figure addressing them, though it was impossible to make out features. Over a backdrop of static, he or she was speaking. Chunks of speech were muffled or distorted, and only scattered fragments came through.

"... returning Lanteans ... list of priorities ... three settlement programs on ... ensure that we ... do not neglect the ... Telion is insistent on ... coordinates in prototype gate device ... do not neglect what we left ..."

Then the voice broke up, and what little picture there was dissolved into a green snowstorm. McKay flicked the display off.

For a moment, there was a hush around the chamber. It wasn't the first time they'd seen footage of Ancients, but the experience never quite lost its air of strangeness.

"Can you get anything more out of the recording?" asked Weir, turning back to the table.

"Believe me, I've tried," said McKay. "That's as good as we're going to get. But it's enough, right? You've figured out what it means?"

"Perhaps you could enlighten us with your opinion," said Teyla.

"Look," explained McKay, giving his favorite wearied expression. "The Lanteans always intended to come back here if they could. This must have been a message to those returnees. Some kind of standing orders, in the event the city was reactivated. Whatever was being worked on in that room need to be revisited. Perhaps they didn't have time to finish off whatever they started."

"You got all that," asked Sheppard, raising an eyebrow, "from *that*?"

"I've had longer to look at it than you," replied McKay. "And, no offense, I really am a whole lot smarter."

Weir looked unconvinced.

"So why the elaborate defense mechanism in that chamber?"

Rodney rolled his eyes.

"You want me to work out every last detail of this? Oh yes. Of course you do." He thought for a second. "I don't know. Maybe it was for Lantean eyes only. Something to stop the Wraith reading the message, in case they ever got down there."

"Or us," said Ronon.

"Quite. But thanks to Colonel Sheppard's acrobatics, we got something out. And now we can use it."

Weir held a warning hand up.

"Whoa. You're going too fast here, Rodney. So far, all we've got is a sealed chamber and a message we can barely understand."

"With respect, Elizabeth, we've got more than that," said McKay. "We've got a gate address, and we've got a theory. We know the gate network isn't perfect. Some destinations seem to require more power to get to than others. The obvious example is the inter-galactic route, which needs huge amounts of juice. But even in the Pegasus galaxy we find some destinations are harder to reach than others. Maybe there are ways around this. My guess is that we stumbled across an attempt to refine the gate technology."

He looked from one member of the team to the others, searching for agreement.

"Interesting," said Weir. She turned to Sheppard. "You got a note of the gate address in the chamber?"

"Oh, I got it. Those little squiggles are pretty well stuck my mind."

"And?"

"I can show you," said McKay, bringing up a galactic map on the display. The map started to zoom. "Here we are, home sweet home, on the galactic rim." The map continued to zoom out. "Any minute now..."

The animation concluded. A red triangle marked Lantea, and a green circle the location of the gate address. The dotted line between them ran the width of the screen.

Weir shook her head. "My God," she breathed. "It's basically out of the galaxy."

"How far *is* that?" said Zelenka.

"In technical terms?" said McKay. "A *really long way*. Further than we've ever been in Pegasus. I looked at the stellar cartography. It's off the scale. The power requirements to get there are pretty scary."

"Yes, but it can't drain more than dialing back to Milky Way," scoffed Radek.

"You know, normally I'd agree with you," said McKay. "But we don't know everything about gate travel, and something's odd about this setup. And there's another thing. Most locations on the Stargate network are accessible from anywhere else. If you know the address, and have some means of dialing, you can jump from anywhere to anywhere. The exceptions are the long hops, like between galaxies. Here's the trick — I think this one's exactly the same. From the database, it seems clear that this node is only accessible from one other place."

Weir let out a deep breath. "I think I know what you're going to say."

Sheppard grinned. "I love it when you're ahead of us."

Weir pursed her lips. She had come to like and respect John in their time serving together on Atlantis, but his endless flippancy could get wearing. She knew that exploration was part of the brief, but it would be nice, just for once, if her senior officers could think about something other than scooting off on a fresh mission as soon as the last one had ended.

"OK, so we have an address, and a mystery device designed to access it," she said, carefully. "What are we going to do about it? Can we access this planet from the regular Stargate? Even if we can, do we want to?"

McKay shrugged. "We'd need to do some work," he said. "I've been thinking of ways to increase the power to the gate mechanism anyway. I'd bet it's possible. As for whether we *should*. That's a different proposition. It's an opportunity to find out what the Ancients were up to in that room. And if it was that heavily shielded, it must be important."

Weir frowned. "We've got our hands full with the Wraith right now," she pointed out. "I can see that there's something interesting going on here, but I'm not sure I'm going to give the green light to this."

Sheppard interjected, looking a little embarrassed to be doing so.

"Er, I know you're not gonna believe this, Elizabeth," he said, "but I reckon Rodney could be on to something here."

She gave him a quizzical look. McKay just looked startled.

"Our situation here's still kinda precarious," he said. "But a gate address on its own, with no other way to get to it? Sounds like a perfect Alpha site to me."

Zelenka shook his head. "This is all still just supposition. We don't really know what that room was used for, and in my experience, gate addresses hidden behind layers of steel tell you one very clear thing: don't go there!"

"Yeah, well that might not be such bad advice," said Sheppard ruefully. "But we did it anyway, and now we've gotta decide what to do with what we found."

Weir turned her attention to Teyla. The Athosian had been uncharacteristically quiet. "What do you think, Teyla?" she said. "You've never heard of this place?"

"No," Teyla replied. "My people have no knowledge of anything that far away. I am not sure whether the risks of going there outweigh the potential benefits." She glanced at the shard still protruding from McKay's laptop. "But we have heard the words of the Ancestors. Though their message was not complete, it seems obvious that they had some important purpose there. I do not think we can ignore that."

Weir saw Sheppard looking at Teyla approvingly. It was what made her so valuable to the team, her willingness to take risks. But the commander had to balance those with the needs of the entire mission. Yet again, the choice was a fine one.

"OK," she said at last. "You can look into this. But we're not going to hurry, and we're not going to get it wrong. McKay, take Zelenka with you and see how feasible it would be to reach this place. Once we know a little more, we can make a decision on what to do next. But if we can't do this safely, we're not doing it at all. Period."

She rose, and the rest of the room did likewise. She could see Zelenka's look of concern, and Sheppard's expression of eager anticipation. They were cut from

very different cloth, those two, and Weir just hoped
she'd chosen wisely.

The screen filled with numbers, filtering downwards rapidly,
before the red lines appeared again. The terminal issued a
perfunctory bleep, then shut down the relay.

"Damn!" hissed McKay.

He was sitting at a computer in the Operations Center,
directly over the gate room. Zelenka was down by the gate
itself, wrestling with thick cables and a battery of routing
equipment. They had been trying for a couple of hours to
get the Stargate to accept the mystery address, but the power
requirements were too large. Every time it was entered, the
system shut down.

"I'm guessing this was why the Ancients decided to use a
replacement!" shouted Zelenka from the bay below.

McKay scowled. He could swear Zelenka was enjoying
this. Despite the best efforts of a dozen technicians, they
were still nowhere near getting the beefed-up Stargate mechanism to work and the ideas had started to run dry.

"OK, let's try again with the re-routed backup supply,"
said McKay over the intercom. "It's all about timing. We
only need a short burst."

The figures on his monitor reset themselves, and down
in the gate room the technicians set about arranging the
equipment again.

McKay looked at the schematics one more time. The issue
wasn't just raw power — now that the ZPM was installed,
they had plenty to spare for the operation of the gate. The
problem was the efficiency of supply, ensuring that the
Stargate's complex and subtle mechanics were fed what
they needed when they needed it. Opening an event horizon was an art that the Atlantis team still barely understood, and it was clear that the existing Stargate had defi-

nite limits. Trying to keep everything within the necessary parameters was like trying to herd cats. In the dark. With oven gloves.

"OK, Rodney," came Zelenka's voice over the intercom. "We're done. Run the sequence when you're ready."

McKay took a deep breath and looked carefully at the command scripts he'd developed. He made a few minor alterations, changing the order in which certain items were run, and then packaged the lot for execution.

"Get your people out of the way," he told Zelenka. "Here we go again. If this doesn't work, we'll have to start over."

The gate room cleared. Once the area was sealed, McKay hit the Enter key on his terminal, and the power sequence activated. Lights danced across the monitor as data was relayed back to the command center. Huge amounts of energy surged down the power cables, each burst timed to what McKay hoped was perfection. A few nanoseconds apart, the carefully placed units powered up. For a moment, very little happened. Then the red lines appeared on the monitor again.

"Oh, please..." groaned McKay, feeling the empty sensation of failure in his stomach. "This should be *working*."

Then the red lines cleared. There was activity in one of the compensators and a series of lights flicked on across the control terminal. With a shudder the gate stuttered into life, the familiar watery surface of the event horizon tearing across the circular aperture. Strange readings lurked at the edges, but those could be tweaked. It had worked!

"Yes!" McKay punched the air in delight. "I knew we were getting close! Oh, I'm good. I'm really good."

"Congratulations, Rodney," said Zelenka over the intercom. He sounded genuinely impressed, albeit grudgingly. "I didn't think we'd squeeze that last bit out."

McKay did his best to calm down. Victory was always

sweet; there was no point milking the moment too much.

"Oh, ye of little faith," he said. "Now we need to tie this down and do a few more tests. We've shown it can work, but Elizabeth will want a repeatable demonstration. I don't want to let her down."

"Very good," said Zelenka, his voice breaking up slightly over the comm link. "I just hope all of this is worth it. You still haven't convinced *me* we should be going there, whatever Elizabeth thinks."

"Well, thankfully you're not in charge of this installation, and she is," said McKay impatiently. "Is the MALP in position?"

"It is. Sending it through now."

Zelenka and his team stood clear as the cumbersome MALP crawled towards the shimmering gate, servos whining as it disappeared into the event horizon. Immediately, more red lights flashed across McKay's console.

"What's that?" said Zelenka, concerned. "We've got some strange readings down here."

"Ignore it," snapped McKay, concentrating on the data stream beginning to emerge from the wormhole. "It's just the power drain from the extra mass in the gate buffers. It'll clear up."

The MALP was gone, sucked into the wormhole and hurled thousands of light years distant in a fraction of a second. The readings on the monitor went back to normal.

"It's through," said McKay over the intercom. "We'll be getting telemetry any second."

He swiveled in his chair to look at the monitor assigned to the video feed. The screen was a snowstorm; clearly the MALP hadn't begun relaying yet.

"What a mess!" said Zelenka, suddenly appearing at McKay's shoulder.

"Don't worry," said McKay, starting to get worried.

"We'll get something through soon." It would be just his luck, after all this effort, that there was a problem with the MALP's transmitters.

Zelenka clapped him hard on the shoulder. "Look again," he said, enjoying the moment. "That's a real snowstorm."

McKay screwed his eyes up and studied the feed more closely. The lines of white and gray were momentarily broken. There was an fleeting image of a vast, open space. A glacier, or perhaps a snowfield of some kind. Then the streaks of snow and ice returned. The camera was rocking badly. The MALP had been sent into the middle of a storm. It looked absolutely filthy.

"Atmospheric readings?" asked Zelenka.

"Usual oxygen/nitrogen mix. Within standard Ancient parameters. Perfectly breathable."

"And the temperature?"

McKay took a look down the screen at the flickering figures being transmitted by the MALP. He let out a low whistle.

"*Cold*. Very cold. That's odd."

Zelenka gave him a quizzical look. "I don't see why. The Czech Republic is cold. Everywhere the Ancients seeded doesn't have to look the same. These are planets we're talking about, not movie sets."

McKay gave him a withering look. "Yes, but the similarity we've noticed between most of the places we've been to is no accident. Surprisingly enough, the Ancients didn't want their populations freezing to death within a generation. So they made their homes as pleasant as possible. And this is way outside the normal envelope."

Zelenka sucked his teeth thoughtfully. "But habitable?"

McKay studied the readings.

"Yeah, I'd say so. Just chilly." He looked suddenly worried. "I'm really not that good in the cold. It's a family thing. My circulation's bad."

Zelenka ignored him. The signal from the MALP began to break up. "You're not the only one. We're losing the MALP."

"We can't be losing the MALP," snapped McKay, frowning. "Those things are tough. It's got to be a transmission problem. In fact, now I look at them, there's something *really* strange about these wormhole integrity indicators..."

The video feed sheered into nothing, and the data readings gave out soon afterwards. McKay looked at the empty screens, suddenly perturbed. The euphoria of getting a MALP to the mysterious gate address had dissolved into a nagging worry about what it had found.

"God, that place looks horrible," he breathed, half to himself.

"Then good luck!" said Zelenka, grinning at him. "You'll need it. This is one mission I'm happy to miss."

CHAPTER TWO

SHEPPARD digested the information on the screens care-fully. There were a lot of numbers he didn't understand, but he could read a temperature gauge. The planet they'd all started to refer to as "Dead End" didn't sound that invit-ing. Teyla and Ronon looked similarly thoughtful. Weir was downright skeptical.

Having finished his demonstration, McKay leaned back in his chair and looked at the others clustered around him in the Operations Center. He looked genuinely torn between his desire to see what the Ancients had been up to and his dislike for the expected conditions.

"It *might* work," he said, giving Weir a sidelong glance. "It's going to be cold. *Very* cold. And we'll need the proper gear."

The mission commander looked back at him sternly. "*If* I authorize this mission, then you'll get all the equipment you need," she said. "But I'm not sure I'm there yet. We've seen the footage from the MALP. We don't know if there's any settlement on this planet, or even if the Ancients actually did anything much there at all. For all we've discovered, this experiment might never have gotten off the ground. I'm all for exploration, but are we taking a sensible risk here?"

Sheppard shot her a winning smile.

"So it's a little chilly," he said. "It's not gonna to be a picnic, but we've experienced worse. Cold weather gear, some extra rations, and we'll be fine. Ronon might have a problem standing up to it, but I'm sure McKay'll show him the way."

Teyla smiled, and looked over at the Satedan, who remained impassive. McKay just rolled his eyes.

"Seriously, we've got to remember why we're here," continued Sheppard. "If we're gonna turn down missions because they look borderline, then we may as well head back to the clubhouse for good. There's something weird about that place, or the Ancients wouldn't have rigged up their magic back-door to it."

"Something *weird?* That's your reason to go?" asked Weir.

"Well, I'm not best qualified on the science stuff. But yeah, that's about the size of it. Rodney'll give you the technical side."

All eyes turned to McKay. He looked uncomfortable.

"Look, I don't like cold. Or hot, come to think of it. But especially not cold. And I get chilblains easy," he said. "But we could certainly use a way to travel around without relying on the *Daedalus*. If there's new gate tech working here, then I'm not going to sleep well until I know how it works. If we can crack it, we could even get the backup link to Earth you've been trying to get me to build since we got here. So that's a reason for checking it out. Not that I'm keen on going myself. I'd be happy to monitor things from here, really I would. But we can't just ignore it."

Sheppard turned back to Weir. "You heard the man," he said. "Now we've got two reasons for going. It's weird, and it's useful."

Weir turned to the other members. "Teyla?"

"I agree with Dr McKay," the Athosian said. "The Ancestors have spoken. If they had come back to Lantea, they would have completed whatever it was they were doing there. There was urgency in their message. We cannot ignore it."

"Ronon?"

The Satedan shrugged. "I'm up for it," he said in his usual expansive way.

Sheppard grinned, feeling things going his way. "You're gonna have to find a reason for us *not* to do this, Elizabeth," he said. "There's a case for a recon, and that's really our job."

Weir looked at him for a few moments, evidently weighing up her options. "I still don't like it," she said, at last. "There's way too much we don't know."

Still she paused. The team waited, saying nothing.

"But I'm mindful of the Ancients' message," she said at last. "They felt it was important, and we have to take that seriously. So take the Jumper — that'll give you some protection. We're breaking new ground here and I want you all back safely."

Sheppard nodded. "Agreed," he said. "No unnecessary risks."

Decision made. Now he'd just have to ensure that something useful came out of it.

McKay picked at his collar nervously. The Jumper was fully loaded, the bulkheads stuffed with cold-weather gear. Like the rest of the team, he was decked out in ECWCS versions of their standard fatigues. In Atlantis's controlled atmosphere they felt close and restrictive, but he knew they'd be needed as soon as they emerged from the other end of the wormhole. It was little comfort. He didn't like the cold any more than he liked the heat, or the damp, or the dry.

He still wasn't sure he'd made the right choice in coming. It was either him or Zelenka, and the battle between his natural fear of the unknown and the chance of his colleague discovering something about the Ancients he didn't know had been close. In the end, his thirst for knowledge had won. But only just. Now the nerves had returned and he felt terrible.

Up in the cockpit, Sheppard ran through the final preflight checks, the translucent screens of the Ancient head-up display floating before him. Teyla sat in the co-pilot's seat, Ronon next to McKay in the rear compartment. He seemed to take up all the spare space.

"This damn thing's too tight!" Rodney mumbled, trying to pull the insulated fabric from his neck.

"Don't pull it, then," said Ronon.

Sheppard spoke into the comm link. "Jumper's good to go."

"Very good," came Weir's voice from the Operations Center. "You're clear to leave when ready."

Sheppard ran his fingers over the Jumper's control mechanism and McKay felt vaguely resentful of the man's easy familiarity with Ancient technology. He didn't seem to realize quite how lucky he was.

"Here we go, boys and girls," Sheppard said, casting a final watchful eye over the diagnostic readings streaming across the lower half of the HUD. "Watch yourselves on the other side. There's a storm blowing."

"Oh, that's just great," muttered McKay. "We had to take off when there's a storm blowing. Would it have been so hard to pick a clear window?"

"From what I can tell, there's *always* a storm blowing," said Sheppard, maneuvering the Jumper into position. "Quit complaining. You're the one that started all of this."

"I'm so glad you're here to point these things out," McKay grumbled.

Sheppard ignored him and continued nudging the Jumper round.

The ship hovered for a moment before powering the thrusters. Ahead, the surface of the Stargate shimmered with the vast energies of the contained event horizon.

"Good luck," Weir said. "Bring back something good."

McKay almost responded with a 'like frostbite' quip, but

bit his tongue. Sheppard gave the necessary command and the Jumper responded with the strange, inertia-less movement so typical of Ancient technology. The sleek craft shot forward, the gate room blurring into the familiar split-second of wild disorientation before they were spat out.

Except they weren't. Something had gone wrong. Instead of emerging into a new world, they were hurtling along a snaking, whirling tube of energy.

"This isn't good," Sheppard growled. "Oh, this is *really* not good…"

The HUD ran with strange figures. The Jumper lurched sideways, scraping along the edge of the wormhole limits. McKay was thrown roughly against Ronon as the Jumper listed crazily.

"What is happening?" Teyla yelled.

"Ask McKay!" Sheppard snapped, battling for control of the Jumper.

"What? This isn't my fault!" McKay protested, heart thumping with alarm. "This didn't happen to the MALP!"

Unbuckling himself with fumbling fingers, he stumbled over to a control panel in the rear of the Jumper — and was nearly hurled straight into it by a fresh yaw sideways. "Keep this thing on the road, will you?"

"You wanna fly?" Sheppard looked like he was struggling to maintain control.

"We've got massive power loss," shouted McKay, desperately flicking a series of controls. "We'll need to use the Jumper's own supply to get us out."

Teyla gave him a sharp look. "Can you do it?"

"If I can't, we're beyond screwed!"

"Any time you're ready…" Sheppard ground out.

John pulled the Jumper into a long, tight arc that rolled waves of nausea around McKay's stomach. He swallowed hard.

"OK, OK! I'm there. Are you getting anything now?" The Jumper swooped dizzyingly and McKay clamped his jaw shut, making a mental note to check the inertial dampeners.

"I've routed all power to navigation," Sheppard barked. "Something's picking up on the display. I think we're on the way out."

McKay slumped back in his seat and attempted to buckle up. "This didn't happen to the MALP," he muttered. "Zelenka must have gotten something wrong with the calculations. I should have run a final check myself. If you want something done…"

He stole a quick glance at Ronon and Teyla. The huge Satedan was untroubled. Nothing seemed to faze him. Teyla was similarly stoic. They were both far too calm. God, he hated that.

The Jumper lurched again. The readings suddenly changed, and a stream of data cascaded across the screen.

"OK, we're getting out of this," announced Sheppard. "Get ready. We'll be coming in hot."

McKay closed his eyes. "Ironic."

The swirling mass of energy in the forward viewscreen coalesced into the more familiar shape of a bubbling event horizon. The Jumper gave a final, bone-shaking shudder, slamming Rodney hard against the hull. A microsecond later, and they were through the gate.

Sheppard felt like whooping.

But it wasn't over yet. Everything skewed, bounced and jumped as the gravitational forces suddenly changed. He compensated. Too late. The Jumper skidded, grazing something jagged and hard, before careering back into the air. The whole ship rolled around like a drunkard.

"For God's sake!" cried McKay, hanging precariously on

to his seat. "Land the damn thing already!"

Sheppard ignored him. The atmospheric readings were crazy, the Jumper's power near zero. Sixty percent of the primary systems were damaged and they'd emerged into the mother of all storms. Perfect.

"I'm gonna have to put her down now!" he cried. "Keep it tight. This is gonna be bumpy."

Flying on little more than gut instinct, Sheppard dipped the nose of the Jumper five degrees. The thick cloud rushing past them got thicker and the Jumper's entire hull began to judder. The shielding was critically weak.

Suddenly, a gap appeared in the cloud ahead. For a split-second Sheppard had sight of an ice field. It was enough to mentally calculate the angle of descent. The Jumper responded instantly and they plummeted downwards, the viewscreen white and useless. Somewhere below, the land was rushing up to meet them.

With a heavy crunch, they hit the ice. Plumes of loose snow billowed up, momentum plowing them onwards, grinding and churning across the ice field. Metal twisted and shrieked, equipment shook loose and crashed into the cabin. Sheppard thought his teeth might rattle loose from his skull. And then the power failed, plunging them into darkness.

It took an eternity, but at last the Jumper slowed to a painful halt. The viewscreen was still obscured by the white-out and they sat for a moment in a shadowy stillness.

Ronon broke it. "Good job, Sheppard."

John just nodded in the dark, not trusting himself to speak; his hands were still shaking.

"That was expert flying," agreed Teyla, unbuckling herself and climbing to her feet. "But I do not believe we are safe here. With power supplies so low, this storm is a danger."

"Reckon you're right." With effort, Sheppard brought his

breathing under control. "Break out the survival suits. If we have to bail, I want something warm and orange to wear."

"Now?" said McKay. "You're *kidding* me. I'm not heading out there until this storm has blown over. Who knows, it might be a short one."

"Or a long one," said Ronon bleakly. "Or maybe it's always like this."

Sheppard nodded. "Can't stay here without power," he said. "No light, no heat, no air. I don't like this any more than you do, but we're gonna suit up now while we have the chance."

McKay looked briefly rebellious, but then a huge surge of wind buffeted the Jumper and the entire ship rocked. From beneath them, came an ominous, echoing sound of ice cracking.

Rodney swallowed nervously. Even Sheppard felt his heart miss a beat. That sounded pretty bad. Jumpers were robust things, but you still didn't want to be inside one, without power, halfway down a crevasse.

McKay began to rummage for his gear. "Having considered the options further, perhaps you're right."

It didn't take long to suit-up, and soon they were ready to evacuate the stricken Jumper.

"Take as many rations as you can carry," Sheppard ordered.

"We're going to freeze," McKay muttered. "More importantly, that gate'll be fried. Fried closed."

There was another long, echoing crack from beneath the Jumper. The cabin shifted slightly to the left and Teyla had to brace in order to keep her footing.

"OK, time's up," said Sheppard sharply. "Let's move."

The rear door opened with a whine. Immediately the interior of the craft was filled with swirling, buffeting snow and sleet. The temperature plummeted. Even inside his suit

Sheppard could feel the sudden chill. It was like a shard of ice right in the guts.

"Out!" he barked.

Ronon produced a line of rope.

"Use this," he said, looping it around his waist and passing the cord to Teyla.

"Nice thinking," said Sheppard, leaning into the wind. Getting separated out there didn't bear thinking about. "Any Eagle Scouts on Sateda?"

Once they were all connected, Ronon strode out into the open. He was followed by McKay and Teyla. Bringing up the rear, Sheppard ducked under the lintel of the Jumper exit. He tried to close the rear door, and failed. No power. It would have to stay open.

He quickly took in the situation. The sky was heavy, low and gray. Visibility was about twenty meters, the air thick with gusting snow. There was no let-up in the gale, and no means of getting oriented. The power of the wind was massive — he had to push hard into the gust to stay on his feet — and there was no chance of being heard over the storm, so he was glad of the comm link built into the hood of his suit and facemask.

For a moment, he wondered if leaving the Jumper was such a good idea. Even without much life support, it was at least shelter from the wind. But then there was another crack and a few meters away a whole tranche of snow sank into the ground. The rocks — or whatever — under his feet tangibly shifted. This was no place to linger.

"OK, guys," he barked. "Let's keep moving and find some shelter."

"What a great idea," came McKay's sarcastic voice. "I mean, I'd never have thought of it. Goddamn it, I can't feel my toes."

"Wrap it up, Rodney," warned Sheppard.

The team began to wade through the knee-deep snow away from the stranded Jumper. Before the machine was lost to view, Sheppard noticed the last lights flicker and die along its flanks. With the Jumper down and the wormhole status unknown, the mission was in danger of degenerating into a deadly farce. He needed some luck, and needed it fast.

Even walking in a straight line was hard. Once they were a few paces from the lee of the Jumper the wind screamed across the ice, throwing the snow up in gusts. The cold was incredible. The USAF cold weather gear was designed for extreme conditions, but it seemed like it was barely there. Sheppard felt himself begin to succumb to shivering. He kept his breathing shallow.

Once away from the landing site, making any sense of their location soon became impossible. Footprints were scoured from the snow almost as soon as they were made. Sheppard looked at the compass built into his wrist-strap — as long as they maintained a constant direction, they wouldn't lose the ship. But that was scant comfort. They needed to get out of the storm.

They plowed on. Only Ronon was strong enough to keep his posture. McKay was bent nearly double into the wind, cursing under this breath as he went, the expletives crackling over the intercom; Sheppard knew he'd be in trouble after too much punishment. Already, he felt his own fingers begin to ache from the cold.

Then, just as Sheppard began to wonder if they'd better head back to the Jumper, Ronon stopped trudging and turned around. He obviously thought the same.

"See anything, Sheppard?" he yelled.

Sheppard shook his head. "Nothing! We've got to go back!"

"Hail, strangers!" came a dim voice from the howling storm.

Sheppard adjusted the comm link in his hood and wiped the visor of his mask with a snow-encrusted glove. "Who said that?"

"*He* did," said Ronon.

Sheppard peered into the white-out as figures emerged from the murk. They were massive and furry, and he immediately thought of the abominable snowman. Only as they came closer did Sheppard see that they were human, but clothed in many layers of thick, white fur. Each of them had a hood over their head and masks over their faces, their voices muffled and indistinct but just audible over the screaming wind.

"After so long!" said one of them, his voice cracking with emotion. "The portal has opened again!"

"You have come back," came another voice, addressing Sheppard. "I knew this day would come."

Sheppard looked at Teyla, then Ronon, then back to the newcomers. Even within the suit he was beginning to shake uncontrollably, the Jumper was wrecked, and the gate inoperable — the situation could hardly have been more desperate. There wasn't really a whole lot of choice. "That's right," he said. "We're back. And right now, we could really use some shelter."

The man's eyes smiled. "Come with us," he said. "We'll lead you to safety." He beckoned the team to follow and turned back the way he'd come.

"Oh good job," sniped McKay. "Make first contact with the locals and impersonate their long lost friends. There's no way that can go wrong. After all, it's never gotten us in trouble before."

"Button it, Rodney, we've got no choice." Sheppard peered through the snow at his team. "But stay sharp, we don't know what we're getting into here."

"Oh I think we do," McKay grumbled as he stomped after the strangers. "And it begins with a capital T."

As the fire did its work, feeling gradually returned to Teyla's feet.

She sat with the others in a chamber set deep underground. A healthy blaze crackled and spat in the central hearth and torches flickered against the rock walls, bathing the room in a gentle ambient light. The surroundings were simple, but clean and warm. A few tapestries hung from the walls and woven mats blunted the worst of the harsh rock floor. Many of the hangings had stylized pictures of animals and hunting scenes. The familiar images reminded Teyla of home.

Around her shoulders Teyla now wore a lavish fur cloak — a gift from their hosts. It was beautifully warm, and it had not taken long for the effects of her brief foray into the storm to abate.

It hadn't been a long trek from the gate to their rescuers' settlement, but they would never have stumbled across the entrance by themselves. The people of the place appeared to live deep within a series of caves and fissures, the entrance to which had been obscured by heaped snowdrifts. The team's attempts to find shelter had in fact taken them some distance in the wrong direction — the underground dwellings were very close to the Stargate, and there'd been a painful trek back the way they'd come before being led out of the wind.

Once through the main gates of the settlement, they had been taken down a series of winding tunnels towards the main living chambers. Fur-clad children had come to gape at them as the team passed the open doorways and halls, still dressed in their snow-covered environment suits. Fires burned in the deep places, keeping the tunnels and rough-hewn chambers both warm and well-lit.

Having given them food and a place to recover, their hosts had left them alone to regain their strength. It was a courteous gesture and one Teyla appreciated. In some ways, their manner reminded her of her own people, as if a splinter group of Athosians had found itself flung across the galactic plane and isolated for many thousands of years. The thought intrigued her; there was no telling what wonders the Ancestors had performed in the days of their hegemony.

With a satisfied sigh, McKay finished the last of his second bowl of soup and sat back against the wall. "This situation is improving," he said. "Definitely improving. I'm almost glad I came. I wonder if we can get more of this soup?"

Sheppard looked less certain. "Enough to keep you happy?" he said. "I doubt it. Any idea what happened back there?"

Rodney shook his head. "Not until I can take a proper look. And, frankly, until that storm blows over I've no intention of finding out."

"The storms must lift," said Ronon. "These people eat, they hunt. They can't hunt in *that*."

From outside the small chamber came the sound of footsteps.

"Remember, we *need* these guys," whispered Sheppard. He shot McKay a hard look. "So let's all be on our best behavior."

Teyla turned to face the low doorway as two men and a woman entered and bowed low. Lean and hardy-looking, they were dressed from head to foot in the pale furs all their people wore. Their skin was milky and their hair dark and straight. The leader, a man, wore a brightly colored torque around his neck and, though clearly old, appeared lively and vigorous.

"Greetings, honored guests," he said, his voice quiet and measured. "I am Aralen Gefal, Foremost of the Forgotten People. This is my daughter, Miruva, and my chief of hunters, Orand Ressalin. You are most welcome here. We have waited long for your coming."

Sheppard inclined his head awkwardly and introduced the team. He wasn't good at formal greetings. "We're pretty pleased to see you too, Aralen," he said. "You guys showed up right on time."

Aralen smiled. "The portal to Sanctuary has not operated for ten generations. Orand witnessed the strange machine come through it some days ago, and then we knew that some work of the Ancestors would not be far behind. Some claimed we'd been abandoned, but others of us have kept the faith. We have been rewarded at last."

Sheppard looked uncomfortable. "Well, we're not exactly—"

"You must be tired after your journey," Aralen interrupted. "Please, sit. We have come to hear what your task is, here on Khost."

"So that's what this place is called," said McKay, sitting down heavily on the pile of mats he'd accumulated. "Nice name. Lousy weather."

"You are far from other worlds," said Teyla, eager to find out more. "We are curious to learn about your people, Aralen."

The leader of the Forgotten frowned. "Surely you know all about us? You came through the portal to Sanctuary. You must have knowledge of the Ancestors, of their plan for us."

Teyla looked at Sheppard. These early moments were always awkward. How much did these people know of the wider galaxy? Where were their allegiances?

"Oh, you bet," he said. "Well, kinda." He paused. "Maybe

you should fill us in on the details."

Aralen looked surprised, but then inclined his head graciously. "Of course," he said. "We are the Forgotten. You may think it a strange name, but it is apt. We have been alone for a long time. Some think we've been abandoned by the Ancestors altogether, but the wise know that cannot be so. The years have been heavy, and much has changed. The lore-keepers tell us that once Khost was green and good, our people flourished and our villages were numerous. The Ancestors walked among us then. We call this the Blessed Time."

Orand gave a skeptical snort. "These are, of course, mere legends," he said. "Not all of us believe them."

"Our young people have their own ways," Aralen said with a tolerant smile. "But the lore-keepers preserve the legends for us, and I trust their wisdom."

McKay frowned. "This place was green once?" he said. "Wow. That's what I call climate change. What happened?"

A shadow passed over Aralen's face. "There was some transgression. Many speculate what it could have been. For myself, I do not claim that knowledge. But the health left this place, the snows came ever more strongly, and then they never left. Life became hard and many died. Now we are cursed by the cold at all times."

He drew closer, his voice low.

"Khost is dying, travelers. You should be careful. If you stay here too long, you'll die too."

It had no name. It knew it had once had a name, but like so much else, that had been forgotten. All that remained was a list of numbers and letters. Even that was corrupt. There was so much that it couldn't do, now. It looked down on the humans clustered below. Most were familiar. Several of them were already requisitioned, stored on the lists for processing. One was earmarked for early removal.

But the others were new. This was outside the generally accepted conditions. It might pose a threat to the Great Work.

It ran over the options. It was always so difficult to think *clearly*. It would need to confer with the others. But that would take time, make it weak. Perhaps the Great Work demanded action now.

It looked down, considering the humans.

Not yet. But it would come soon. It could feel itself weakening. There was only so long it could watch and wait without acting.

Very soon it would make a decision. Then it would come for the names on the list. They would scream, just like they always did. That had never stopped it before. Nothing could stop it. The only thing was timing.

It watched, and waited.

"What do you mean, *dying*?" said Sheppard. He didn't like the gleam in Aralen's eye.

"The storms get worse. Every time we have a big one, we think it will be the last. And there are other things…"

"You think the Ancestors abandoned you?" interrupted McKay. "Because that's interesting. There was a recording we saw before we — "

He bit his lip, looking at Sheppard. John shot him an irritated look.

Aralen shook his head. "They will never abandon us. There is the portal, the passage to Sanctuary. That knowledge is preserved among us. We know that one day we shall be gathered up in the halls of restitution, so you must know why you are such a sign of hope for us. Never in ten generations has the portal opened! Now you come. Surely, you will teach us the route to Sanctuary, and what we must do to restore the favor of the Ancestors."

Sheppard looked awkward. "Well, perhaps we can get on to that later," he said. "I've gotta be honest, it's a bit… colder than we're used to out there. It'll take us time to orient ourselves."

"Of course. I can see that you are not used to the ice. No doubt Sanctuary is more pleasant. Khost is a hard place to live."

"And yet you survive," said Teyla. She felt a strange and unexpected kinship with the Forgotten; the stories of her people and theirs were different, but each had survived against the odds.

The woman, Miruva, turned to her with pride in her eyes.

"We endure," she said. "We are strong and can sustain much hardship." She waved at the stone walls around them. "We learned the arts of carving the ice from the caves and keeping them warm. This place was once a network of dark and empty caverns, choked with snow. We have turned it into our city. This is where the remnants of our people live, harboring what we have left from the endless storms above. We make the best life we can."

"Interesting," mused Rodney. "A totally troglodytic lifestyle. Like the Genii, at a lower level of technology. But how do you source your fuel? And keep the air filtered?"

Aralen raised an eyebrow. "We can explain all these things, and more, in due course. But though you are most welcome here, you must understand that your presence amongst us has caused much excitement. You have come through the portal. There are some who say that you are from the Ancestors, ready to lead us to a new paradise. I am afraid that others have more superstitious beliefs, and fear your intentions. Forgive my candor, but I must tell the people something. My own belief is that you are indeed from Lantea. Is this the truth?"

Sheppard shot Teyla a quick look. "Look, I hate to break it to you," he said, "but if you think we're Ancients, you're gonna be disappointed. They don't get around much any more. You should just think of us as… travelers."

"So you're not from the Ancestors?" Aralen looked deflated. Orand just gave a bitter, knowing smile. "When I heard the portal had revived, I was so sure…"

"I'm sorry." Sheppard scrubbed a hand through his hair. "Real sorry. But if we can help you, we will — and that includes fighting the Wraith."

Aralen hardly seemed to hear him. He was crushed. Orand, however, looked curious.

"The Wraith?" he said. "What is the Wraith?"

Ronon looked up, his eyes flickering darkly. "You never heard of the Wraith?" asked the Runner.

Orand shook his head, surprised by Ronon's vehemence. "The Foremost told you, we are alone here. There is just us, the snow, and the White Buffalo. That is all. We know nothing of your Wraith."

"It is good that you know nothing of the Wraith," Teyla said. "Consider that the greatest of blessings."

There was a difficult pause, but Miruva was quick to smile again. "Clearly, we have much to learn from one another," she said. "I am not sure why you have come, nor what your arrival means for us, but it must presage some good for us. I am glad I lived to see this day."

"So am I," said Teyla, seeing much in the girl's quick, lively expression to like. It was rare to find a people the Wraith had not ravaged. Rare, and refreshing.

The old man, Aralen, roused himself. His earlier satisfied pleasure had evaporated.

"So be it," he said, and his voice was quiet. "You are not the emissaries from the Ancestors I had hoped for. But travelers you are, and such a thing has not been known on Khost in memory. We have not forgotten our hospitality, whatever else may have been cast aside. Perhaps in time you will see that your coming is indeed part of the Ancestors' plan after all." Orand looked dubious, but Aralen ignored him. "Now that you have rested, may we show you more of our home? My people are anxious to meet you."

Sheppard shrugged. "Sure, that'd be great." As they filed out of the chamber behind Aralen, he drew close to Teyla and whispered in her ear. "This is going pretty well, don't you think?"

"I like these people, Colonel," she said. "Perhaps there will be something we can do to ease their plight."

"Well, that's a lovely idea, it really is," hissed McKay from behind her. "But let's remember what we're here for; the Ancients were up to something on this planet and I'll bet the changing climate is part of it. And if there are any more of them who think we're messengers from the gods, then things are going to get tricky."

"Keep your pants on," said Sheppard under his breath. "One step at a time. Let's hang tight for a while and find out a bit more. It's not like I'm real keen on going outside again."

McKay shuddered and drew his furs close. "You may have a point," he agreed. "But remember, if we don't fix the Jumper, we're never getting out of here. We've seen no sign of a DHD anywhere, and even if we had there's *no way* I'm walking through that wormhole of madness without a working ship around me."

"No argument," said Sheppard. "We'll check out the gate when we can. For now, be glad you're not still out there."

With that, the whole group moved down the corridor and deeper into the underground settlement. Far above them, the wind howled and moaned, and the fury of the storm continued unabated.

CHAPTER THREE

"ALRIGHT, *what* just happened?"

Weir spun round to face Zelenka.

"It wasn't us!" Zelenka protested, fingers flying across the keyboard in front of him. "We just lost the signal. I've never seen it happen before. It was almost as if — But that's impossible."

"What's impossible, Dr Zelenka?"

Radek ran his hands through his hair.

"OK, I'll tell you what this computer tells me," he said. "It looks like there was a power failure. The drain on the system was too much. They were stuck in the wormhole for a short period of time. Physically stuck. Now, don't tell me that can't happen, I know it can't, but then readings end. Either they got out, or…"

He tailed off, distraught.

Weir took a deep breath. She was angry with him for having no answers, angry with Sheppard for talking her into the mission, and angry with herself for going along with him. But self-recrimination could come later, all that mattered now was getting her people home.

"OK, what are our options?" she said. "Have we got anything from the planet at all?"

Zelenka studied the screen, face creased into a frown. "No telemetry. Nothing. Wormhole has collapsed. And there are strange readings here. It looks like the gate at the other end has suffered some kind of malfunction. I can't re-establish the wormhole. We need to study this."

"That isn't very helpful, Radek," she snapped. "I need options. *Fast.*"

"I know," Zelenka said, already on his feet. "I'm on it."

Ronon walked easily through the narrow corridors. Orand walked beside him, with Teyla and Miruva close behind. The group had separated. Sheppard and McKay had been taken in one direction by Aralen, while he and Teyla had been invited to see the lower levels of the settlement.

As he walked, Ronon found himself enjoying the freedom afforded by the lack of a bulky environment suit. He never liked wearing the synthetic uniforms of the Tauri if he could help it, but felt very much at home in the furs and leather of the Forgotten. From what he had seen of these people, they were admirably strong and capable. With no fear of the Wraith, they had been forced to take on the elements of their homeworld instead. As an enemy, the endless cold of Khost was possibly just as formidable. The fact that the Forgotten refused to buckle and give-up impressed him.

"These are our living areas," said Orand, gesturing to either side of the party.

Every few yards the walls of the corridor were broken by low entrances, the light was low and they looked dark and dingy. But when Orand pulled aside the tapestry hanging over one of the doorways, a cheery light escaped from the chamber beyond.

"Please, enter," he said. "These are my quarters."

Stooping, Ronon and Teyla stepped inside. Orand and Miruva followed them, walking with a supple grace. All of the Forgotten were lean, and despite their underground lifestyle there was little sign of sickness among them. Orand was tall and wiry, with dark hair and quick-moving brown eyes. His face seemed ready to crease into a smile at any moment. Miruva looked similar, though slimmer. If she was slightly less ready to talk than Orand, she seemed to weigh her words more carefully. Ronon thought he saw something of Weir in her calm demeanor.

The space beyond the hanging was not large, but capable of comfortably accommodating a small family. The walls were bare rock, but everything was tidy and well-kept. There were obviously more rooms branching off from the main chamber. As ever, these were screened by the embroidered hangings. Mats covered the floor, decorated with images of massive beasts — the White Buffalo, he presumed. Ronon studied the handiwork. On many worlds, such fine artifacts would fetch a rare price.

"How do you make these things?" he said, running the tapestry through his fingers.

"Our women weave the patterns from the plains grass," Orand said, motioning for them to sit on the mats. "The White Buffalo graze on the plains, and so it sustains everything. But the winters have been harsher lately. The snows linger nearly the whole year, and the grass dies. The Buffalo travel further to find it, and so do we. As a result, these things are increasingly valuable. We make fewer every year."

Miruva nodded. "They still provide meat for our tables, and fur to clothe our bodies. We use their bones and horn for our tools: an axe made from Buffalo horn can carve rock. In the summer season, their waste fertilizes our fields. We can cure their meat for the long winter months. They are everything for us."

"Some speculate that the Ancestors created the Buffalo purely to serve our needs," said Orand. "Without them, we would have perished many years ago."

Ronon raised his eyebrow. "I would like to see these animals."

Orand's eyes lit up. "I hoped you would say so, as soon as I saw you. We could use a man like you. When the storm abates, the great hunt will begin again. Our stocks of food are low, and the deep winter is nearly upon us. We must make a kill, or our city will suffer. Will you come with us?"

Ronon looked at Teyla, unwilling to commit without consulting the rest of the team. But the thought of testing himself against the creatures was tempting. He was already feeling the need to flex his muscles.

The Athosian smiled back at him. "How much use are you going to be fixing the Jumper, Ronon?" she said. "We are going to have to remain here for some time. You should go with these people. You might even learn something."

"It'd be a good test," he said. "You should come too."

Miruva's eyes widened. "But you are a woman!" she said, laughing. "Women do not hunt the buffalo. Such a thing has never been done."

Ronon knew this would irritate Teyla. To her credit, her feelings did not show on her face. "Where we are from," she said, her voice icy calm, "women do all that men do. I fight with my team, just as Ronon does."

Orand started to laugh, but was cut short by a glare from Teyla. Seeing the look on her face, he quickly let his eyes fall to the floor.

"Your people have strange ways!" Miruva said, delighted. "Perhaps we can indeed learn from you. I have often thought it unfair that the menfolk must take on all the risk of the great hunt. There is no longer enough grass for us to weave here."

Orand looked skeptical. Ronon could see that he was protective of her and wondered if they were a couple. If they weren't, then he guessed Orand would like them to be.

"You'd have to get past your father, first," said the young hunter. There was an edge to his voice.

"He is old-fashioned, then?" said Teyla, gently probing for information.

This was what Teyla was good at, thought Ronon, gaining people's trust, finding out more about the situation without causing offense. She was a natural diplomat.

Miruva let slip a sad smile. "My father is a good man. He's guided us for many years, and our people have survived thanks to his planning and dedication. But he is old. He believes that the Ancestors have ordained everything. And so there is no change, and we cling to tradition in all things."

"Not all of us feel the same way," interjected Orand. "Some have called for a great exodus, to try and find better hunting grounds and warmer weather."

"But you've chosen to stay?" said Ronon.

Miruva nodded. "Most of the people are with my father. They have always trusted in the portal to Sanctuary, believing that help will come from it one day. And now your coming has given them hope."

Teyla frowned. "We are not gods, and we are not the Ancestors. We have many troubles of our own. Our vessel is damaged, and unless we can find a way to restore power to it, there is little hope we can help you."

Orand shrugged. "Whether or not you're Ancestors, your coming will change things here," he said. "We need change. We can't keep hiding in these caves forever."

Miruva looked uneasy at his proud words.

"We will have to see what develops," said Teyla, heading off discussion of their role in a potential revolution. "For now, we are your guests, and we would like to hear more of your ways."

"Of course," Orand said. "Do you need more to eat? I have some stew, and *heruek* — water flavored with berry-essence. Will you take some?"

At the prospect of food, Ronon's mood instantly improved. "Sounds good," he said. "You'd better tell me how you hunt, too. I've got my own weapons, but I'd rather use yours."

Orand looked at the big Satedan with approval.

"I'd like that," he said. "I can see already you'll be a valuable addition to our hunting party. When the time comes, we'll be sorry to see you go, Ronon."

The Runner inclined his head at the compliment, but he couldn't entirely share the sentiment. If McKay couldn't fix the Jumper soon, then they'd be staying a lot longer than any of them wanted.

"I think we've made some progress."

Zelenka's head poked around the door to Weir's office, and she turned away from the window and her silent contemplation of the Stargate. "Let me hear it," she said, giving him her full attention.

Radek stepped into the room. He looked exhausted. "We've done some calculations," he said. "There's a power drain for every object moving through the gate network. The larger the object, the greater the drain. If we establish a wormhole but send *nothing* through, we'll at least be able to start measuring the tolerances involved. It may be that the Jumper itself was the cause."

"OK. What are the risks?"

Zelenka took a deep breath. "That we fry the Stargate on Dead End entirely," he said. "I think it's already been damaged. But we have to try."

Weir let some of her frustration enter her voice. "Do we have a Plan B?"

"At this stage, no."

"Do it," she said, at last. "But if you start to lose control again, abort at once. We'll take this one step at a time. I'm not losing my team on a frozen pile of rock in the middle of nowhere."

McKay, Sheppard and Aralen walked down the long, snaking corridors. After a few minutes walking in the opposite direction to that taken by the others, the true scale of the settlement began to become apparent. Looking up at the careful engineering of the roofs and doorways, Rodney found himself more and more appreciative of their skills.

"You've got quite a place here, Aralen," he said, and there wasn't a trace of sarcasm in his voice.

Aralen looked pleased. Despite being told that the team weren't Ancients, or even their servants, the Foremost seemed keen to impress them. McKay guessed he didn't get to show visitors around very often.

"You haven't seen the best of it yet," Aralen said, gesturing for McKay and Sheppard to walk ahead.

The corridor continued for a few meters, after which it opened up into a vast chamber. They stepped through.

"Whoa!" Sheppard gasped. "Now *that's* worth seeing!"

It was as huge as a cathedral, the roof disappearing into darkness despite the many torches set into the stone walls. Mighty pillars of living rock descended from the distant heights. Massive tapestries and decorative banners hung from the walls, each of them showing the ubiquitous hunting scenes, and all around was the sound of murmuring, which rose in volume as the two men walked in.

"My people are eager to greet you," said Aralen.

The place was packed and when the people caught sight of the newcomers, a spontaneous cheer erupted. McKay shot a concerned glance to Sheppard.

"Did I mention I don't like crowds?" he whispered. "What *is* this? Do they still think we're Ancients or something?"

"Just nod and smile, Rodney," Sheppard said, through clenched teeth. "When in Rome…"

Rodney rolled his eyes and gave an awkward wave to the masses, who responded with eager applause.

Aralen beamed. "This is our Hall of Meeting," he said. "The center of our city. It was once a natural cavern, but we have fashioned it into the spiritual home of our people. The finest examples of our skill may be found here."

Rodney looked up towards the distant ceiling, lost in shadows, noticing the tips of jagged stalactites lancing downwards from the gloom.

"Is it safe?" he asked, only half-meaning to speak aloud.

Aralen laughed. "Perfectly. We have held our gatherings here for a hundred years. This rock is as hard as iron. It is difficult to carve, but never fails us."

Sheppard looked at the sea of expectant faces. "Looks like you've got a pretty good thing going here."

Aralen's expression faltered. "Do not be deceived, Colonel Sheppard. Life is hard, and getting harder. The White Buffalo provide all we need, but even they struggle to survive in the growing cold. We have to travel further each season to track them. It exhausts the hunters, and the returns dwindle."

"Forgive me, but why not follow the herds?" asked McKay, remembering his first grade lessons on the plains Indians. "If they head south, you could go after them."

Aralen shook his head. "We must stay close to the portal. I have always told the people that the Ancestors would return and deliver us from this place. That is our hope, whatever you may say about them. It is our only hope."

Sheppard sighed. "Look, Aralen," he said. "I'm not sure that's such a great idea. The Ancestors aren't gonna come any time soon. They've... got a lot on their plate."

"Your coming gives me confidence, Colonel John Sheppard," he said. "I know why you tell me these things, but you will not dent my faith. This is the beginning of something new."

Sheppard and McKay shared an uneasy silence. "Well, that's nice," said Rodney at last. "Really, it is. There may be things we can do to help your people. But, as you might have noticed, we've got a few problems of our own. The vessel we arrived in has sustained a lot of damage. If we're going to fix it, we'll need help. And preferably power."

Aralen looked concerned for the first time. "I'm not sure what we can offer you. As I told you, everything we have is provided by the cave and by the White Buffalo. I don't believe much of what we have would be of any use in repairing your vessel."

"But there must be something else here," McKay persisted. "Something the Ancestors left behind. A building of some sort, or a special chamber? Or maybe a glass column, that glows in a strange way? Or some kind of crystal polarization centrifuge?"

Sheppard rolled his eyes. Aralen merely frowned. "I'm sorry. We are all that is here."

"That's not possible," McKay retorted, his voice rising. "There has to be something. Little blinky lights? A glowing—"

"I think the answer's no, Rodney." Sheppard's tone was light, but his expression said 'Shut the hell up'.

Grudgingly, McKay shut the hell up.

"You'll have to forgive my friend," said Sheppard. "He gets a little excited. We just need to know when this storm's gonna blow over."

"A day or two, I would guess," said Aralen. "It is rare, even now, for a storm to last more than a week, and this one has been raging for several days already. When the air is clear, we can take you back to your vessel. Perhaps a solution will present itself."

"Maybe it'll come gift-wrapped too," McKay muttered, not quiet enough to avoid a sharp look from Sheppard.

But McKay didn't care; they were screwed. Totally screwed. If the best this ice-cube of a planet had to offer was cow hide and a T-bone steak, then they might as well give up now. There was no way they were getting home.

CHAPTER FOUR

SHEPPARD awoke abruptly, shaken from dreams of piloting Jumpers down infinitely long tunnels of plasma. He blinked and rubbed his eyes. With relief, he saw that he was still in the caves of the Forgotten. The light was low, drowsy flames flickering in the braziers above him.

John pulled himself upright and rolled his shoulders. The mats were firm, but there wasn't much of them between him and the rock floor. There was a niggling stiffness in his lower back, but otherwise he felt thoroughly rested. He looked around the small chamber he'd been given to use. There was something different about it. Somehow, his body knew that it was morning, even though he was closeted many feet underground. Then he realized what it was; there was natural light filtering down from the ceiling.

Sunlight-traps were embedded far up into the uneven roof of the rocky chamber. Each of them sparkled with a fresh, pure light. The cold gleam complemented the warm glow of the embers in the torches, lending the room a gentle sheen.

There was a bowl of frigid water and some linen on a low rock shelf nearby. He washed as quickly as possible, and then donned the fur wrappings over his fatigues once more. The hides of the White Buffalo were incredible things; light enough to enable normal movement, but extremely well insulated. Sheppard smiled to himself, thinking how Rodney would spend his time analyzing the properties of the material when they got back to Atlantis. If they got back to Atlantis.

He slipped his pistol into its holster and pulled the hangings over the entrance aside. McKay was waiting for him in the antechamber beyond, his room built into the opposite wall. A third door led to the corridor outside.

"So, how d'you reckon we get hold of food here?" he said, scratching his stubbly chin. "I'd kill for a coffee and a Danish. The nice ones. With pecan on them."

Sheppard shrugged. "Guess we go and find out," he said. "Good news is, I reckon we'll get outside today. There's sunlight coming down from somewhere — the storm must be over."

"Yes, ingenious, aren't they, those sun-traps?" McKay said. "I'm not sure how they do it. There's so little glass around. They must've placed lenses at the top and bottom of shafts in the rock. They're clever, these Forgotten, I'll give them that."

There was a polite cough from the corridor outside and Miruva came in, bearing bowls of steaming stew.

"Forgive me, but when I heard noises I prepared you some breakfast," she said. "I hope it will be pleasing."

McKay wrinkled his nose at the thick gravy. "Hey, I don't suppose you'd have something a bit less... meaty? I mean, it's a little early for me, and to be honest my digestion needs — "

He was cut off by Sheppard reaching across to take the two bowls. "That'll be perfect," he said, pointedly. "Thanks."

Miruva smiled, bowed, and left the room.

Sheppard glared at McKay. "For God's sake, Rodney, we've got to get along with these people. It's not like we're in Trump Tower here, and they've given us a lot."

McKay took one of the bowls and sniffed it suspiciously. "Alright," he said. "But if I don't get something green soon, there'll be consequences. And you won't like them any more than I will."

There was the sound of footsteps outside, and Ronon and Teyla entered. The Runner had to duck some distance under the low entrance to the antechamber. It looked like he was getting used to doing it.

"Morning," said Sheppard. "How's the accommodation?"

"Same as this," said Ronon, looking grumpier than normal. "I like these people, but they're too short."

Sheppard took a mouthful of stew, and with some difficulty swallowed it down. Much as he hated to admit it, Rodney had a point about buffalo meat so early in the day.

"OK, we've gotta start planning our next move," he said, still chewing. "Priority one: salvaging what we can from the Jumper and working out how we get home."

"Agreed," Rodney said. "We need to get the Jumper systems operational as soon as possible, and then I need to take a look at that gate. I don't know what we did to it, but it won't be pretty."

"There is little Ronon and I can do to help you with that," said Teyla. "We need to find out more about these Forgotten. I sense that there is much about this people that is still hidden. If the Ancestors have achieved something here, then we will need to use their expertise to locate it."

"That's your area," agreed Sheppard. "Any ideas?"

"Nothing has come to light. But the girl Miruva is perceptive and she has undertaken to show me more of these dwellings. I will spend today with her, discovering as much as I can."

"And I'm going hunting," said Ronon. "The place needs more supplies."

Rodney rolled his eyes. "Oh, and how, exactly, is that going to help the mission? That's all we need right now — a jolly jaunt across the ice after some giant space cows. C'mon, guys. This isn't a galactic safari. If we can't get ourselves back into shape soon, we'll be in serious trouble."

Ronon glowered at him. "They need to eat," he said. "We need to eat. I don't hear you offering to give up your food."

McKay started to reply, but choked on a rogue piece of buffalo gristle. Sheppard stepped in. "Alright guys, no need to get all antsy," he said. "We can't all work on the same thing at once. Rodney and I'll take a look at the Jumper and the gate. Ronon, do what you gotta do to get alongside these people. Just be careful."

Ronon shot McKay a satisfied look. "Don't worry about me," he said. "I can look after myself."

"Madness," McKay mumbled, grimacing as he worked his way through the stringy meat. "Just total, screwed-up madness."

"Right, let's get going," said Sheppard, putting down his bowl with some relief. "We don't know how long we'll get before the weather closes in, and before then I want some answers."

Zelenka was tired, hungry, and irritable. He'd worked through the night and was no closer to finding a solution. The situation was bad and, even after several hours of brainstorming, the numbers still didn't add up.

Weir walked into the operations room, and Zelenka could see the lines of weariness around her eyes. With no news of the team, he doubted she'd slept well.

"Alright, where are we?" she asked.

Zelenka coughed an apology. "We've made some progress," he said. "But not much. We still have no idea why the Jumper seemed to re-materialize within the wormhole vortex. My only guess is that the Stargate on the far side works differently to the ones we're used to. That would fit in with Dr McKay's hypothesis that the Ancients were working on a new method of interstellar propulsion."

"So our gate and theirs were incompatible?" asked Weir, looking alarmed at the prospect.

"I don't think so," said Zelenka. "Not quite. We've been working hard, and we think we can re-establish the link. On your command, we'll run a test. It's likely that the problem was one of power — we're theorizing that the gate at the other end experienced a major failure, causing it to attempt to abort the transit while the Jumper was still inside the wormhole. The energy burst containing the mass information for the Jumper could have rematerialized in something like real space. I'd never have believed it if I hadn't seen the data, but we think — "

"We *think*?" said Weir. "It's *likely*? These aren't very helpful words, Dr Zelenka."

"I know," he said. "For what it's worth, I believe they got out at the far end. My working hypothesis is this: the Stargate on the other side has suffered a catastrophic failure and lost a key component. Maybe the power drain was too much, and some critical circuit failed. Normally, it would be able to draw on the gate at this end to compensate, but for some reason it didn't. If we're going to get the team back, we'll need to find a way to power up the gate remotely. Or they'll have to find a way. Until then, we can't establish a wormhole, and neither can they."

Weir took a deep breath. "No other options?"

Zelenka shrugged. "We'll keep working on the numbers. If that gate can't power up or take power from us, it can't maintain a wormhole. End of story. But there might be some means of making contact with it. I'll let you know. In the meantime, you could get some more people working on excavating that chamber Dr McKay discovered. Get through that shielding, and we might be able to find some more clues. Something very odd is happening here."

Weir nodded. "I'll do that. God, if only the *Daedalus*

were here…"

Zelenka looked up at her, feeling a flicker of hope. "How long before it's back?"

Weir shook her head. "Two weeks. If we're still talking about this by then, I'm afraid we'll be looking at recovering bodies rather than personnel."

Zelenka's heart sank. Every avenue seemed to be closing down on them.

"You never know," he said. "There may be shelter there. Even people. This was an Ancient world, after all."

"I hope you're right, Radek," said Weir. "In the meantime, find me some better numbers. We're working in the warm here. They're not."

CHAPTER FIVE

THE SUN burned coldly. Ice wastes stretched away in every direction, bleak and harsh. Ronon had to shade his eyes against the glare, even with his hood pulled far down over his face. The sky was clear and almost unbroken, the palest blue he had ever seen. Faint streaks of bright white cloud marked the eastern horizon, but otherwise there was no sign at all of the storm which had kept them locked underground for the night.

"Tough country," he said to himself.

Orand came up to him, grinning. In the fine weather, the hunters eschewed the face masks they usually wore and their pale features were exposed. Each of the hunting party wore carefully bleached outer furs, and looked almost like they were carved from ice themselves. There were a dozen of them in the party, all young men, all eager to be off.

"Not too cold for you, big man?" said Orand, good-naturedly.

If Ronon had been honest, it was crushingly cold. Despite several layers of fur cladding, the chill sank deep into his bones. With difficulty, he had managed to suppress any visible shivers, but he longed to get underway and moving. Standing around waiting for the hunting party to assemble had been difficult, even for him.

"No problem," he lied.

Orand grinned again, clearly skeptical.

"Good," he said. "But don't worry, it'll warm up once we're underway. The sun's strong, and the light on your back will heat you soon enough."

Ronon looked up into the washed-out sky, covering his eyes with his palm. If this was strong sunlight, he wondered what weak was. Even though the sky was clear, the light was oddly diffuse. He had traveled on a hundred worlds, and this was the palest light he had ever seen. There was something strangely ineffective about Khost's sun.

Orand offered him a weapon. It was a long wooden shaft, tipped with an ornately carved blade. Ronon took it in both hands. It was light, but felt strong and well-made. He hefted it powerfully, noting the way the wood of the shaft flexed.

"This is a *jar'hram*," said Orand, proudly. "My father's. He no longer joins the hunt so, as our guest, you shall use it."

Ronon looked at the young man carefully. "You sure?" As a warrior himself, he knew the importance of an ancestral weapon. He wouldn't have parted with his own Traveler gun for all the ZPMs in the galaxy.

Orand studied the blade with a pinched expression. "He has no use for it any more," he said. "Say no more about it."

Ronon nodded. "Thanks."

There was a long leather strap attached to the base of the shaft and tethered to the point at which the wood gave way to steel. Seeing how the other hunters were arrayed, Ronon strapped the spear to his back. As he did so, he felt the reassuring weight of his pistol against his thigh, buried in layers of fur. Swords and sticks were all very well, but it was good to know he had a force weapon available if need be.

"When do we go?" he said, still trying to hide his sensitivity to the cold.

Orand looked around at the party, fully clad for the conditions and standing expectantly.

"No time like the present," he said. "There was a time when my people used to ride across the plains. But the horses couldn't take the cold and there are none left. Now it's just us and the Buffalo. That alright with you?"

The Satedan shrugged. "Sounds 'bout right," he said.

"Let's get started."

Ronon pulled the radio from his furs. "You picking me up, Sheppard?"

"Loud and clear, Ronon. Stay in contact."

Orand gave a signal, and the hunters began to move off towards the wasteland ahead. They didn't assume any particular formation, but walked easily in ones and twos. Ronon cast a look over his shoulder. The barely-visible entrance to the cave complex was several yards distant. Beyond that was the snowfield where the Jumper had landed, and past that stood the Stargate. It all looked very insubstantial compared to the endless expanse of ice and snow around them.

"You'll be able to get us back?" he said to Orand.

The hunter laughed. "I've pursued the White Buffalo on dozens of hunts. I've not lost my way yet."

Orand was young and fresh-faced, but he had an air of calm confidence about him.

"Good," said the Satedan, grimly. "If we get lost out here, I'll never hear the last of it from McKay."

Teyla looked across at Miruva as the young woman stripped dried grass stems into narrow ribbons. The Forgotten worked quickly and surely. Her fingers danced in the firelight, weaving the strands into ever more complicated patterns.

Teyla appreciated Miruva's art. Her own people back on Athos had been more used to the skills of farming and craft-making than high technology. Teyla even thought she recognized some of the Forgotten girl's techniques from her homeworld. Though older members of her village had retained many of the Athosian ancestral skills, and no doubt still did so on Atlantis, she had never had the patience or the time to learn. Hers had always been the way of the warrior, the leader. Perhaps the presence of Wraith DNA in her body had driven her that way, to a rootless existence, trading where possible, fighting where necessary. Now, looking at Miruva contently working, she saw a vision of a different life, one that she might have had. That is, if the Wraith had never existed.

She shook herself free of her introspection. It did no good to speculate on what might have been.

Teyla looked around the chamber. It was much like all the other Forgotten dwelling places: clean, basic, well-kept. Even though it was now mid-morning, the torches still burned. They seemed never to be extinguished. Every so often, she saw attendants pour a little more of the mysterious oil into the base of the lamps. When this was done, there was a faint acrid smell, but otherwise the fuel burned with remarkably little residue.

Aside from the ever-present torches, the room was lit with trapped sunlight filtered down from the sky above. They burned as brightly as any of the synthetic lighting on Atlantis, and did much to relieve the feeling of closeness engendered by the subterranean environment.

"The sun-traps," said Teyla to Miruva. "They are artfully made. How did your people construct such things?"

Miruva sighed. "The secret to making them is lost," she said. "We have legends amongst us, about the first attempts to carve out a life in the caves. This was in the days when the winters were short. Back then, the secrets of the Ancestors were better known. The tale is told of the master glassmaker, who constructed the shafts of light in the underground places. We benefit from his foresight, but we cannot replicate it."

"That is a shame," Teyla said. "You could make your living quarters more comfortable with more such devices."

Miruva put down her weaving and looked at the twinkling points of light herself. "You're right," she said, as if considering the possibility for the first time. "But where would we get the glass? We can still delve the tunnels, but many of the materials our people once used have left us. We make use of what we have, repairing what is broken, but we do not create new things."

Teyla found this idea disturbing. The galaxy was torn by war and conflict. There was no place for such gentle people, stuck in their ways and reluctant to try new things. If they didn't find some way of moving forward, they would surely be swept aside. Even if the Wraith didn't know they were there yet, there was no hiding from them forever.

"The changing climate has no doubt limited what your people can do," she said, anxious not to offend. "But are you not concerned that if you stick to your traditions, then you may be at risk? The Tauri are not perfect, but you have seen that they are restlessly curious. Where there is a problem, they try and solve it. That is why they are so strong."

Miruva looked puzzled. "The Tauri?" she said. "Is that the name you give to your men?"

Teyla smiled. It was easy to forget how isolated these people were. "No," she said. "It is the name of their people, the ones I travel with. And you must put aside the notion that only the menfolk are responsible for our achievements. Our commander is a woman, and I am as much a part of the team as my colleagues."

Miruva looked at her with admiration. "It is not like that with us," she said. "I wish it were. But while our men have the honor of hunting the Buffalo, we have little to do but tend the dwellings and ensure that all is kept in order for their return."

"Such things are important, to be sure," Teyla said. "But you are an intelligent woman, you can see the problems your people face. Can you not help them do something about them? I've seen the way Orand looks at you. You have a follower there, at least."

Teyla smiled as Miruva blushed deeply. "It's not that easy. My father…"

"He seems like a good man," Teyla said, not wanting to cause a family rift.

"Oh, he is," Miruva said, with feeling. "But perhaps age has not been kind to him. My mother was taken many years ago…"

A note of grief marked her voice, and she trailed into silence. Teyla felt awkward. She had no business interfering. "I am sorry," she said. "I have been discourteous."

"No, you haven't," said Miruva. "You're making me think, Teyla."

She looked up at the Athosian, and her smile returned. Her face was lit by the sunlight coming from above and, despite her slender features, she looked strong and determined. Like all the Forgotten, she clearly possessed resilience.

"Maybe we should be looking to make changes," she said. "But for now, there are tapestries to be woven. Let us keep talking. Your ideas will find their ways into the designs, if nothing else."

Teyla smiled. "I would like that."

It studied the two subjects. One was outside the parameters, and no analysis had yielded any helpful results. The delay had caused problems. There was chatter over the data-streams.

You are wasting resources. Act.

It hung, immobile, invisible. Not yet. Information was invaluable. There were fragments, snatches. Some of them reminded it of events a long time ago. Some words were…

So much had been lost. Something like anger coursed through its cortex. Not real anger, of course. Even when things had been better, they had only been a sham set of emotions. The program couldn't change that.

The time was coming. Power levels had fallen again, and the recovery had to commence. With every passing hour, the chatter grew.

What do I do about the newcomer?

There was no answer. They didn't know any more than it did. The days of being able to process creatively were long gone. It was all blind interpretation now. Cold and blind, like the planet itself.

I have set the sequence in motion.

That finally shut them up. They would be getting what they wanted.

It gazed down at the scene, half regretfully. Only a matter of time now. They wouldn't like it, of course. But it had to do it. It had to come for them.

It had to perform the cull.

McKay was cold. Seriously cold. It didn't seem to matter how many layers of furs he had on, the freezing air took his breath away. He stood in front of the stricken Jumper, slapping his hands together in a vain attempt to keep them warm.

"Looks pretty bad," said Sheppard.

McKay fixed him with his most withering stare. "Well, that's an astute comment, if ever I heard one," he said, acidly. "Why don't you take over the repairs? Perhaps I could hand you a wrench from time to time and make the coffee?"

"Maybe you should," Sheppard said, dryly. "Might get this thing fixed a damn sight quicker."

The Jumper looked as if it had been through an inferno. The curved sides were blackened and scored. Many of the Ancient-designed patterns on the flanks had been razed from the superstructure. There were several places where it seemed as if explosions or heat had nearly penetrated the shielding. The windscreen, remarkably, had remained relatively unscathed. Clearly, the damage had been done as the Jumper had careered into the edges of the wormhole anomaly. There were no lights working. The vessel lay nose-first in a snowdrift, its cockpit buried deep. Fresh snow from the storm had piled up around the open rear bay, obscuring any footprints from their hasty exit. The door had been frozen in place, leaving the innards of the vessel open to the elements.

The Stargate had been the same. It looked like had been burned, and badly. There hadn't been a flicker of life from the chevrons, and some of the inner panels were cracked. That alone was worrying. It was naquadah, for God's sake. That stuff didn't crack easy. What was worse, there was no sign of a DHD, nor the MALP. If a dial home device had existed in the past, it sure didn't now. As for the MALP, there was no telling where it had ended up — probably destroyed, or buried deep in a snowdrift.

McKay sighed; once again, the entire galaxy had conspired against him.

"Well, I suppose we'd better make a start," he said.

The two men ducked into the Jumper. Soon McKay had pulled out an array of transparent panels. He looked at them in disgust, tutting to himself as he carried out basic diagnostic tests. "Well, this is shot. So's this. That's totally zeroed, and I don't even know what that does."

Irritation began to boil inside him. The cold was part of it. Having to exist on a diet of pure meat was another factor. It seemed that whatever situation the team got itself into, it was always he who had to perform the necessary magic to get them out. And yet, who emerged with the plaudits? Most likely Sheppard, or perhaps Weir. Without McKay's in-depth knowledge of Ancient artifacts and power systems, virtually every mission they had ever been on would have ended in failure. And the few times he got it wrong, such as the unfortunate business on Doranda, were never quite forgotten. It was unjust, and irritating, and constant.

He sighed, and stomped through the open bulkhead to the cockpit. Sheppard was sitting in the pilot's seat, aimlessly trying a few controls.

"Nothing," he said. "Nada. Zilch. This baby's going nowhere."

McKay gave him a wintry smile. "This endless positivity is really helping. Honestly, you should think about becoming a motivational speaker or something. You'd be a blast."

"Hey!" Sheppard swung around in the seat and scowled at him. "Just what is it with you this morning? You've been even more grouchy than normal, which is saying something."

"*Grouchy?*"

"You heard me. *Grouchy.*"

"Oh, let me see," McKay snapped. "We're stuck on a god-forsaken rock on the edge of the galaxy with no supplies and no power. We can't send as much as a shopping-list back through the gate to Atlantis because the gate's been served-up well-done and we've got the only DHD on the whole damn planet and that's toast too. The people here are about to freeze themselves to death because they're too stupid to look for somewhere else to live. It's freezing cold. And I've got massive indigestion. So, yes, I'm not exactly the happiest I've ever been. But thanks a lot for asking."

McKay picked up a loose circuit board and started poking at it.

"Oh, give it a rest, Rodney," Sheppard snapped. "If these people hadn't been here waiting for us, we'd be deep frozen by now. And if we can't generate enough power to get back in the Jumper, Elizabeth will send the *Daedalus*. You're worrying over nothing."

"Am I?" The circuit board suddenly gave a fizz, and a shower of sparks burst from the housing. "Dammit!" McKay yanked his hand back. His mood was getting worse all the time, and Sheppard's admonishment hadn't helped. "The *Daedalus* isn't available, which you'd know if you'd looked at the schedule more carefully. We're on our own. And maybe I wouldn't mind that if, for once, it wasn't me in charge of getting us back."

"You know, Rodney, you've really got the knack of looking on the dark side of life."

"Well that might have something to do with being stuck here with a bunch of primitives who haven't mastered the basic techniques of Jell-O making yet, and who seem to think the height of architectural achievement is a bunch of caves with — "

Sheppard's eyes widened and he shot a warning look towards the back of the Jumper. With a sudden lurch of embarrassment in the pit of his stomach, McKay turned around. Aralen was standing in the open bay, observing.

"Greetings," the Forgotten leader said, unperturbed. "I trust things are going well?"

McKay felt his face redden, despite the cold. Why could he never learn to keep his mouth shut?

"Ah, Foremost," he said. "Didn't see ya there. Did you, ah, hear much of the conversation?"

The Forgotten walked towards them, looking at the interior of the Jumper with intent interest. "I assumed you were discussing the means by which to restore your vessel."

Sheppard gave Rodney a look which said *you got away with that one*. "Something like that," he said. "We've just made a start."

Aralen stared at the cockpit viewscreen with undisguised wonder; there was little glass on Khost and it must have looked like something out of the legendary past. "I am glad you're moving toward a solution," he said. "Surely this machine will soon be operational."

Feeling he needed to claw back some dignity, McKay put on his most authoritative voice. "Perhaps," he said. "There's relatively little structural damage, but there are some important systems which might take a while to bring back on line. One problem we have is power. We don't have any. And I fear that your Starga... — sorry, *portal* — might have been damaged by whatever it was we did in that wormhole. I'll need to look into it. Whether it's the distance, or some other problem, I don't know yet."

Aralen looked troubled at McKay's downbeat assessment. Perhaps the old man thought that the visitors should be capable of fixing anything. Rodney wasn't convinced that Aralen had entirely given up on idea that they were Ancients.

"That sounds grave," the leader of the Forgotten said. "May we help?"

McKay couldn't help but let a sarcastic smile slip through. "Not unless you've got a ZPM," he said. "Or maybe a stash of ZPMs?"

"Forgive me, I don't understand..."

Sheppard coughed significantly.

"Not unless you've got access to more power," said McKay. "And from what I've seen — with all due respect — you don't. So we may be here a while."

Aralen nodded. "Very well. Then I will leave you to your work. But if there is anything else..."

McKay was prepared to give him his version of a polite refusal, when suddenly there was a grinding sound deep beneath them. It echoed inside the Jumper bay ominously.

"What the...?" started Sheppard, rising from his seat.

It sounded like someone was using a circular saw on metal, directly below. Aralen looked around, his face stricken with panic. The Jumper started to rock and McKay grabbed on to a bulkhead, heart hammering.

Then, as suddenly as it had started, the noise ceased. The Jumper settled back into position, listing a little further to port and embedded deeper in the snow.

"And that was?" said McKay, his voice shaky.

Sheppard looked at Aralen. "Felt like a tremor," he said. "You get earthquakes here?"

Aralen, recovering himself, sank back against the wall of the Jumper cabin. "From time to time," he said. "Some of the ice is less stable than the rest. Perhaps your descent has disturbed something." He looked troubled. "But they have been increasing in recent months. Another of the many curses we have had to endure."

"Oh, great," said McKay, glancing towards the heavens. "Now we're on thin ice. And I mean that, of course, *entirely literally.*"

"Sure puts a new spin on things," Sheppard agreed, clearly uneasy. "If this thing disappears beneath the ice, then I start getting worried. We're gonna have to work quicker."

McKay shook his head bitterly. "And by *we*, you mean *me*, I take it?"

"Just get working, Rodney. If we lose the Jumper, you'll be eating buffalo for a lot longer than you're gonna like."

The wind tore from the east. It was unrelenting. Despite the heavy furs, Ronon felt his legs begin to go numb. He had pulled his hood down as far as it would go, and still the chill air found its way under his collar. His fingers had long since lost most of their feeling. He wondered how useful he would be once the hunting party reached its destination. He stamped as he walked, trying to generate some blood flow. He was tightening up, and if that continued he would be worse than useless once the action began.

They'd been walking for over an hour. In the clear daylight, Ronon could see that the Forgotten settlement had been built in the center of a wide, near-circular depression. The land was broken and rocky, ideal for delving their subterranean dwellings. The going was treacherous, and would have been near-impossible had it not been for the experienced guides. Pristine snow-drifts hid knife-sharp rows of rocks or bottomless crevasses. Orand had pointed these out to Ronon as they had passed them, regaling him with stories of lost travelers blundering to their deaths in the unforgiving wastes. That had, of course, been in the days when there had been travelers abroad in Khost. Now, none went across the snowfields unless they had important business. The conditions had just become too dangerous.

From those lower regions, the hunting party had ascended narrow and winding paths and emerged on to a high plateau. The effort of climbing up to the highlands had restored much of Ronon's body warmth, but once out on to the exposed terrain the true meaning of cold had become apparent. The wind moaned and rolled across the flat, featureless plains with no interruptions. In the far distance, Ronon could see the low outline of what might have been mountains. Otherwise, there was nothing. Just a huge, flat, empty field of dazzling white ice stretching in every direction. It looked like a vision of some frigid hell. As he trudged along, willing his body to cope with the frozen temperatures, he wondered how anything could possibly survive in such a place.

Orand walked by his side. He had long since lost his smile. Even the hunters, used to such conditions, were finding the going tough. They had wrapped leather masks around their faces and only their eyes remained exposed. Just as they had been when rescuing the crew of the Jumper, they looked like pale ghosts toiling across the harsh landscape.

"How're you doing?" said Orand to Ronon. His voice was

muffled by the facemask and the wind.

"Fine," said Ronon. "Don't worry about me."

Orand nodded. "You've done well," he said. "Lapraik and Fai thought you'd have turned back by now. You're made of strong stuff. Not like the others, I'm guessing."

"I dunno," Ronon shrugged. "Colonel Sheppard's hard to wear down. And I'd trust Teyla with my life."

"And the fat one? The one who eats all the time?"

Ronon smiled under his facemask. "He's OK," he said. "Maybe not the toughest."

Orand pulled the top of his facemask down a little and peered ahead. The flat ice yawned away into the distance. Then, suddenly, there was a whistle from one of the hunters up ahead. Orand immediately pulled his facemask down again and screwed up his narrow eyes at the horizon.

Ronon did likewise, but could see little. Nothing appeared to have changed. The weak sun was still high in the sky, the landscape bathed in its pale light. The ice shimmered coldly and the wind continued its endless bluster. Aside from some jagged cracks in the surface of the ice, there was almost no break in the flat landscape.

"What did you see, Lapraik?" hissed Orand to one of his companions.

"Northwest," came a voice from up ahead. "A big herd. They're heading west. We can catch them."

Orand nodded sharply. He cupped his hands to his mouth, and gave a low call through them. The hunting party immediately broke into a loping run. Ronon joined them, feeling his stiff limbs gradually respond. His blood began to pump a little more strongly. This was good. With the prospect of action, the cold was easier to bear.

"You came looking for excitement," said Orand, sounding much happier. "I think we'll find it for you."

The team went quickly but stealthily, keeping their

hunched bodies as low to the ice as possible. Ronon couldn't match their stooping gait, but was nearly as invisible against the ice, covered as he was in the bleached furs. As they ran, the hunters slid their spears from their backs, and carried them in both hands, swaying as they went. Ronon did likewise, nearly losing the shaft in his frost-numbed hands.

They began to pick up speed. The outlying hunters drew together, and soon the dozen young men were running in a tight pack, guided by the instincts of the one called Lapraik. The snow crunched under their fur-lined boots, flying in little spurts behind them as they closed in on the distant prey.

Ronon still struggled with the light. It was near-blinding if he looked directly at the shimmering horizon. But as he ran, the objective began to become apparent. In the far distance, there did seem to be a break in the flawless sheets of ice. At first it looked like a rocky outcrop, a narrow fringe of dark against the glass-like terrain. But soon there was no mistaking it. There were huge objects, and they were moving. From such a range Ronon couldn't make out much detail, but it was clear that they were big.

He kept running, determined not to fall behind the more experienced hunters. Now that they were on the move, his longer legs gave him an advantage. The *jar'hram* felt light and supple in his hands. Just as it had done many times when hunting Wraith in far-flung worlds across the galaxy, the thrill of the chase began to take control of him. He felt his heart beating, his lungs working powerfully. The last of the chill left him and a savage heat kindled in his heart.

The Buffalo had seen them and the nearest of them began to break into a lumbering run. They were still some distance away.

Orand looked over at Ronon as he ran. He had a feral expression of joy in his eyes.

"This is it, big man!" he cried, whirling the *jar'hram* loosely around him as he loped. "Are you prepared?"

"Believe it," growled Ronon, picking up the pace.

The hunt had begun.

Unlike Ronon, Teyla had no trouble slipping under the low doorways and between the various chambers of the settlement. The big Satedan had taken several bruises with him on the hunt. Teyla found herself wondering how he was fairing. With any luck, he was enjoying the sun on his skin. She was glad to be in the relative warmth for once, not chasing around and having to use her own considerable martial skills. The chance to immerse herself in an alien culture, to take some time to try and understand how the people of another world ordered themselves, was a rare privilege. She intended to exploit it to the full.

"Where are we taking this?" she said to Miruva.

The Forgotten woman carried the product of her labor, a circular mat made from the dried plains grass. It was much smaller than others Teyla had seen. She guessed that the scarcity of materials forced compromises to be made.

"This is to be placed in the Hall of the Artisans," said Miruva, proud of her creation. "There will be many other items there. In due course, the Elders will come to judge their merit. Those deemed worthy will grace the dwellings of our leaders. I am hoping that mine will be chosen." She slid Teyla a rueful smile. "My position is somewhat difficult, of course. My father heads the ruling council, and is a fair-minded man. As a result, he has never used his vote in my favor, and others have taken the prize. But I'm proud of this one. You never know."

Teyla looked at the woven disk again. Miruva had created a ring of geometric shapes around the rim, all of which tessellated with each other wonderfully. In the center of the mat, there was a depiction of a hunting scene, as there seemed to be in all the Forgotten artwork. The White Buffalo was woven using a series of swirls to indicate movement. The diminutive figures of hunters surrounded the great animal in heavily stylized form. The colors Miruva had chosen were muted and subtle. Each hunter was a different shade, though it was difficult to make out in the flickering torchlight.

"Look carefully," she said to Teyla, her eyes shining. "What do you make of the blue hunter?"

Teyla took the mat from Miruva and held it up to the light. The figure was almost the same as the others, except that it had a female shape. The Athosian smiled, and handed the mat back. "Will you get in trouble for that?"

Miruva shrugged. "What if I do? I told you your ideas were beginning to have an effect on me. For the time being, women hunters will only exist in tapestries and weaving. Maybe one day they'll take their places in the real world."

Teyla wondered if Miruva herself could make such a leap. Though outwardly shy and deferential, there seemed to be a core of steel to the young woman.

"I hope that is so, Miruva," she said, placing her hand on the girl's shoulder.

"We are here," Miruva said, and pulled aside a hanging from the entrance in front of them.

They entered a wide hall, somewhat like the assembly chamber, but smaller and lower. Elaborate drapes covered every wall, and the floor was strewn with mats and weavings of many shapes. Miruva's wasn't the smallest, but it wasn't far off. Many of the other items seemed to use grass recycled from previous artifacts. The hall could have held twice the number assembled there with room to spare.

Miruva looked confident as she placed her mat near the center of the chamber.

"This is all new grass," she said, proudly. "I walked long

and far to find it before the snow came for good. The key to this competition is detail. A larger object will not necessarily win the prize."

Teyla nodded in appreciation. She cast her gaze across the panoply of woven artifacts, admiring the consistent skill. As she did so, she noticed something strange, high up on the bare rock walls.

"What is that?" she said to Miruva, pointing at an ornate shape engraved on the surface.

The Forgotten looked at it casually. It looked like it had once been carved deep into the unyielding rock, but was now faint and indistinct. The shape was complex. It could have been an inscription, or maybe a diagram.

"I don't know," she said. "There are marks of this kind scattered throughout the settlement. I have always assumed they were placed there by the builders of this place."

Teyla strained her eyes to see more clearly. "Maybe so," she said. "But I have seen such marks elsewhere. On my home planet, there is a place where engravings are commonplace. Dr McKay has studied the technology of the Ancients, perhaps he will be able to decipher it."

For some reason, as she spoke, a chill passed through her. The glyph had an unsettling aura. She turned her gaze from it. Something to raise with Aralen, perhaps.

Miruva smiled at the mention of Rodney. "Is that the angry man?" she said, suppressing a laugh. "He is very popular here amongst the young people. They are calling him the Greedy One. He finished twice the normal portion of stew in his first night here."

"I am sure he will appreciate the gesture," Teyla said, knowing full well he wouldn't. "He is an interesting man. Despite his... foibles, he is steeped in the ways of the Ancestors. If any of us are able to decipher it, it is he."

Miruva paused, and looked at Teyla with a searching

expression. "You speak of the Ancestors as if they were far away, and yet as if you were intimately connected with them."

Teyla felt a little uncomfortable. The fiction that Atlantis was destroyed would one day surely come out into the open. For now, however, the Wraith had still to discover their error. Until that day came, they all had to be careful.

"We have traveled widely," said Teyla, choosing her words carefully. "The Ancestors left their mark in many places, and we have learned much of their ways. There are some of us capable of using their technology with the power of the mind alone. Colonel Sheppard is one such man. Even those without the gift can now be helped to understand the Ancestor's technology. We are not the Ancestors, Miruva. But we are moving closer to understanding their secrets."

Miruva looked thoughtful.

"To use the Ancestor's machines using only your mind..." she murmured, clearly pondering the possibilities. "That would be marvelous indeed."

The young woman lapsed into thoughtfulness. Teyla regarded her carefully. It was entirely possible that some of the Forgotten possessed the ATA gene. If there were any descendants of the Ancestors among them, then such a thing should have been possible. However, as the only Ancient artifact they knew about — the Stargate — had been lifeless for generations, they could have had no way of knowing.

"I will leave this here until the judging session," said Miruva, looking carefully at the rival artworks. "Where would you like to go now?"

Teyla paused, taking in her surroundings, pondering what she wanted to know most about the Forgotten and their ways. As she thought, the sound of children laughing filtered down the maze of tunnels. It came from far off, but was as unmistakable as the sound of falling rain. It warmed her heart to hear it.

"Show me your young people," she said to Miruva. "It has been too long since I heard laughter — our travels have been too full of danger and loss. It would be good to be reminded that there is still hope in the galaxy."

They left the room. Above them, the symbol gazed down on the empty room, impassive and cold.

CHAPTER SIX

THE WHITE Buffalo were magnificent animals. They were entirely covered in thick fur which hung down from their flanks in straggling tresses. Their massive shoulders were easily twice the height of a man. Even draped in such thick layers of insulating fat, their powerful muscles were evident. As they galloped, huge plumes of ice and slush were thrown up behind them. The giant bulls had long, wickedly-curved horns, which they used to plough through the top layers of snow and throw waves of it over themselves.

As their hooves thundered against the terrain, Ronon felt the earth vibrate like a drum. The noise of their bellows was deafening. These indeed were worthy foes. As he ran to keep up with the herd, he realized just how brave Orand and his fellow hunters were to take on such beasts. Despite himself, he felt a sliver of fear. He would have to be at the very top of his game.

The herd numbered perhaps twenty animals. All of them were now lumbering through the ice fields, startled by the near-invisible hunters around them. There were calves among them, protected by a ring of the bulky adult animals. Most of the bulls were juveniles, but there was one truly huge creature at the head of the herd who must have been the patriarch. Every so often, it would issue a great bellow of rage. The noise was incredible.

"Stay close to me!" yelled Orand. "If we get charged, run as fast as you can! They move quick when they're angry!"

Ronon nodded. It was as much as he could do to just keep up with the sprinting pack of hunters. Despite their heavy furs and the layers of snow they waded through, they seemed able to go on forever. They were now within

a spear's throw of the nearest animals. The pursuers had
spread out around the lumbering herd. Their objective was
to separate the animals from each other. Some of the giant
creatures looked in better condition than others. Ronon
guessed that the hunters would keep forcing them to run
until one of the weaker or older animals fell behind. Then
the killing would start. He just hoped it was the hunters
who did it, and not the buffalo.

He looked up ahead. The featureless plains rolled into
the distance. The ground had become more broken. They
were heading for what looked like a low range of hills. The
peaks were flat and snowbound, but at least they provided
some break from the endless ice plains.

"Watch that one!" cried Orand.

One of the buffalo veered suddenly to the left. As if aware
that he was the weak link, the vast creature headed straight
for Ronon. Hooves thundered, and snow shook from the creature's flanks. The gap between them narrowed frighteningly
quickly. For a brief instant, the Satedan looked directly into
its eyes. They were tiny and red with rage. Its huge shaggy
flanks shook as it plowed heavily through the snow, throwing up torrents of ice. It was coming straight for him.

His legs feeling like lead, Ronon turned and ran. He
powered clumsily through the snow, following Orand's
course as best he could. The buffalo bore down on him and
Ronon could feel the spatters of snow as they were thrown
against his back. Despite the cold, sweat pooled against his
back. His heart hammered, and his lungs strained. This
was too close.

Suddenly, there was an echoing cry of distress from the
charging beast. Ronon risked a look over his shoulder. A
spear had been thrown. The buffalo listed to its right, limping suddenly on its forelegs. The shaft of a *jar'hram* protruded from its shoulder. The spear must have been thrown

with amazing force to penetrate the hide of the beast.

Ronon stumbled, trying to get his bearings. The rest of the herd was still close, but their formation had become confused. The wounded buffalo was separated from the others, but not by very much. Everything was still in motion. Hunters darted around the fringes of the herd. The animals themselves still lumbered onwards, desperate to escape the pack of predators in their midst.

"This is the one!" shouted Orand, gesturing towards the buffalo with the spear in its flank.

The other animals seemed to sense it. The juveniles headed away from the stricken creature as quickly as they could. The herd was still determined to get away. Some of the hunters ran between the body of the herd and the separated animal, waving their spears and whooping wildly. It looked insanely dangerous, but their daring runs did the trick; the herd was splintering, losing its cohesion and allowing the other hunters to have a free run at the isolated buffalo.

A second *jar'hram* was hurled up at the lone beast. Ronon saw the shaft shiver as it hit, and the razor-sharp blade sunk deep into the buffalo's heavy stomach. A huge roar went up, and the creature turned to face its tormentor. The spear-thrower, now bereft of his weapon, danced away and shrank back into the snow. With his white furs on, even Ronon had difficulty seeing where he'd gone.

The buffalo was becoming enraged. It reared up on its massive hind legs, before crashing its hooves back to earth. The snow flew up, and the earth shuddered under the impact. Ronon had difficulty keeping his feet. Out of immediate danger, he crouched down in the ice, panting for breath, looking for a chance to get involved.

The bulk of the herd was now moving away. Despite their huge size, the creatures seemed terrified of the hunters. Some of Orand's group were driving them further off.

Others were ensuring the separated animal couldn't get back to rejoin the herd. More *jar'hram* flew through the air. Each time they landed, a fresh bellow of pain and rage rose from the lone buffalo.

Ronon rose, hefting his shaft lightly in his hands. Adrenalin had kicked in. Despite the long chase he found he still had reserves of strength. It was time for him to make a contribution. He pulled his spear back over his shoulder and hurled it at the buffalo with an almighty heave. The blade flew in a spinning arc, before clattering uselessly against the animal's thick hide. With dismay, Ronon saw the *jar'hram* slide ineffectually down the buffalo's flanks and into the snow.

There was no scorn from the others. Some of their spears had also failed to penetrate the animal's protective layers of fur, and the remaining hunters were too busy keeping themselves alive to pay much attention to Ronon's actions. Despite this, the Satedan felt a burning sense of failure. Without his spear, he was useless to the hunt. He shrank back away from the beast, wondering what to do.

"Stay in the circle!" cried Orand sharply.

The young hunter was to Ronon's right, and hadn't dispatched his spear yet. Ronon looked quickly across at the others, and saw that the party had formed into a wide ring. With the bulk of the herd driven off, the isolated animal was surrounded. There was no escape. The lone buffalo seemed confused and weary. Every so often it would make an attempt to charge free of its tormentors. When it did so, a fresh spear would spin up from a hidden hand, provoking a fresh lurch and stagger from the wounded animal. The snow was now stained with dark blood, and the bellows from the creature were becoming strangled and hoarse.

Ronon stayed where he was, watching the buffalo warily. It was a precarious occupation, being part of a living barrier. There were now half a dozen spears sticking from the buffalo's body, and they swayed strangely as the beast wallowed and reared. Despite its wounds, the vast creature was still on its feet. The bellows rising from its cavernous ribcage now sounded more like pleas for help than roars of aggression. They were not answered. The rest of the herd had been driven some distance away. The hunters who had chased them off were returning. The game was entering its final stages.

The wounded buffalo turned away from Ronon, and challenged the hunters on the other side of the circle. There were few *jar'hram* left to throw. Then the Satedan spotted something lying in the churned-up snow. It was his blade, miraculously unbroken by the trampling hooves of the buffalo. With a sudden inspiration, Ronon realized he could get it. He stole a glance towards Orand, but the hunter was preoccupied with maintaining the stranglehold on the prey. Without waiting for doubt to cloud his judgment, Ronon sprinted forward. The spear was only a few yards ahead, half buried by the blood-stained slush.

As he did so, the buffalo turned. Its enraged eyes flashed, and it bore down on him. Ronon normally thought of himself as a big man; under the gaze of a rampaging White Buffalo he felt like an insect. This was dangerous. The Runner half-heard Orand's urgent shout, but there was no choice, he was committed. The buffalo careered towards him, throwing slush into the air like a ship surging through the waves.

Ronon stooped down and picked up the *jar'hram* while still at full-tilt. He could smell the acrid musk of the wounded buffalo, its fur waving wildly as it careered onwards. Sliding and skidding, Ronon changed direction, scrabbling to get away. The thud of the creature's hooves shook the ground beneath him.

He lost his footing on the churned-up snow, staggering

as he ran. The gap closed. He felt his heart thumping heavily in his chest, he dreadlocks flailing, his furs streaming out behind him as he ran.

He was too close. The buffalo was on him. He could feel its bellowing breath against his shoulders. His legs burned, his arms pumped, but he knew it was no good.

He was going to get run down.

Teyla sat against the rough-cut stone wall, enjoying the warmth of the fire. There were voices all around. The womenfolk and children of the settlement had gathered in one of the larger chambers and were chatting and laughing amiably. The smaller boys ran around with sticks, mimicking the actions of the great hunt. The girls sat quietly, absorbing the deft movements of their mothers as they wove more plains-grass artifacts.

There seemed remarkably little disharmony in the Forgotten, Teyla thought. There were few quarrels, and no raised voices. The entire settlement seemed to realize their debt to one another. Perhaps the harshness of their predicament had forced them to become a uniquely cooperative people. Or maybe the absence of the Wraith had enabled them to lead lives of relative peace and security. But Teyla felt there was something more to it; they seemed almost too passive, too secure in their settled ways. Even during the team's short stay on Khost, Teyla had seen that their situation was hopeless. If the winters carried on getting worse, then the Forgotten way of life would soon be wiped out.

Teyla watched Miruva laughing and gossiping with her friends as she wove. The girl's face was alive with delight, and her smooth features were illuminated by the flickering light of the hearth. Teyla knew that she had potential. Not all the Forgotten women were destined to live their lives sewing and darning the furs of their men.

The Forgotten girl seemed to sense she was being watched, and turned to look at Teyla. The Athosian smiled, pushed herself up from the wall, and walked over to Miruva, picking her way past the scurrying children carefully.

"It is easy to lose track of time in this place," said Teyla. "How long have we been here?"

Miruva looked up at the light-traps in the rock ceiling.

"It is now late afternoon," she said. "You have seen a typical morning in this settlement. If you want to leave and help your friends, I won't be offended."

Teyla shook her head. "There is not much I can do to assist Dr McKay and Colonel Sheppard," she said. "And it is just as useful for us to learn more about your situation here."

Miruva put her weaving down. "Is there anything in particular you'd like to know?"

"There is one thing," Teyla said, sitting down beside her. "We are here because we believe the Ancestors may have had something special planned for you and your people. This planet is the furthest we have ever traveled within the Pegasus galaxy. There seems to be something unique about your world. Do your people have any histories concerning the plans of the Ancestors?"

Miruva shook her head. "To be honest, until you arrived, I had begun to doubt whether they even existed at all."

"Oh, they do exist," said Teyla. "The full story is somewhat complicated, but there are many worlds throughout this galaxy which bear their mark. Your portal is not the only one. If your gate were working properly, you too could leave Khost and seek a better home."

Miruva's eyes lit up briefly. "Is that why you're here? To lead us away from Khost?"

Teyla began to wonder if she'd suggested too much. Sheppard wouldn't thank her for planting ideas in the heads of the Forgotten. "We will have to consult with your leaders first," she said. "But Dr McKay and Colonel Sheppard are working to repair your portal. Once this is done, we will have to see what we can do to help you. You can be assured of one thing: we will not stand by while your people are driven to starvation."

Miruva took Teyla's hand in hers. "From the moment I saw you, I knew that you were here to lead us to freedom," she said. "This is the time our people have been waiting for."

Teyla felt uncomfortable; she had allowed her liking for the Forgotten to get the better of her. Once people thought you were their redeemer, then things became difficult. "Well…" she began.

But then there was a sudden loud swishing noise. All around her, women and children jumped to their feet in panic. The flames in the hearth guttered and waved wildly.

"What is happening?" asked Teyla with alarm.

Miruva looked back at her in terror, scrambling to her feet. "Banshees!" she cried. "Run! The Banshees have come for us!"

Sheppard took a good look at the scenery. The air was as clear as glass, the sky an icy blue, almost green at the furthest point from the horizon. The only sign of cloud was in the far distance. Beneath the sky's wide dome the mighty ice sheets sprawled, and in the weak sunlight they sparkled like swathes of diamond. Mighty snowdrifts were piled up against each other in the lee of the rock formations around the settlement. Out on the flats, the exposed ice mirrored the cool blue of the sky. Sheppard was not a man given to hyperbole or artistic reflection, but even he had to admit that the view was something close to pretty special. He wondered why he never remembered to take a camera out on these trips. One day, when he was surrounded by grandkids in a rocking chair, he'd regret it.

The thought of kids brought painful memories of Nancy to the surface almost at once. This was unusual; he didn't think of her often. But that didn't mean his failure with her didn't rankle. Occasionally, it occurred to him that his career had finished off pretty much every relationship he'd ever had: his father, his ex-wife, even the burgeoning friendship he'd enjoyed with Lieutenant Ford. As the sun bathed the ice before him in a frigid light, he found himself wondering whether it was all worth it. Was the chance to die on an ice-ball at the wrong end of a distant galaxy really worth losing everyone he cared about? It was a question he didn't like to think about too much.

"Colonel, may I ask if you're here to help, or is your primary function on this mission to admire the view, lovely as it is?"

The acidic sound of Rodney's sarcasm broke his train of thought. With a weary sigh, Sheppard turned from the vista before him and re-entered the Jumper rear bay.

"If I remember," he said, "it was *you* who told me to get the hell outta your way while you did… whatever it is you did. Again."

McKay scowled. "That was then. This is now. And right *now*, I need your help."

McKay looked back over the mess of instrumentation cluttering the cramped interior of the Jumper. Most of it had been pulled from panels in the interior wall — the craft looked as if it had had its guts torn out — and the rest had come with McKay, part of the Swiss Army knife of tools and spare parts he always had stowed away somewhere.

"We've got some burned-out sections of transmission circuitry here," said McKay, scowling at the twisted wires in front of them. "Even I can't do much with those. But, as I like to say on such occasions, where there's a Rodney, there's a way. I've bypassed a couple of the worst affected systems and rigged up some proxy solutions to cope with the gaps. It's fiendishly complicated, but I reckon it's all in place now."

"*Fiendishly* complicated, eh?"

McKay gave a smug smile and turned back to the tangle of electronics. Like a worried mother adjusting her son's clothing on his first day in school, he tweaked at a few nodes and adjusted a pair of esoteric-looking crystals. The mix of Ancient technology and Earth engineering made an unusual pairing, but for all the man's bluster, Sheppard knew that McKay was the foremost expert on such things in the galaxy.

"Now, I've not tried to get everything up and running at once," said McKay, looking nervously at his jury-rigged contraption. "Just primary life support and some core structural functions. Trying to get it to fly might blow the few remaining circuits for good, so we've got to be careful."

"Careful. Right," said Sheppard. "What do I do?"

McKay handed him a couple of transparent rods. They were clearly of Ancient design, though they were plugged into a collection of McKay's own pieces of kit.

"This is a replacement for your normal mode of interface," he explained. "I don't want anyone trying to use the main instrument panel yet. Think of it as a bypass into the basic systems of the Jumper."

Sheppard frowned. He had the uncomfortable feeling he was being wired for an experiment, and wouldn't have been surprised if the electrodes had given him a shock.

"You're making me nervous, Rodney," he said, taking a rod in each hand. "What's the drill? Click my heels and say 'There's no place like home?'"

"Nice," said McKay. "Now listen. I'm going to feed a little power to the system now. It's more or less all we've got left in the portable units, so it needs to kick-start the reserve packs in the Jumper. When I say 'Go', do whatever it is you do that starts-up the Jumper."

Sheppard lifted an eyebrow. "Whatever it is I *do*? You want to be more precise?"

McKay scowled. "Just remember, if you leave it too late we'll lose the power. Lose the power and we could damage the Jumper's few remaining relays. Damage those, then we…"

"I get it. Flip the switch, Dr Frankenstein."

McKay shook his head and delved back into the heap of wires. After a few more moments of fiddling and tweaking, he stood back. "Alright," he said. "Here we go. Three, two, one… zero!"

Nothing happened.

McKay stood back, scratching his head.

"That's odd. I could've sworn —"

Suddenly, a spasm of power surged through the rods in Sheppard's hands. Pain bloomed up from the conductor, and he had to fight not to drop them like red-hot pokers. But the flash of power began to ebb almost as soon as it had begun and he scrambled to summon the mental activation commands. Normally, it was so easy. A second or two passed, and the power flow ebbed further.

There was a bang, and one of McKay's linked machines started to bleed smoke. A power cable snapped free of its moorings and snaked towards Sheppard, spitting sparks. Another unit burst into flame, and a shower of red-hot metal exploded from one of the ceiling compartments.

Sheppard staggered backwards, caught his heel on something and fell heavily. The rods clattered to the floor as he sprawled backwards, cracking his head on a bulkhead, and crumpled to the floor. As abruptly as it had been established, the link severed.

McKay stumbled over to him, waving fronds of smoke away. "Are you OK?"

Sheppard shook his head, groggy. "Yeah, reckon so," he mumbled. His vision was shaky. Or was that the smoke? "Sorry. Guess I blew it."

McKay squatted down beside him, looking at Sheppard's head with some concern. "Well, you certainly produced some fireworks," he said. "That was unexpected. But otherwise I'm pretty happy with the way things worked out."

Sheppard stared. "Happy?" He pushed himself upright, shaking his head to clear his vision. There was a throb in the back of his skull, but he ignored it as he looked over at the McKay's cluster of equipment. Against all his expectations, a series of lights were happily twinkling. There was a faint hum. Systems were operational. There was even a low heat returning to the air around them. "Well, I'll be..."

McKay patted him on the shoulder. That was unusual, the man was clearly pleased with himself. "See? What did I tell you? Genius."

Ronon didn't see his life flash before him. All he felt was frustration. This was a *bad* way to die.

A few more paces, and he saw the shadow of the beast fall over him. He screwed his eyes closed, gritting his teeth and waiting for the lancing of the hooves.

It never came. There was an almighty bellow, rending the air around him, and the pursuit suddenly stopped. Ronon kept going, legs scything through the snow. Only after he'd covered another few meters did he slow, finally turning to see what had happened. His heart was hammering

The White Buffalo was writing in pain, twisting and shaking its head frantically. A *jar'hram* protruded from one of its eyes. Orand let slip a cry of triumph, and the hunters cheered. Ronon bent double, leaning the shaft of the *jar'hram* against his knees, gasping for breath. The cold air made his lungs ache, but he was just glad to be breathing. That had been *too* risky.

But it wasn't over. The buffalo was sent mad by Orand's spear. The bellows became a frenzied trumpeting, and it reared again on its massive hindquarters, waving its head from side to side in agony.

"Fall back!" cried Orand, seeing the danger.

It was too late. Blind to all but its fury and pain, the buffalo crashed back on to four legs and charged headlong at the source of its misery. Orand, now empty-handed, turned to flee. Like Ronon before him, he was too slow, and too near. The Buffalo surged towards him, head low, streaming blood from its sides.

Despite his condition, Ronon stumbled into action again, running back toward the rampaging buffalo. He still had the *jar'hram* in his hands, though he didn't trust a throw. There wasn't time. Orand was just yards away from the slicing, churning hooves, moments from being crushed. All depended on a clean thrust.

Ronon held the *jar'hram* high over his head with both hands. He closed fast. Half of him screamed to retreat — this was the monster than had just nearly killed him. The other half, the warrior half, kept him going. Never leave your comrades behind. That's what he'd learned on Sateda, and the principle didn't change with the planet.

With a cry, he hurled himself into the air, straight at the charging beast. The spear-tip plunged deep into the side of the buffalo. With a sickening lurch, Ronon was torn from his feet. The *jar'hram* broke free, swaying in the air, and he staggered and fell back into the snow. Hurled to the earth again, he had a confused impression of movement. The musk was almost overpowering. Barely knowing what he was doing, he scrambled backwards through the trodden mire frantically, expecting at any moment to feel the crushing weight of the buffalo come down on him. The sound of the animal's death throes was deafening, snow falling in heavy gouts around him, thrown up by the frantic wallowing of the buffalo.

He wiped the slush from his eyes, still scrambling clear. The vast animal had fallen on its side, writhing in agony. *Jar'hram* protruded from its hide in every direction and the snow was dark and thick with blood. Ronon's own spear stuck from its stricken flank, buried deep into the flesh.

Several yards away, Orand regained his feet. His face had the pallor of a man who had stared death in the face too closely. Without saying a word, he pulled a long dagger from his furs. The buffalo seemed no longer capable of gaining its feet. Its bellows sank into long, rumbling cries of distress.

Orand waited for a few moments while the rest of the hunters approached the wounded animal. With effort, Ronon pulled himself to his feet. His vision still swam, but he kept upright, determined not to show weakness in front of the others. Orand walked forward, holding the knife aloft as the rest of the hunting party watched in silence. The only sound was the moan of the endless wind and the increasingly shallow suffering of the buffalo.

Orand approached the huge head of the animal. It had sunk to the ground and was now moving only listlessly. The creature was having trouble breathing, and its flanks shivered as it attempted to suck in the frigid air. Orand positioned himself over its thick neck, and held the knife motionless for a moment. The hunters all bowed their heads. Orand himself seemed to be mouthing a few words under his breath. It looked like he was praying.

Then, in an instant, the knife came down. There was no sound, no cry of distress. The animal died quickly. There was a momentary twitching along its flank, and then it lay still. Orand pulled the knife clear, and withdrew. He wiped the blade carefully in the snow and re-sheathed it.

Ronon felt his body begin to recover. His breathing returned to normal and his vision cleared. He walked over to the Forgotten hunter and Orand came to meet him, smiling broadly. He seized the Satedan in a sudden bear hug, and held him long before releasing him.

"Well fought!" laughed Orand. "That was a mighty blow. I would have died, had you not intervened when you did. You have my thanks."

"No problem," Ronon said, embarrassed by the hunter's effusive praise. "You did the same for me."

Orand turned to look over the huge carcass.

"It fought well," he said, quietly. "We honor the buffalo after death. It sustains us. In its death is our life, and we do not forget it."

The rest of the hunters were gathering together. Each had taken out a long knife.

"There is no time to lose," he said, in a more matter-of-fact voice. "We'll butcher the carcass now. If we leave it too long then the meat will freeze solid. There is a cache nearby which we often use. We'll store the cuts of meat there, and others will come and collect it for storage in the settlement."

"You leave the meat out here?" asked Ronon. "How come it doesn't —"

Then he realized what he was saying. Orand laughed.

"Who would take it?" he said. "No animals but the buffalo can survive out here. And we share everything we have. That is our way."

"Then we'd better get to work," Ronon said, looking at the massive carcass. "Got a spare knife?"

Orand drew a second blade from his furs, gave it to him

and walked over to the carcass. Ronon paused before following him, checking his equipment. His sidearm was unharmed by the experience of being thrown against the ice by an enraged buffalo. He reached for his radio.

It was gone. At some point in the excitement it must have fallen loose. His stomach suddenly tight, Ronon jogged back the way he'd been chased, feeling the muscles in his legs tighten against the cold.

The snow behind the carcass was a bloody mess of slush and ice-crystals. Broken *jar'hram* shafts littered its path. And there, sitting in the middle of them, was his radio. The buffalo's hooves had made short work of it.

Ronon stopped to pick up what was left. The casing fell apart in his hands, spilling fragments of circuit board. Not even McKay could have fixed that.

"Hey, big man!" Orand beckoned him over to the buffalo. "You're wasting that knife."

Ronon dropped the remnants of his radio back into the snow, and trudged toward the butchery. It was a waste of a functioning radio, but that was nothing to get too upset about. They'd be back at the settlement before long. No problem.

As he walked, he looked up at the skies. There were heavy black clouds banked up against the horizon. They looked pretty big.

Nothing to worry about.

CHAPTER SEVEN

WEIR strode down the corridor toward the Operations Center. When she arrived she saw Zelenka and his coterie of scientists hunched over flickering screens. He looked even more disheveled than usual. Weir wondered how much sleep he'd gotten over the past forty-eight hours.

"So what have we got, people?" she said, with deliberate brightness. Zelenka and the others couldn't be allowed to see how much this was affecting her.

Zelenka looked up from his panel. His eyes were red-rimmed, and his face gray. Had he even gone to bed since the Jumper left?

"We're in a better place than we were," he yawned. "But not much."

Stretching in his chair, he managed to pull a little of his crumpled uniform into shape as he climbed to his feet. "We've succeeded in salvaging some equipment from the chamber McKay stumbled into," he said. "That's been a help. These things have been the most interesting of all."

He gestured to a series of objects, each about two feet tall and surrounded by complicated-looking electronics. They looked for all the world like one of McKay's half-baked engineering projects. None of them seemed finished, or even capable of powering-up.

"They're not complete, as you can see," said Zelenka, looking at them with ill-disguised irritation. "But we've learned quite a lot about them. They're remote power-relays — and there are similar mechanisms in the Stargate here."

Weir regarded the semi-complete devices carefully.

"OK, so the Ancients were working on the Stargate tech," she said, trying to sound encouraging. "How does that help us?"

"We've run some simulations of their potential function." Zelenka ran his hand through his hair. "We've made some guesses, cut some corners, and I'm reasonably sure these were designed to be used on the Jumpers themselves."

He pressed a button on the console before him, and a graphical simulation appeared on the monitors. "Here," he said, motioning towards a rolling series of power bars. "When a Jumper enters the Stargate network, the storage and transmission of the energy produces a drain on the system power levels."

As he spoke, the bars dipped a little.

"Normally, the connected Stargates would compensate almost immediately," he went on. "There should never, *never*, be a case of a Jumper materializing within an event horizon. Under normal conditions, it wouldn't even be physically possible — a transiting object is just a stream of mass converted into pure energy."

He pressed a second button, and the display changed again. "In this case, the gates were so far apart that the system wasn't able to adjust. But it seems to me that there was a deliberate partial materialization on this jump. My speculation is that the distance was too great for a standard Stargate node to use, so the system scheduled a 'drop' out of the wormhole, ready for a second leg."

The lines on the computer screen shrank, glowed red, and died. Whether or not Zelenka was right, obviously the numbers on his simulation didn't add up. Beyond that, the readings were opaque. Weir was no one's fool, but wormhole physics had never made much sense to her.

"So it didn't work?" she said.

Zelenka shook his head.

"I believe the Stargate at the other end has not been used for a long time. Possibly hundreds of years. It may have been damaged from other source — perhaps the extreme cold. In any case, our attempt to create the wormhole placed a strain on the fragile system. Even the MALP, which has much less mass and complexity than a loaded Jumper, might have been enough to cause a failure at the other end. It seems likely that this Ancient booster mechanism was needed. Frankly, I'm surprised they got out the other end at all."

A chill passed through her body. "But they did, right? They got out?"

"From what we can tell from the buffer records, yes. We're working with fragments of information here, but something got them out. *How...?* That I don't know."

Questions bubbled up inside, but she kept a lid on them for now.

"When they dropped back into real space," continued Zelenka, "there was no power left in the loop to complete the transit. We know they got through, so Rodney must have found some means of generating a little extra zip."

"Where from?"

Zelenka shrugged. "The only source he had available was within the Jumper itself," he said. "Propulsion systems, life support, etc. The point is, if he used those to get them out of the other end, the ship will be in bad shape. My guess is, it's as dead as the gate."

Weir sighed, and rolled her shoulders slightly to ease their tension. The longer this conversation continued, the worse things seemed to get.

"Right, I'm gonna need some good news now," she said. "Give it your best shot."

Zelenka gave a tired smile, and ran some new figures through the computer simulation.

"The best I can do is this," he said. "We think that these Ancient devices are a means of bolstering the power to maintain wormhole integrity from within a Jumper, without risking a catastrophic drain on resources. Think of them as an extra battery, but one with a specific function. In a normal transit, the process might take fragments of milliseconds."

This time, the bar chart on the computer monitor didn't shrink when the sequence was run. As the power levels fell, there was a boost just when it was needed.

"If *this* was wired into the Jumper's power systems," said Zelenka, watching the dancing figures on his screen carefully, "there would have been enough energy to enable safe passage. That must have been what the Ancients were working on. A method of extending the range of gate travel from within the system. The implications of the research are impressive. Imagine, the intergalactic route could be opened-up without the use of ZPMs — "

"I get it. Does it help us?"

"My hope is yes," said Zelenka. "There might be some way of using the modules we have here to restore the link to Dead End."

Weir frowned. "But I thought we couldn't send anything through the gate? You told me we couldn't re-establish a connection."

"That's right," Zelenka admitted. "At the moment."

Anxiety had already worn her patience thin, and Weir felt it beginning to fray. "Then perhaps we should be working on a way to do that first, rather than — "

"Please!" Zelenka snapped. "What do you think I'm doing here? Or perhaps you have some solutions I've not considered. Do you?"

A shocked silence fell across the operations center. The scientists clustered around Zelenka looked away, awkward and embarrassed; no one spoke to the mission commander like that. For a moment, Weir thought about giving as good back.

She shelved that idea. The man was exhausted. "I'm sorry,

Radek," she said, placing a hand on his shoulder. "This situation is affecting all of us, and you've been working hard. Forgive me, I didn't mean to interfere."

Zelenka drew a deep breath. "No, no, I'm sorry," he said. "It's been a tough puzzle to crack." He looked over at the Ancient devices. "But I feel sure there's something important here. If Rodney were here, he'd agree."

Weir gave his shoulder a reassuring squeeze. "I'm sure he would. And after you've gotten some sleep, you can get back to work on it."

Zelenka looked at her, briefly rebellious. But then the fight left his eyes. He was on his last legs, and he knew it. "Very well," he mumbled. "Just a couple of hours. Then I'm back on it."

"Good," said Weir, looking at him with approval. "I know I can count on you."

Teyla sprang up beside Miruva, instantly alert. She had seen this terror all across the galaxy. The faces of the people around her said one thing: cull. Had the Wraith followed them somehow? She had thought Khost was free of them.

"What is happening?" The hall had dissolved into a mass of fleeing people. The children were screaming, some of their guardians had pushed themselves up against the walls, staring wildly into space as if unseen enemies were in the air in front of them.

"There are Banshees coming!" cried Miruva, ghost-white. "We have to escape!" But she seemed paralyzed by fear and did not move.

Teyla looked around, trying to see what was causing the panic. There was nothing visible in the chamber, but the swishing sound was getting louder. Some of the Forgotten had rushed out into the corridors beyond, others stood still, awaiting their fate.

"This is no good," muttered Teyla. "If there are Wraith here, we at least have to fight. Come with me."

She pulled Miruva close to her, and half-jostled, half-dragged her to the chamber entrance. The girl recovered slightly and started to run alongside her.

"Where are we going?" she said, her voice clipped with anxiety.

"Back to my quarters," said Teyla. "My weapon is there. Whatever these Banshees are, they will regret attacking this place while I was in it."

Miruva looked doubtful, but said nothing. The two of them pushed their way back to Teyla's quarters. The corridors were full of people running in all directions, bereft of a plan. In their fright, they were charging into each other or down dead ends. The swishing rose in volume. It was impossible to tell where it was coming from; it sounded as if it was all around them.

They reached Teyla's room and she grabbed her P90 from under the bed. The cool weight of the submachine gun reassured her, but Miruva looked at the weapon with a horrified expression.

"What's that?"

"Insurance," snapped Teyla. "Tell me what you can. What are the Banshees?"

Miruva whirled around quickly. The swishing had now become painfully loud and cries of distress echoed along the corridors of the settlement. The Forgotten seemed to have lost their sense entirely.

"You can't fight them!" cried Miruva, scampering over to the chamber entrance. "It's no good! They just keep coming!"

Teyla gave up on Miruva and snatched her radio from her shoulder. "John, can you read me?"

Nothing. Just a hiss of static.

"John?"

Whatever else they could do, the Banshees could clearly jam her communication.

Teyla ran to catch Miruva up, her mind racing. Her Wraith-sense remained dead, which was a relief. But the panic sweeping through the Forgotten was infectious. She had to make a conscious effort to control herself. Hefting her P90 purposefully, she followed Miruva into the corridor and scoured the dim recesses of the tunnels for any sign of movement.

"What do they look like?" Teyla hissed. "What are we fighting?"

Miruva turned to face her, eyes wide and staring. "Don't you understand?" she cried. "They look like nothing! You can't fight them! They're Banshees!"

Suddenly, the swishing vanished with a echoing snap. The fires in the hearths flickered and dimmed. Teyla thought she caught sight of an ephemeral shape flitting across her field of vision. She raised her gun, but it was gone. Despite herself, she felt a cold grip of fear around her stomach. How could you fight something you couldn't see?

She spun around, trying to catch a glimpse of what was terrifying the people. There was movement, but it was impossible to see. She had an almost overwhelming urge to spray bullets indiscriminately at the shadows. Only her training and discipline prevented her. Why was she so scared? Screams echoed down the narrow tunnels, heightening the febrile atmosphere. Miruva had fallen to her knees and had her hands over her ears.

"Miruva!" shouted Teyla. "Stand up! I need your—"

But then a shuddering wave of nausea reared up inside her. She felt her vision dim and her head throbbed. Teyla reeled, and felt the P90 slip from her fingers. She fought to retain consciousness, but something was pulling the life out of her.

For a brief moment she thought she saw something. A

face: metallic, cold, severe. It seemed to be leaning over her. There was something familiar about it, something very familiar...

But then the darkness took her. The screams and wails of the Forgotten echoed away and Teyla collapsed. Her last awareness was of Miruva calling her name, but then she fell heavily and knew nothing more.

McKay pushed a series of panels back into place. One of them fizzed and popped back out again. The others stayed where they were and a propulsion sub-system came back online. A bank of lights illuminated, went red, and flashed out again. The system shut down and a sigh shuddered through the engine chamber below.

Rodney scowled. He felt like he was trying to reconstruct the Jumper more or less from scratch. Using novelty tools out of a kindergarten. As soon as one thing went right, another would go wrong. Even for someone with as much faith in his own abilities as he, there were moments when he wondered if he was attempting the impossible. At least the heating was still working. He'd just about managed to take off a top layer of furs.

Sheppard stomped back into the Jumper after a quick recon around the vessel, stamping snow from his boots. "Rodney, I need an sitrep."

Irritated, Rodney put his work down. "I'd go a lot quicker if I could work for five minutes without —" He stopped, catching the anxious look on the Colonel's face. "What is it?"

"Storm coming," said Sheppard. "You don't really want to see it. Sky's pretty black. A few more minutes, then we need to bail."

McKay let slip a despondent groan. The sound was slightly more despairing than he'd intended, but it captured his mood pretty well. "I could use a few more hours," he said. It sometimes seemed like his whole life was spent asking for a few more hours when he only ever ended up being given seconds. Scotty could go eat his heart out.

Sheppard glanced at the open rear doors. The wind was picking up already. He unclipped his radio.

"Ronon? You copy?"

Silence.

"Dammit, Ronon," Sheppard muttered to himself. "I told you to stay in touch."

"Could be the storm," said McKay, looking up from his work.

"Yeah, I figured. Where are we up to with Frankenstein's monster?"

"You're still on that riff, eh?" McKay replied. "Here's the good news: life support's back up. But I'm not sure for how much longer. We've got fairly consistent power and the reserves are recharging. But I'm a long way off getting the drive systems online, and we've got no back-up at all. Another day, perhaps two, and I might be able to give you a working Jumper. But I wouldn't bet the farm on it."

Sheppard frowned. "That's not good."

As if to reinforce his pessimism, suddenly there was a great crack from beneath them. Sheppard staggered and reached for a bulkhead.

The Jumper shifted and came to rest an inch or so lower. There was a echoing sound from far beneath them — it took a long time to die away. Neither McKay nor Sheppard said a word until the noise had faded. They both knew what it meant.

"Uh, should we really have the heating on in here, Rodney?"

McKay felt a twang of irritation, the same feeling he got whenever the non-scientists on the mission tried to tell him his job. "For God's sake, nothing's escaping through the hull of the Jumper," he said. "These things are designed to fly through space, as you might have observed."

Sheppard held up his hands. "OK. My bad. No need to get snitchy." He looked warily at the open rear doors. "But you gotta see the problem. If this ice keeps moving, we're gonna have to think about leaving the Jumper behind."

"*What*?" McKay fixed him with an incredulous stare. "Leave the Jumper and walk home?"

"Gate's on the surface."

McKay rolled his eyes. "Oh, I see," he said, caustically. "We don't need to worry about the fact that the gate's got no power. Because, if getting this thing working is a problem, getting a 10,000 year old experimental Stargate operational will just be a cinch. Ignoring the fact that it's got no DHD and the only means of dialing we have is right here. And, above all, we don't need to worry about materializing in the middle of a wormhole in just a HAZMAT suit and a prayer, because *that never happens, does it*?"

The first flush of anger rose in Sheppard's face. Words began to form in his mouth that began with *Now listen, you little*...

Before he could speak there was another booming crack. This time it came from above, rather than below. The storm was right above them. The Jumper began to sway slightly as the wind outside rose in speed.

"Let's do this another time," Sheppard snapped. "Secure this thing as best you can, we gotta go. Now."

For once, McKay said nothing. There was a time for bickering, and this wasn't it. He scrambled to get the haphazard systems ready for a period of hibernation. Most things responded as he expected them to. Control over the rear door was, predictably, still flaky.

"OK, you should get out of here now," said McKay, grimly.

"I'm going to have to set the rear hatch to close from here, and then try and get out before it shuts. Things are still a bit... basic."

"You want me to handle that?" Sheppard looked doubtful. "You're not exactly quick on your feet."

McKay gave a dry smile. "Thanks, but no thanks. As if you'd know where to start with this stuff."

Sheppard took one look at the morass of wires and electronics tumbling out of the Jumper's internal structure, and the argument seemed to have been made. "OK, but be quick," he said, turning to head out into the gathering storm. "I don't want to have to break you out of this tin can on my own. I left my opener on Atlantis."

The Jumper swayed again. The storm was now howling outside, and McKay could feel the snow thumping against the sides of the vessel. Sheppard leapt out of the Jumper and disappeared at once. As he did so, McKay made a few last-minute adjustments. Then he took a deep breath, got into position and set the door to close.

He scrambled to his feet as quickly as his heavy furs would allow and sped towards the door. As he did so, a gout of crimson smoke escaped from one of the pistons driving the doors. The exit suddenly began to shrink rapidly as the heavy external panel started to slam.

"Oh, sweet quantum fluctuations..." McKay yelled, flinging himself forward.

He managed to get his head and shoulders out of the gap, but the rapidly ascending doors clamped firmly on his heavily-clad waist. He felt the metal grip his body like a pair of very heavy, very uncomfortable calipers.

"John!" he cried, though his voice was swept away by the wind. The Colonel was nowhere to be seen, and the air was rapidly filling with snow and sleet.

McKay wriggled furiously and made some headway. The

door mechanism, still imperfectly powered, was struggling to close properly, With a final heave, he thrust himself out of the grip of the Jumper and on to the snow beyond. Behind him, the door slammed shut. A row of lights flickered briefly and then extinguished. The Jumper was sealed. As long as the ice sheet beneath didn't give way, it would be safe.

Unlike him. Sheppard hadn't been exaggerating about the storm. The entire horizon was dominated by a filthy wall of near-black cloud. The wind screamed around him, throwing snow into the air, and visibility was reducing rapidly. Even within his layers of buffalo hide, McKay shuddered. He'd gotten used to the warmth of the Jumper's internal heating very quickly.

"You OK?" came Sheppard's voice from the blizzard.

For a moment, McKay couldn't see where he was, but then the shape of the Colonel came blundering out of the snow. His furs were encrusted in a layer of ice.

"I am now!" yelled McKay, still shaken by his narrow escape from the Jumper. "Where the hell were you?"

"Trying to spot the route back!" shouted Sheppard over the increasing roar of the wind. "It's this way! Let's go!"

McKay staggered to his feet. He pulled his hood down low, and replaced the leather face guard. Only a few moments into the storm, and he was already chilled to the core. He trudged after Sheppard's silhouette, now just vaguely visible through sheets of whirling snow and ice.

After a few moments walking, the form of the Jumper was lost in a cloud of white and McKay's entire world drifted into a freezing nightmare of shapeless ice. The more he thought about it, the more he hated this planet.

Zelenka half-awoke from a particularly pleasant dream involving a flower meadow in the mountains of the Śnieżnik massif and a very attractive woman called Magdalena.

Dragging himself away from it was really quite painful, especially as the two of them were getting on so well. Strangely, there was an incessant beeping coming from somewhere in the sky. Blearily, he dragged his eyes open, and the spartan interior of his room on Atlantis materialized around him. The alarm clanged irritatingly. With a sigh, Zelenka reached out and silenced it. Magdalena would have to wait.

He lay for a moment in the dark, gathering his strength. Getting out of bed was always difficult, especially when he'd only had two hours of sleep. Then he remembered what he'd been working on.

Zelenka hastily pushed the covers off and pulled some clothes on. A few moments to splash water over his face and soften the worst excesses of his unruly hair, and he was out of his room and striding back towards operations.

When he arrived, most of his team was still at work. They'd been working shifts under his direction and most had got considerably more sleep. Despite that, they looked as crumpled as he. What was it about scientists?

"*Dobrý den, tým,*" he said, as cheerily as he could. His colleagues had gotten used to his Czech 'Hello, team' greetings, and responded with tolerant smiles. "Now, where are we on this?"

One of the modules retrieved from the experimental chamber lay on a table, looking like a dissected carcass. He'd left orders for the modules to be taken apart in the hope that they would discover something useful. A slim chance, but one worth taking.

One of his colleagues, Watson, came forward.

"We've made some progress," he said, looking proud of himself. "Come and look at the module."

The Ancient device had been thoroughly pulled apart. What had initially looked like a monolithic structure had turned out to be a collection of smaller machines, encased

in a thick layer of shielding. Zelenka cast his expert eye
over the detritus. "It looks hastily assembled," he mused.
"I'd say a collection of pre-existing parts. Fair enough. I
was experiment."

Watson nodded. "Like many of the projects from the
last days of the city, it looks like they were in a hurry. The
system is composed of about twelve separate devices, each
connected to each other with some fairly simple logic. I
they'd had more time, this machine could have been half
the size."

Zelenka looked over the components with interest. They
were all standard-looking Ancient constructions: angu-
lar, well-finished, with that esoteric patterning they were
so fond of.

"This might be helpful," Zelenka agreed, noting the way
the various parts seemed to fit together. "If we could just
find a way to get them through the gate to McKay..."

Watson could barely contain his excitement. "Take a
closer look."

Frowning, Zelenka cast his gaze back over the pile of
machinery. For a moment, he couldn't see anything particularly special. Then, as his sleepy brain finally hit full
speed, he saw what Watson was so excited about. "These
are standard Jumper parts!"

One by one, he recognized the pieces of machinery: there
was a plasma transfuser straight out of the main drive system, and a crystal relay matrix that must have come from
the cockpit HUD unit. "Are these all pieces cannibalized
from one of the city's Jumpers?"

"All but one," said Watson. "Apart from the connecting
equipment, there's one component that I've not seen before
No doubt that's the one that does the magic. But we've had
a look at it and it doesn't look that complicated. My guess
is that things were pretty tight when this device was being

designed. They had to use whatever they could lay their hands on. We might be able to reproduce it."

Zelenka clapped the scientist on the shoulder. This was very good news. "Right, this is a start," he said. "Good start. We need to figure out if there's way of reconstructing this thing within a standard Jumper. If we can, then so can they. And that might just bring them home."

"We're on it," Watson said. "There's a Jumper kitted out in the bay, ready for work. It's got the standard issue stuff in it, plus a few things we think Dr McKay would have had with him."

"I'll go to it," said Zelenka. "I want you too, and anyone else you can spare. If we can create one of these units from the material the team will have available, we're half-way towards getting them back."

"That's true." Watson gave him a warning look. "But we've still got no way of communicating with them. And we have no idea how these things work."

Zelenka waved away his concern. He was feeling full of energy, despite his lack of sleep. Once he had something to get his teeth into, there was nothing he liked better than meddling in Ancient technology. "One thing at a time!" he said. "For now, we have a power module to build."

CHAPTER EIGHT

SHEPPARD screwed his eyes up. It was almost impossible to see where he was going, and he was navigating on instinct alone.

"Are we there yet?" shouted McKay. In the howling gale, his yell was not much more audible than a whisper.

"Sure," said Sheppard, hoping he was right. "Any minute now."

"That's what you said ten minutes ago."

"Yeah, well this time I mean it."

He powered on ahead, more relieved than he'd admit when he felt the ground rising beneath his feet. Within a few moments he spotted a dim light up ahead. In the ferocious storm, it looked as faint as candle flame.

"Bingo!" he shouted to McKay. "Let's pick up the pace!"

Easier said than done. Despite his heavy clothing, his limbs already felt heavy and sluggish; the middle of the storm was no place for a man to be, buffalo hide or no, and he could hardly wait to get inside the Forgotten's hidden city.

But when they reached the entrance to the cave complex, the heavy external doors were shut. Light leaked from the cracks in the wood. Sheppard hammered on the weather-worn wooden portal, the dull sound of his banging snatched away by the wind. But there was no answer and the door did not open.

The storm howled in delight, throwing all its terrible might against them, and it was hard to keep his feet even in the lee of the rock face.

"So, you want to fill me in here?" cried McKay, huddled and miserable in the shadow of the rocks. "This party season, or something?"

"Didn't strike me as party people," Sheppard shouted. "I don't like it. Aralen told me these gates were always manned."

He retrieved his P90 from deep within the furs covering him. As he did so, the icy wind wormed its way inside and he gasped from the cold.

"We're not going to last much longer out here!" Sheppard yelled. "Get back!" He raised the gun to fire at the heavy lock. Using a submachine gun to pick a lock was hardly an elegant solution, but the cold was crippling and there weren't many options left.

"Tell me you're not going to do what I think you're going to do…" groaned Rodney.

"Time to knock a little louder. You might want to get clear."

Rodney scampered out of range, back into the fury of the storm. Sheppard took a few paces back, took aim and issued a controlled burst.

The ancient wood around the lock shredded instantly, and the heavy door swung open. From the other side, warm torchlight flooded out on to the snow.

"Typical military," muttered McKay. "See a problem. Shoot at it."

"Got us in, didn't it?" snapped Sheppard, feeling his limbs begin to seize up from the cold. "Now let's find out what the hell happened here."

The two of them staggered through the broken doorway and did their best to close the door behind them. The freedom from the howl of the snow-laced wind was a huge relief — Sheppard found his ears still ringing even after it had been shut out.

"Stay close," he warned, keeping the P90 raised.

McKay, for once, had nothing smart to say. The corridor

was deserted. Even though the torches still burned, there was no sign of movement.

They crept down the tunnel watchfully. As they went, the noise of some commotion echoed up at them from further ahead.

"What's that?" hissed Rodney, starting to look agitated.

The noise got louder. There was the sound of running feet thudding against the rock, shouts of alarm, stuff breaking.

"I dunno, but we're headed right for it."

Sheppard picked up the pace. They turned a corner and walked into a scene of chaos. The hall in front of them was one of the minor audience chambers of the settlement, and it was full of people. Men, women and children staggered aimlessly about, some moaning, others weeping. A few of them saw Sheppard and McKay enter and pointed accusatory fingers.

"Why didn't you stop them?" they cried. Some Forgotten men began to advance on them menacingly, their eyes wild. The transformation from their earlier placid nature could not have been more pronounced.

"Whoa!" said Sheppard, eager to keep the situation from boiling over. "Stop who?"

One of the Forgotten, an older man with graying hair, pointed his finger at Sheppard.

"The Banshees! They came again. The Foremost told us you Ancestors had come to free us from their menace. You lied!"

McKay groaned. "I mean, we *told* him we weren't Ancients," he complained. "What more do we have to do?"

Sheppard raised the muzzle of his gun to the roof. He *really* didn't want to use it in such a confined space, but the mood of the crowd in front of him looked ugly. He'd seen this in Afghanistan, in villages after an atrocity had been committed.

"Now slow down," he warned, looking directly at the old man and holding his gaze. "I've got no idea what you're talking about. How about you explain this, nice and slow?"

Something in Sheppard's voice seemed to cut through the worst of the anger. The crowd wasn't really furious with the two of them. The target of their rage was elsewhere.

"The Banshees came for us again," the man said, bitterly. Wails of despair echoed up from corridors beyond the chamber. "We've been culled."

As the man said 'culled', Sheppard's blood turned to ice. He turned to Rodney.

"I thought..." McKay started.

"Yeah, me too," said Sheppard. His voice was grim. "God, those guys get everywhere."

"And what about...?" McKay started again.

"That too." Sheppard was ahead of him. Teyla had been in the settlement. "Let's go. Find her first, and *then* we'll worry about the Wraith."

Ronon staggered onwards through the blizzard, gritting his teeth against the pain in his legs.

The wind tore across the plains, ripping and buffeting everything in its path. The noise was overwhelming, visibility was down to a few meters, and the snow had begun to pile up in massive drifts. The entire landscape had transformed into an icy hell.

Each member of the team had been given massive cuts of meat to transport. The hunters had brought with them long poles stitched into sheets of leather. These had been quickly arranged to form makeshift sleds, and the now hard-frozen chunks of buffalo carcass had been piled on each one. Much meat had been left behind on the ice, ready to be picked up by a future expedition. The rest, seemingly enough to feed an army, had been loaded on to the sleds. Now each hunter dragged it through the storm, hauling the heavy burden against the crushing power of the wind and the deadening layers of snow at their feet. The going was tough. Very tough.

Ronon couldn't remember a time when he'd been so exhausted. There'd been many occasions when fleeing from the Wraith (or hunting them — it was much the same thing) when he'd gone without food for days and trekked across harsh terrain. But Khost was something else. His lungs labored against the icy air, his fingers and toes had lost sensation, and his exposed cheeks and eyebrows were covered in a painful lattice of ice.

The hunters clustered closely together, taking turns to shoulder the worst of the wind. Ronon could see that many of them were near the end of their strength. All conversation had ceased. The storm had them in its grasp, and it wasn't letting go.

"We close?" Ronon yelled at Orand, who was trudging along by his side.

"Nearly there!" It was hard to read the hunter's expression. Almost his entire face was covered in his leather mask, now encrusted with layers of snow. "This storm's a big one! They've been getting worse!"

Orand sounded worried. Up until now, he had laughed at nearly every challenge Khost had thrown at them. Now it looked as if they might have bitten off more than they could chew. Ronon had been reluctant to question Orand's leadership up until that point, feeling himself a newcomer and not wanting to admit weakness. But it was clear now that the hunt was in danger of becoming their final adventure.

"We've gotta leave this meat!" shouted Ronon. "It's weighing us down!"

Orand paused, panting heavily from the exertion. He looked in two minds. "We'll never find it again! The snow will cover it!"

Ronon looked around at the rest of the party. They had also stopped in their tracks, some leaning heavily forward, hands on their knees.

"You think we have a choice?" he shouted. "Better to lose the meat than lose ourselves!"

For a moment longer, Orand hesitated. But he knew as well as the others that dithering out on the ice-sheets was the surest way to die. "Untie the sleds!" he bellowed. "We'll pile them together and leave a *jar'hram* at the top. I don't want these to be buried forever."

With clear relief, the hunters unhooked the heavy loads from their waistbands and began to haul them into a cairn-shaped pile. The work was slow and difficult, frozen hands slipped and tired legs stumbled. By the time they had finished, the chill in Ronon's bones had set in. They needed shelter, and fast.

"Let's go!" The fear in Orand's voice was palpable.

The party clustered together once more and battled onward through the snow. The absence of the load was a relief, but Ronon was dog-tired. Merely making progress against the inexorable storm was an achievement and the hunters leaned heavily into the wind, fighting against it just as they had done against the buffalo. But they were tiring, the slips became more common and every time one of them stumbled it took longer for them to get back up.

"We're nearly there!" cried Orand, desperately trying to rally the group. But his voice had a hysterical edge to it and the effect was not comforting.

Ronon squared his shoulder to the storm, clenching his fists. He was coming down to the last reserves of strength, but was damned if he was going to give up. As long as there was icy breath in his body he would keep fighting.

Then the world lurched and everything changed. His foot, rather than crunching into a thick layer of snow, plunged deep into the ice beneath. He flailed and immediately sank up to his waist. A sudden wave of panic took over and he cried out in alarm. Hands reached for him, but it was too late. There was the sound of cracking ice, and everything below him seemed to disintegrate.

"Crevasse!" he heard someone shout, but there was nothing he could do. In a frenzied whirl of snow and ice, he plummeted downwards. He frantically tried to protect himself, cradling his arms around his head, but he was thrown in every direction by the tumbling snow. Rock tore at his thick fur hides, and then there was a shuddering crack as he hit something hard. Then everything went black.

CHAPTER NINE

TEYLA was swimming, far out in the warm, balmy ocean. As she swam, schools of tropical fish slid past her, flicking their tails in unison. She smiled with delight and reached out to touch one. As her fingers closed over the darting shape, the water turned cold. She shivered and looked up. A massive storm cloud loomed on the far horizon, lightning lancing down from the skies. The blue waters turned gray, and the waves chopped in the rising wind. Panic seized her and she began to sink. She tried to cry out, but the words were drowned. She went deeper. Colder. Her temples thumped, her lungs ached. She tried to shout again, and this time a strangled sound burst from her lips. She broke the surface again. Ahead of her was the shape, the terrible face that had taken her...

Covered in sweat and shaking, Teyla woke into darkness and silence. She pulled her furs closely round her shoulders, trying to shake off the lingering sense of fear. She had no idea how long she'd been out, or where she was, or what had happened. The feeling of dislocation was oppressive.

Sitting up, she tried to get her bearings. There was very little light, just a faint red glow. Despite the fact she was clearly still underground, the surroundings were not at all like the settlement. The floor and walls were rock, but they'd been finely carved. The surfaces were as smooth as glass, reflecting the ruddy light. The air was clean and tasted wholesome; there was no aroma of buffalo tallow to taint it. Just on the edge of hearing, Teyla thought she could detect a low hum. Somewhere, there was machinery operating.

She looked around her and realized she was surrounded by about a dozen of the Forgotten. Miruva was among them, lying deeply unconscious like the rest. They looked unharmed and all were wearing their own clothes. Some even clutched what they had been working on when the Banshees came: bits of tapestry, bindings for the hunting spears, sewn leather shoes. All of the abductees were women and children. Had the Banshees ignored the men? Or was it just because most of the hunters had been out chasing the White Buffalo?

Teyla felt her equilibrium returning. Whatever had happened had left no obvious effects. She had only the dimmest memory of the Banshee itself. The shape had been insubstantial and hard to pick out. There *was* something familiar about it, but even now she couldn't place it. Just like the dream she had awoken from: a faint memory, confused with other things, impossible to retrieve.

Miruva stirred and Teyla placed a hand on her shoulder. The Forgotten girl gave a frightened moan, then awoke sharply. For an instant she stared into Teyla's eyes, looking terrified, then the fear subsided. Perhaps the bad dreams were all a part of the process.

"Do not fear," said Teyla. "I do not believe we are hurt. We have been taken somewhere, but that appears to be all."

Miruva looked around her, wide-eyed. "I remember the Banshee…"

"What do you remember about it?" Teyla said. "My recollection is unclear."

Miruva paused and then shook her head. "It's so hard. They were coming down the tunnels. You had your weapon, but it seemed to do no good. I can't even remember whether you used it."

Teyla looked around her, hoping against hope that the P90 had come with them. Unsurprisingly, it hadn't. Whoever had abducted them wasn't foolish enough to leave them their weapons.

"What did they look like?" said Teyla. "And why can't I

remember?"

"That is the way with the Banshees," Miruva said. "Whenever they've come before, everything is confused afterwards. We can only recall our fear." She looked down at her lap, ashamed. "I just ran. I cared nothing for anyone but myself."

Teyla shook her head. "I do not believe you were a coward," she mused. "I ran myself, and that is unusual. I suspect that these Banshees have some kind of power over people, a power over their minds. We shall no doubt find out more."

All around them, the remaining Forgotten were beginning to stir. Some of them were very young, and cried out in fear when they awoke.

"Calm yourselves!" ordered Miruva. She didn't speak harshly, but there was a tone of command in her voice. "We must remain in control. We don't know where we are, or when those things might come back. So let's keep quiet."

The Forgotten listened to her, and roused themselves more quietly. The few remaining sleepers were gently awoken, and soon the entire band was fully aware, huddled together like children in the night. Teyla was impressed by Miruva's air of leadership. Not for the first time, she wondered whether the next generation of Forgotten would lead their people more ably than the last.

"Let us take heart," Teyla said, addressing the group. "None of us seem to be hurt. Whatever has taken us here clearly has no immediate desire to harm us. We are also together. I have traveled across many planets, and been in many dangerous situations. Believe me, if we stick together and do not lose hope, we stand every chance of coming safely back to the settlement and being reunited with our loved ones."

The Forgotten looked back at her calmly. The first blush of fear on awaking seemed to have passed. They were refusing panic. This was good.

Teyla turned to Miruva. "We need to find out more about this place," she said. "Without food and water we will soon begin to suffer. I should begin to explore."

"I will come with you," she said. "But what of the others? Some of them are merely children."

Teyla smiled wryly. "Believe it or not, there are some worlds in this galaxy where children are all there are," she said. "But I agree with you. We cannot all go together. The two of us should scout ahead, and return when we have found something of use. Is there someone among this group who can lead in your absence?"

Miruva looked over the huddled band. "Gretta," she said. "Teyla and I are going to explore our surroundings, to see what kind of place we have been taken to. You will stay here and look after the young ones. We will not be long."

A young woman with mouse-brown hair and a sensible look about her nodded in assent. Teyla and Miruva rose. There were walls around them on three sides, but in one direction the chamber simply disappeared into darkness. There was only one way to go.

"Keep close to me," said Teyla, as they started out. The thought of running into the Banshees again was not a pleasant one, but at least she had some degree of martial arts training.

Miruva raised an eyebrow at the condescension. "And you to me," she said. "I know how to look after myself."

Teyla noted the gentle reprimand. "Then we should be well together."

Together, the two women crept forward. After only a few paces, they were lost in shadows.

Sheppard jogged down the passageways of the settlement, McKay in tow. Things were calming down around them. The corridors were still full of grieving Forgotten, but they were less manic. He tried the radio again.

"Teyla," he barked. "You copy?"

Nothing.

"Ronon?" he tried. "Anybody?"

And things had been going so well. Now half his team was missing and out of radio contact, and they were still no closer to getting the Jumper back working.

"This looks familiar," said McKay from behind him.

Sheppard stopped, following Rodney's pointing finger. The problem with the Forgotten dwelling chambers is that they *all* looked the same.

"You may enter, Colonel Sheppard," came a familiar voice from inside.

He ducked under the low doorway, followed by McKay.

Aralen sat in the center of his modest quarters, clearly distraught. A few of his advisors clustered around him, also seated. None of them looked in great shape.

When he saw them enter, a cold smile crossed the old man's features. "So you are safe," he said. "You may sit."

Sheppard didn't feel like sitting. He found himself bursting with questions. While all hell was breaking out across the settlement, he couldn't believe the Foremost was sitting quietly on his own with his council. This thing needed leadership, direction.

"We're fine," he said, staying on his feet. "But what the hell's been going on here? And where's Teyla?"

Aralen looked down at his feet. "I am sorry. Your friend Teyla has been taken. There was nothing we could do."

John felt like he'd been kicked in the stomach. For a moment, he struggled to find the words to respond.

"Taken? What do you mean, *taken*?"

"She is not the first. There are many…"

Sheppard held his hand up. "I don't care about that!" he snapped. "Where's she gone?"

Aralen's face was hollow and Sheppard suddenly realized that all of the Forgotten seemed stricken with loss.

"My daughter was one of those taken," Aralen said. "Just as her mother was before her. So you see, I have as much cause for grief as you. And others of my people have gone. We will never see them again."

"The Wraith," Sheppard breathed.

Aralen looked uncertain. "When you first arrived, you spoke of these Wraith. This term was unfamiliar to our people, but perhaps it signifies the same thing. Perhaps I should have told you of this earlier…"

"Damn straight," Sheppard scowled. "Perhaps you should."

"But we have no means of knowing when they will strike! We always hope they will leave us alone. When you arrived, I thought that perhaps they would no longer dare to come." Aralen shook his head bitterly. "While you were away they swept through the whole place. I have never seen so many of them."

Sheppard clutched the sides of his chair. If there were Wraith here, then things just got a whole lot worse…

"You'd better tell me everything," he said, with a touch of steel in his voice. He didn't like things being concealed from him, and now his team were suffering.

"We call them 'Banshees'," said Aralen. "They have been coming for us more and more. Even as the storms grow worse, so they plague us in greater numbers. At first, the few reports of them sounded like ghost stories. I myself was slow to believe the tales. Perhaps my faith in the Ancestors blinded me. It matters not. None of us question their existence now." He looked up at Sheppard, his eyes imploring. "Truly, has any people had to endure as we have endured?"

Sheppard worked to curb his impatience. He needed to

know about Teyla, but Aralen seemed crushed by Miruva's loss. He had to tread carefully. "I've been on a few planets in my time," he said. "You've got some problems, sure. But I've seen worse."

"What were these… Banshees like?" asked McKay. "Did they come in ships? Wear armor? Did you get a look at their weapons?"

"Ships? No, they are ghosts, flitting between the rocks like a gust of wind. Every attempt to engage with them fails. We never know when they'll come. Sometimes weeks pass with no visitation. Other times they are here for days on end. All we know is that they steal our loved ones away."

McKay looked at Sheppard. "That doesn't sound much like the Wraith to me."

"Except the part about people going missing," John agreed. He turned back to Aralen. "Look, if we're gonna help you, you're gonna have to help us. Can't you fight back?"

"When the Banshees come into the caves, there's panic. It's only once we've recovered ourselves that we're able to take stock. Then we notice the missing ones. They never come back."

"You must see *something*," McKay objected. "I can't believe that in a place like this no one even catches a glimpse of what these things are doing."

"You've never been present during a raid by the Banshees," Aralen said tolerantly, "so your ignorance is forgivable. But, believe me, there is no time to watch. When they come, we all run for our lives. All of us."

Sheppard saw McKay's face redden at the word 'ignorance', and moved quickly to prevent him replying. "Do you have *any* idea what these things want?"

Aralen shook his head.

"No," he said. "If I did, believe me I would tell you. Perhaps there is a link between them and the storms, perhaps not. Whatever the truth, it underlines how much we need the Ancestors. They will listen to our prayers. Whatever you say, Colonel Sheppard, I still believe your coming has something to do with our faith in them."

Sheppard shifted uneasily in his seat. It was never fun being mistaken for emissaries from the gods. You were always liable to disappoint.

"Yeah, well maybe we'll see about that," he said. "Right now we need to figure out a way to do something about these Banshees."

He hefted his P90 and gave Aralen a hard look that said, 'Sitting around on your behind ain't gonna get this sorted'. "Where I come from, we leave *no one* behind," he said, his voice bleak. "I promise you this, Aralen. We're getting Teyla back, and the rest of your people. I don't care how big and scary these monsters are. We're going after them."

Teyla and Miruva crept forward. The light was so low that it was hard to see where they were putting their feet, and the ambient glow seemed to be unevenly distributed. It was relatively strong in the area where they had awoken, but the further they went, the dimmer it got. After some distance, the level surface beneath their feet began to slope downwards. It remained smooth and unblemished, and several times they nearly slipped on its flawless surface. The walls and ceiling were the same. It felt as if they had ended up in a beautifully carved black marble tomb. That wasn't an image that Teyla enjoyed, and she worked to put it out of her mind.

After a while, the faint hum that had been audible in the chamber became more pronounced. The light increased, the size of the corridor grew and openings gaped on either side of them. Just as in the settlement, it was clear that they were in a substantial underground complex.

"Whoever made this must have been highly advanced," whispered Teyla. "To carve the rock in this way requires extensive technology."

"The Ancestors?" Miruva's hope echoed in the corridor, the light gleaming in her eyes.

Teyla dared not answer and they kept walking in silence. Keeping to the central corridor, they continued to descend. After a while, the light grew bright enough that they were easily able to see each other's faces again; it seemed to emanate from the smooth black walls, but it was impossible to see exactly how it was made.

From somewhere ahead there came a low noise, the ceiling rising with each step. Teyla reached out a hand to slow Miruva. "We must approach with caution."

Miruva took a deep breath. "I agree."

They carried on until the corridor turned to the right. Keeping Miruva behind her, Teyla peered around the corner and gasped at the sight before her.

The corridor opened onto a vast hall. The light was much greater and filled the entire space with a dull red glow. Mighty pillars, each three times the width of a person, soared upwards towards the distant rock ceiling. Every surface was the same as before: smooth, dark, and flawless. There was no decoration, no softening of the harshness, just endless, perfect stone. The tiniest noise — their footfalls, their whispered conversation — echoed around the huge emptiness.

Stepping into the hall, Teyla marveled at the engineering required to create such a space in the heart of the living rock. She had seen nothing quite like it in all her travels. Even the subterranean city of the Genii, despite its enormous size, was not quite as impressive. That was a natural cave system which had been appropriated by the people; this bore the look of something created from scratch, honed and carved to perfection.

Miruva looked awe-struck. The silent splendor of the austere hall was mightily impressive. "Who could have created this, on Khost?"

Teyla was going to reply, when a stranger's voice broke in. Suddenly, Teyla realized that there were figures in the shadows, wreathed in darkness.

"Who says you are still on Khost?" The voice was harsh. "You have been taken by the Banshees, and your fate is sealed. This is the Land of the Dead — get used to it, you'll be here forever."

Ronon came round. It felt like he'd been out just a few moments — just a thump on the head, not major trauma. He blinked, watching his surroundings resolve back into focus. He was winded, his head was banging with pain and he saw a whole constellation spin before his eyes. But he was stationary, and alive. That was something.

The cascade of snow around him had ceased. Ronon had come to a halt on solid ground. Apparently solid, anyway. Gingerly, he looked around him. He was on a wide rocky shelf. Cliffs of ice reared up on either side, dark and slick, and the only light was from cracks deep within the glassy surface. Eerily, it glowed blue. For a moment, he thought he'd been transported to a Wraith Hiveship. He shook his head angrily. Now was not the time to hallucinate. The sudden movement send fresh spears of pain shooting behind his eyes.

"Ronon!" An anxious shout drifted down from the gap above. It must have been twenty feet or so. "Can you hear me?"

"I'm OK!" he bellowed back, before realizing that shouting his head off in an unstable ice cave was possibly not the wisest move.

A few moments passed. The chill lay heavy in the crevasse,

but at least Ronon was protected from the searing wind. He shifted slightly, trying to take some pressure off his bruised ribs. As far as he could tell, the rock beneath was solid. In fact, now that the adrenalin was wearing off, he could see how fortunate he'd been. Instead of a yawning chasm to nowhere, the entire floor of the crevasse looked like solid granite. It was hard to make out much detail in the gloom, but it looked as if he'd broken through the ceiling of a cave rather than into the mouth of a bottomless pit.

Something brushed against his cheek. He slapped it away quickly, before realizing it was the end of a cord. The Forgotten made their ropes from strips of leather bound together with worked strands of plains grass. It made for a surprisingly sturdy construction. Before Ronon had time to react, there was a flurry of snow. Orand came down the slender lifeline and landed heavily by his side on the rocky shelf.

"Are you alright?"

"I'm fine," said Ronon, ignoring the throbbing in his ribs and head. "You shouldn't have come down. It's not safe."

Orand cast an expert eye around him. He reached deep into his furs and pulled out a small candle. With a strike of a flint and a deft flick of the wick, the candle lit, throwing a weak light across the subterranean space.

"Interesting," he mused. "This place might just be the safest option we have right now. That storm will kill us if we stay out there much longer."

He swept the candle around, checking the floor of the cave and scrutinizing it carefully.

"This is good," he said. "You're bringing us luck today, Ronon."

"Don't feel much like *good* luck."

Orand tugged on the rope, and the silhouette of a head appeared at the gap above.

"Make sure the rope's secure, and bring the lads down," ordered Orand. "This is a shelter."

The hunters out on the surface hastened to obey. One by one, they slid down the rope. Even in the dim light of the candle, Ronon could see they were in a bad way. All of them limped, and some looked like the extreme cold had bent them double in pain. Eventually, the entire party assembled in the cave. It still wasn't warm, but at least it wasn't lethal.

"You sure about this?" Ronon asked. "That opening doesn't look too secure."

"Relax, big man," Orand said, lighting more candles and passing them around. "If I know anything about this country, this cave will be linked with others. In some places, there are tunnels which go on for miles. Besides, we couldn't have lasted for any time above ground."

Ronon looked around him doubtfully. There were dark recesses ahead. Some of them might well lead deeper into the rock. Going farther into the shadowy recesses of Khost was not something that filled him with enthusiasm.

"You're planning on going down there?"

"Possibly," said Orand. "This chamber looks stable enough to light a small fire. We've got some food, and can melt snow. Unless this storm lasts for long, we can wait it out, but we might have to do some exploring if it's a big one."

The rest of the hunters shuffled further down into the cave. There was room enough for the dozen of them, but not much more. Icy blasts came through the serrated opening, and it was still deathly cold. Getting away from the gap caused by Ronon's descent was in all their interests. Orand moved further down, holding his candle low to show up the uneven floor. Ronon took one last look up, before hauling himself to his feet. He went carefully, feeling for any damage.

He'd been lucky. A few bruised ribs and a headache seemed to be the worst of his injuries. He followed Orand and the others away from the crevasse entrance.

It proved to be a wise move. Seconds after shuffling down into the deeper area of the cave, there was a shuddering crack from above. Part of the hole briefly widened, before a cascade of loose snow slumped down the cliff side.

"Get back!" cried Orand, pushing his men deeper into the cave.

They could barely scramble fast enough. More cracking sounds came echoing down from above and it seemed as if the entire shaft was collapsing. Ronon staggered after Orand, his limbs stiff and unresponsive. More snow and ice tumbled in, dragging the rope after it. There was what felt like a minor tremor, and then the landslide settled.

"Everyone alright?" enquired Orand, his face a bobbing island of light in a sea of darkness. Murmured voices of assent rose out of the shadowy rear of the cave.

Ronon felt his earlier sense of relief evaporate instantly. He looked back, peering at the dark rock against the low light of the candles.

He didn't like what he saw. The cave walls around them seemed perfectly solid and reliable, but that was no longer his chief concern. The jagged gap to the surface, their only means of escape, had just become choked with snow and ice. He didn't need to have the skill of the Forgotten to know that there was no digging through that pile of freezing debris.

They were trapped, stuck under the surface of the planet, and there was no way out.

Sheppard looked down at the floor. McKay stood at his side, doing the same. There, discarded on the stone, lay a P90 and a radio. There were scorch marks around the two items, some other artifacts of Forgotten origin, and nothing else.

Beyond the two of them, people still milled in the corridor, lost in their own concerns. They were still gray-faced, but at least they weren't wailing anymore. Slowly, with difficulty, the settlement was returning to normal.

"That's hers," said Sheppard.

"Well, *of course*," replied McKay. "Unless the Forgotten have learned how to make their own P90s." He gazed at the objects thoughtfully. "Interesting. Did she just drop them before she was taken?"

"Unlikely. She wouldn't have given in without a fight."

"Agreed," said McKay. "So they've got some means of disarming their victims. It doesn't look like Wraith; no one here's been fed on and I don't see any real signs of a struggle."

"I don't see any real signs of *anything*."

Sheppard cast his gaze around the site of the Banshee attack. The remains removed any doubt in his mind that the Banshees were dangerous. Teyla would not have allowed herself to be taken by a mere phantasm.

"There must be something here. Some kind of clue."

McKay stooped down and looked at the scorch-marks. There wasn't much to them, just a random pattern burned into the stone. "OK, let's work with what we've got," he said, brow furrowed in concentration. "These 'Banshees' must be using some kind of teleportation device — there's only one physical way out of the settlement, and we came through it. For that they need power, and we've not seen anything capable of running a teleporter here."

"So they came from off-world."

"Possible. They'd need hyper-drive capable ships to get here — trust me, there's no way anything came through the gate. If they were operating from Khost, it seems unlikely the

Forgotten wouldn't have come across them."

Sheppard felt his frustration rise.

"Dammit!" he snapped, thumping the wall beside him.

McKay rose. "I'm not sure that adds anything to the discussion."

"Well, I'm pissed. Real pissed. We can't go back out, we can't get the Jumper working, we can't use the gate. And I have no clue where Ronon is either."

McKay gave one his rare looks of sympathetic understanding. Being cooped up in the warren of the settlement was frustrating for both of them.

"Look," he said. "Ronon's as tough as that buffalo-slop they keep giving us. If anyone can make it through that storm, he can. And when the gale's over, we can get back to working on the Jumper. That's our best chance of finding both of them."

Sheppard shook his head.

"Negative," he said. "Soon as we can, I'm going out on the ice."

McKay lost his look of sympathetic understanding, and reverted to the more usual unsympathetic exasperation. "You're *kidding* me. John, that's not going to do any good. It'll be like looking for a needle in a Hiveship. A big one."

"Well, what do you expect me to do?" snapped Sheppard. "Sit here twiddling my thumbs while half my team is missing?"

"No, I expect you to help me get the Jumper back online. *Then* we can do something about both of them."

Sheppard started to reply, but the words died in his mouth. Much as he hated to admit it, McKay had a point. There was nothing they could do until the storm blew over. And once it did, their first priority had to be the Jumper. Without its range, a search would most likely be fruitless.

"How close are you to getting the Jumper back on its feet?"

"Always with the impossible questions," said McKay,

shaking his head. "I don't know. Could be a couple of hours, could be much longer. The conditions I'm working under…"

"Yeah, you mentioned it." Sheppard felt torn between a couple of equally bad options. "But you've made your point. When the storm lifts, we'll try to get the Jumper back in the air."

McKay seemed about to launch into another tirade when he realized Sheppard was agreeing with him. "I… oh. Yes, very wise decision. And anyway, I'm probably closer than I think to fixing it."

Sheppard gave him a warning look. "You've got me for a couple of hours, no more," he said. "Then I'm going after Ronon, power or no power. We've been in tight spots before, and this is no different. We've just gotta pull ourselves together, and we'll be back up and running in no time."

But as he spoke the words he wondered whether he really believed them. Something about the cold had seeped into his soul. It was corrosive, it sapped the spirit. And the longer his team was on Khost, the more Sheppard wondered how they were ever going to get home again.

CHAPTER TEN

"SO WHAT do we do now?" Ronon said, not liking the fact he could barely see his own hands in the dark. More candles were quickly lit, but there weren't enough of them to do more than faintly light up the narrow space.

"We can't get back up," said Orand, darkly. "Even if we could shovel all that snow out, we've lost the rope. And anyway, that whole ascent is clearly unstable."

There were murmurings from the hunters behind him. It seemed like every decision that was made brought them into fresh danger.

"You said there would be tunnels to other caves," said Ronon, trying to stay positive.

Orand nodded. "I'd stake my life on it," he said — a poor choice of words. "The rock round here is like a buffalo's heart: full of holes." He raised his candle into the air. The weak light showed up more dark cracks in the rock and ice walls. Some of them were clearly wide enough to walk through. "We've got to pick one of those and see where it leads us."

Ronon cast his eyes over the evil-looking gaps with distaste. However bad it had been on the surface, at least they had been out in the open with the sky over their heads. That was a kind of danger he was used to. Creeping like ants through the narrow tunnels under the ground was an entirely different proposition.

He took a deep breath and tried to push the worst of his fatigue to the back of his mind. He could cope with the aches and the cold. It was the uncertainty that he didn't like.

"OK," he said, firmly. "Let's do it."

Teyla felt her heart miss a beat. The Land of the Dead. A

name which had chilled her since she'd been a child on Athos. Was there any culture in any part of the galaxy that didn't fear the afterlife? Normally, she would have pushed such ridiculous talk from her mind in an instant, but the dark walls, the oppressive silence, the strange red light... As the stranger uttered his words, a part of her believed him and lost hope. It took a few moments for her rational side to reassert itself.

"I am very much alive," she said firmly, trying to convince herself. "As is my friend. Perhaps I will indeed find myself in the promised halls of the Ancestors one day. But not today. You must be mistaken."

The figure standing before her remained in the shadows. Teyla peered into the gloom with difficulty. Who was this man? Was he even human?

"So say all who first arrive here," he said. "But wishing things were different won't change the facts. When have you ever seen a place like this in all Khost? We are on another world. We will never return."

Teyla had to admit the man had a point. No one on Khost had the technology to create such a place. Whoever had made this place, it wasn't the Forgotten.

"I know this feels like the end of the world to you," she said, trying not to offend him. "But you can trust me. I have visited many worlds, and seen many strange things. It is only when we lose hope that we are truly lost. Whatever secret force has brought us here, there will be a way of countering it. There always is."

"I once thought the same thing," he said. "No longer."

The man came forward, and a faint light fell across him. He was tall, built like the Forgotten. It was difficult to make out his features in the gloom, but he seemed human. No vengeful angel, then. And not an Ancestor either, by his demeanor.

"Geran!" exclaimed Miruva.

The man nodded. "When I was a living man, my name was Geran. That past is all but forgotten to me now."

"You were lost three years ago! Are all those taken by the Banshees here?"

"Yes, they are, Miruva," he said. "At first there was a culling every few months. We would wait a long time for more to join us. Then it was every few weeks. Now it is even more frequent. Those that come tell us of the approaching End Times. The land of the living is being destroyed by the creators. Soon enough, all of our people will be taken here, or will perish forever in the ice. You are merely the latest."

Teyla didn't like the use of the word 'culling'. Compared to what the Wraith did to their victims, the Banshees seemed far more benign. At least for now.

"Have you seen the Banshees since they brought you here?" she asked.

Geran shook his head. "They are our jailors, not our tormentors. Some of the younger claim to have seen them from time to time, but, as for myself, I don't believe they live down here with us. They are merely the messengers of the underworld."

Teyla looked at Miruva. She seemed to have recovered some of her composure, but her face was still pale. Perhaps whatever underworld her people believed in did indeed resemble this dark, silent place. As the shock of Geran's arrival had worn off, Teyla was becoming more convinced that it was a highly-advanced remnant of Khost's past. Teleportation was a technology with which she was familiar, even though these people could not have been so acquainted. That meant they were probably still on the planet, although she couldn't discount the possibility they were somewhere off-world. In either case, it was hopeful. If there were beings still capable of using such mechanisms, that offered some chance of solving their predicament.

At that thought, she suddenly recalled the fleeting glimpse of the Banshee. She shuddered slightly. Whatever those things were, it seemed unlikely their motives were purely altruistic.

"Did you come alone?" asked Geran. The grim edge in his voice had begun to recede. Perhaps he greeted all new arrivals in such a manner.

"There are more, back in the tunnels," said Miruva. "We thought it best to explore ahead."

Geran motioned towards two of his companions, and they silently melted into the darkness.

"They will retrieve them," he said. "You needn't fear us: we are Forgotten, just like you. All our squabbles have been put aside now — we must look after one another here."

At that, he looked quizzically at Teyla. "I knew of Miruva before I was taken," he said. "Of you, though, I have no recollection. Which family are you from?"

Teyla returned his gaze flatly. "I am a traveler," she said. "Miruva and her people have given me shelter. I am one of them now."

Geran looked at Miruva, and then back at her. "Strange," he said, suspicion heavy in his voice. "There have not been travelers on Khost for a generation or more."

Teyla found herself unwilling to get into a discussion of her origins, and moved to change the subject. "You say you have been here for three years?" she asked. "How do you sustain yourselves? Where do you get your food?"

Geran looked like he might press his earlier question, but then appeared to relent. "We will show you," he said. "Come with me. If you have any doubt now that this place is indeed the resting place of the dead, you will soon lose it."

The storm blew over far quicker than Sheppard had feared, and the tearing wind seemed to hurl the clouds across the sky. After a frustrating wait cooped up underground, the whole place became a hive of activity as the inhabitants prepared to make use of the break in the weather. No one knew how long it would last, and the people were clearly determined to restore some sense of equilibrium after the Banshee raid.

Sheppard donned his furs and went to find Rodney. The enforced break had at least allowed them to eat something and prepare for the cold again. The morning was not yet over, though they'd lost precious time.

McKay was waiting for him, sitting on the floor of the corridor near the entrance, adjusting some of his instruments and muttering irritably to himself.

"Hey," said Sheppard. "Ready to go back out?"

McKay winced, and struggled to his feet. "Oh yes," he said. "I've just managed to defrost the last of my fingers, so it'll be good to freeze them up again. By the way, were you aware that this place is falling apart?"

"Looks pretty solid to me."

"Well, I guess that's the level of observation I've come to expect. During my only partially successful attempts to warm up, I logged three tremors. *Three.* That's why I came out here. It's frankly a marvel that I'm alive at all, let alone capable of reactivating the Jumper, fixing the Stargate, locating Teyla and Ronon, getting us out again, and... what's next? Oh yes, no doubt we'll be fixing Khost's climatic model so that none of the little children die. Really, I'm very pleased by how things are going."

"Keep it together," warned Sheppard, opening the heavy doors leading out into the wilderness. "I don't need you going all crazy-eyed on me."

"*Crazy-eyed?*"

Sheppard shrugged. "Yeah. You've started looking a little... crazy-eyed."

McKay placed his fingers on his cheek, feeling gently. "You think so? God, that'll be the cold. I mean, my eyes are my best feature. Apart from my hair. And Jeannie always said I had a cute smile. When she was talking to me, that is…"

Sheppard shook his head and walked out into the snow. One day he'd like to meet McKay's sister. The woman deserved a medal.

After the latest storm, the ground was swept clean. Any residual footprints near the settlement entrance had been buried. Just as before, the vista before them was magnificent: sweeping arcs of glittering ice interposed with isolated craggy outcrops, all watched by the insipid sky. It was frightening how quickly the scene could change into one of utter desolation.

"Anyway, I was talking about those tremors," said McKay as they trudged through the snow.

"Don't get jumpy. We can cope with a little jiggling about."

"I had time to take a few readings when I was in the Jumper," said Rodney. "Seismic read-outs. Some basic meteorological scans. Nothing very detailed — nothing was working properly. But I didn't like what I saw."

"Why do I get the feeling I'm not going to like it either?"

"Look, I'm not sure. We've not been here long enough. But the shakes we felt when we arrived? They're getting closer together. And those storms — they're building up to something."

"OK, quit beating about the bush. What're you telling me here?"

McKay shrugged. The gesture was almost entirely absorbed by his thick layers of clothing. "I don't really know yet," he said. "I'll take more readings when I can. But I've got to say it: from what I've seen, this place is falling apart.

The storms, the earth shifting. Something very bad is happening here. It could be coming to a head."

"Why is it that we seem to arrive places just as everything's kicking off?" Sheppard sighed.

"Well, in this case, we've got the whole nine yards. We already knew about storms, ice-shifting, no power, dead Stargate, missing team. You can add earthquakes to the list now."

"Great," said Sheppard, grimacing as the icy wind scoured his exposed skin. "Just great."

Weir forced her attention back to her paperwork with difficulty. There were things that really needed her attention — there were always things that really needed her attention — but it was hard to concentrate on them when she knew there was a team stranded off-world. Just as her weary eyes started scanning the opening lines of a report on food supply in the Athosian settlement, Zelenka's voice crackled over the intercom.

"Dr Weir? I think we've got something. Do you have time?"

"You bet," snapped Elizabeth. She flipped the report into her 'pending' tray, and made her way quickly down to the Jumper bay.

When she arrived, the place was a mess. Cables connected to various diagnostic instruments trailed all over the floor. One of the Jumpers had been moved into the central area, like a patient on a surgeon's table. All of its various panels had been opened or removed and Zelenka's team were crawling over it like blowflies on a wound.

"I see you've been busy," said Weir.

Zelenka looked up and gave her a satisfied smile. His fingers were black with engine oil. Which was odd, because as far as Weir knew, Jumpers didn't use engine oil.

"We have!" he said. "And I think we've done it. If Rodney were here, he'd be proud."

The Czech scientist wiped his grimy hands and took her around to the rear of the Jumper. Within the exposed bay, the scene was even more chaotic than outside the vessel. Most of the internal panels had been pulled open. The equipment inside them had been taken out, mixed-up, and put back again in various configurations. It all looked extremely confused.

"It's possible," he said, gesturing to mass of electronics. "It's really possible. The power module used to negotiate the long link can be constructed using standard Jumper internals. Presumably, this was a design goal of the original project. We should think of the experiment as a way of boosting the Jumper's own systems, rather than a replacement for them. So the team should be able to modify their systems, and augment their vessel for the journey home."

"That's good, Radek," said Weir, trying to keep her voice neutral. It was important not to get carried away. "I thought we couldn't make contact with the gate?"

"Yes, that is still true — at least partly," Zelenka said. "But it's progress, nonetheless. Come."

Weir followed him into the Jumper's open bay. "Assembly process for the module isn't too difficult in itself," he explained, gesturing to a relatively small set of components connected by a cluster of wires. "The problem is ensuring that the Jumper's basic systems remain fully functional in the absence of the instruments needed for the power boost. It can be done, but getting the bypass circuitry right is tricky. It's taken us a while, but we've shown it can be done. I've run a hundred tests on this Jumper. If we could get it through the gate in one piece, I've no doubt that it would be able to travel all the way to Khost."

Weir pursed her lips, impatient to know more but aware

that she had to give Zelenka time to explain his achievement. "Well done, Radek," she said. "This is good work, but…" It felt cruel to puncture his bubble, but it had to be done. "It doesn't solve our main problem. We know how to avoid premature materialization, but we still can't communicate with the team, nor reach them. Unless they somehow stumble on the same conclusion as you, we're as stuck as we were before."

At that, Zelenka shook his head. "I've been looking at the data from the first journey again," he said. "What is clear is that the gate at the far end has been damaged, both by our actions and by its environment. We can't simply fly a second Jumper through the gate to rescue them. The stress of opening a fully-functional wormhole, with all the power demands we'd need, risks irreparable damage being done. However, do you remember when Dr McKay managed to open the intergalactic gate for just a second or two on very low power? When we thought our days on Atlantis were numbered?"

"Of course I do." How could she forget? "But how does it help us?"

Zelenka walked over to a monitor wired into the cannibalized Jumper bay. He pressed a button and streams of data began scrolling down it. "We've managed to put the instructions for enabling the module, plus everything we know about the power systems in the gate route, in a highly compressed data file," he said. "Sending a Jumper through the Stargate might be impossible, but there's a chance there's just enough residual power in the receiving gate to get a short databurst across. Think of it like a ping."

Weir felt her heart jump. With the schematics available to them, the chances of getting the team home were suddenly looking much better. "What kind of a chance?"

Zelenka looked uneasy. "If everything works as I think

it will, McKay will be able to modify his Jumper to make the trip back. If he can find a way to get the Stargate even minimally operational, he'll be able to break the event horizon at that end. Once inside the wormhole, there'll be a critical power failure, just as before. That might damage the gate on Dead End even further as it attempts to compensate, but that's OK, because the Jumper will now have the additional module onboard. It should kick in immediately, giving the craft just enough energy to exit the gate at this end. We'll have destroyed whatever Stargate technology the Ancients were working on, but at least we'll have our people back."

"That's good enough for me," said Weir. "We've got to take the risk."

Zelenka nodded. "It's all ready. Just give the word."

Weir looked back over the chaotic piles of instruments and equipment. It was hard to imagine anyone being able to assemble a workable module of such complexity from a simple set of instructions, and when she imagined the conditions McKay would have to work in, she shuddered. Zelenka's plan was a shot in the dark, but it was the only plan on the table and dithering over it would do no one any good.

"You've got it," she said, her voice betraying none of the doubts in her mind. "Let's go."

Ronon cast a wary eye over his surroundings. All the hunters now carried the little tallow candles; they burned slowly and with a minimum of smoke, but the light was feeble. The ground was uneven and slick with iron-hard sheets of ice. Even the practiced hunters slipped and fell occasionally; Ronon had been on his backside more than once and his body ached from the sudden impacts. They inched along in the dark, trying to ignore the distant sighs and cracks deep within the ice. It was like being buried alive, with just a glimmer of hope to keep you going.

The network of fissures and caves might lead nowhere and this could very well be their grave.

He put the thought to the back of his mind. That kind of speculation could prove fatal. Instead, he concentrated on Orand's optimism. The leader of the hunters seemed unperturbed, confident that the warren of narrow subterranean passages would lead to the surface. Even after an hour of painstaking progress, though, they were no nearer to finding an exit. Ronon's sense of direction had totally abandoned him in the darkness and he hoped that Orand had a better idea of where they were.

Occasionally, a dim blue light filtered down from the ice above and Ronon caught a glimpse of the tiny stalactites encrusting the roof of their strange underground world. The caves were not entirely devoid of life — there were patches of luminous algae on some of the rocks on either side of them — but mostly it was a barren place, shrouded in unremitting darkness and cold.

"How are you doing, big man?" came a whisper from beside him. Orand was there, insubstantial in the shadows.

"No need to worry about me," said Ronon. "I'd rather be here than in that storm."

"Some of these systems go on for miles," Orand said. "But that's a good thing. The longer we keep going, the more likely we are to find a route back up to the surface. If we're lucky, the storm will have blown out. If we're unlucky, we'll have another trek in the wind. I hope we're back soon, though — I'm beginning to get hungry."

The hunter grinned in the dark, and the faint blue light picked out his teeth. Ronon found himself regretting the loss of all that meat, now no doubt frozen solid on the surface. It was unlikely they'd ever see it again.

"Orand!" came a low voice from up ahead. "You should look at this."

They had entered a slightly larger section of cave and the ceiling rose high above them. One of the hunters crouched next to a dark fissure in the wall.

"What is it, Haruev?" said Orand.

At first glance, it looked little different from the many narrow gaps they had clambered through. But Haruev ran a hand along the edge of the rock. "That's not natural." As soon as the man spoke, Ronon saw that he was right. The shape was too regular, too smooth. It looked as if a doorway had been carved into the rock and ice. Even with the candle flames it was difficult to see too much, but there was no mistaking it — the fissure had been manufactured.

Orand stood before the gap for a few moments, thinking. "It must be an abandoned settlement from the old times," he said eventually. "And if it's a settlement, then there must be a way out the far end." He turned to Ronon. "What do you think?"

Ronon shrugged. "Not much choice, I reckon."

"Agreed. Then we go this way."

With a slight hesitation, the hunters began to file through the narrow opening, only to be consumed by the darkness beyond. A bobbing line of little flames was the only evidence of their progress on the other side.

"They're afraid," Ronon observed. "Of the dark?"

"No," said Orand, preparing to squeeze himself through the opening. "Of what lives in the dark."

Saying no more, Orand slipped through the fissure and vanished into the shadow. With a muttered curse, Ronon followed; not for the first time that day, he was glad of the weapon concealed beneath his furs.

Geran led Teyla and Miruva back along the length of the massive hall. His companions fanned out on either side of them, saying nothing. In the dim light, it was certainly possible to imagine them as silent servants of the gods. Even Teyla had to work to keep her imagination from running away with itself. Miruva was more subdued. That was to be expected. To be reunited with colleagues who had been missing for several years was a difficult adjustment, and the bizarre surroundings didn't make it easier. Teyla resolved to keep her skepticism to herself. There would be plenty of time later to investigate what this 'underworld' really was.

Traversing the hall took some time. It seemed to go on forever. Rows of pillars marched away into the darkness on either side of them, glinting dully in the half-light. It was gloomy and silent. Teyla wished she had her sidearm with her, despite its lack of effectiveness against the Banshees. Even a dagger would have been something of a comfort.

"This is the Hall of Arrivals," said Geran as they walked. "At least, that's what we call it. None amongst us knows why it's so big, or why it is kept in darkness the whole time. There are some areas where the shadows are absolute. Many think there are hidden rooms leading from the far walls. If so, then we have no business investigating them."

Teyla found such an attitude disappointing, and made a mental note to come back and have a scout around as soon as she was able. The Forgotten had the unfortunate tendency to accept their fate, which was perhaps the only feature she disliked in their character.

"So the entire... 'underworld' is not as dark as this place?" she asked.

"No," replied Geran. "If it were, we could hardly survive. You asked me about our food supplies. This is the answer you seek."

They had reached the end of the austere hall. The light had been growing slowly as they walked, and now the oppressive red glow gave way to a more healthy, natural illumination. Ahead of them there was a high doorway. There was no mark on it, and it was made from the same smooth dark substance as the rest of the hall.

As they approached the door, Geran pushed it open. Light flooded in and Teyla had to shield her eyes from the glare. It took a few moments to adjust. When she did, she couldn't suppress a gasp of wonder. Miruva, standing beside her, looked rapt.

"Behold," cried Geran. "Sanctuary!"

CHAPTER ELEVEN

AFTER a heavy slog through the ice, Sheppard and McKay approached the Stargate. The edifice stood defiantly in the middle of a wide depression. It was the only structure for miles around that dared poke its head over the bleak horizon. The grounded Jumper was visible about a mile in the distance, now half-buried in piles of snow.

Despite the millennia of ferocious storms the Stargate must have endured, it was barely marked. The Ancients certainly knew how to build things, Sheppard thought. Worryingly, though, he also noticed that it wasn't quite level with the horizon.

He cocked his head. "Hey, you think this thing's leaning over?"

"Possibly," McKay said, looking rather annoyed. "When you get a tremor in the settlement, the Stargate is likely to be affected too."

"Gotta wonder why the Ancients built this thing in earthquake central."

McKay shrugged. "The gate's been here over ten-thousand years. Things change." He squinted up at the Stargate. "But whatever's causing this instability, I don't want to make it worse. If we power the gate up again, even assuming we can figure out how, we risk cracking the ice further. Sending the Stargate into an ice fissure isn't going to get us home any time soon."

McKay turned back to Sheppard. His eyes were rimmed with red. He looked tired. Really tired. The stress of trying to square the circle was clearly getting to him. John regretted his earlier comments about crazy eyes.

"We should press on with the Jumper," McKay said. "One

thing at a time. If we get that working, at least it's a start."

"Right," John said, forcing himself to sound cheerful. "Anything you say."

They turned their backs on the Stargate and trudged the short distance to the downed Jumper. The deep furrows plowed by their chaotic descent had been completely erased by the actions of the wind and the snow. When they came nearer, it looked for all the world as if the spacecraft had simply been deposited on the plain by an absentminded pilot.

Thankfully, it had not been completely buried by the fury of the recent blizzard. The front half of the craft, still more or less completely out of action, was inaccessible, but the rear bay poked up out of the snow as if proud of its elevated status.

Sheppard looked at the damaged craft with a little concern. "Uh, you know you said the door controls weren't working yet?"

"Yeah?" muttered McKay, breaking out his tools.

"Well, how're we gonna get in?"

McKay took what looked like a massive TV remote out of the leather bag he was carrying. "You really think I'd forget about something like that?"

"Seems not. What *is* that?"

"The keys," said McKay, sounding satisfied with himself. "You didn't think I was just twiddling my thumbs while that storm was blowing over, did you? I mean, once you've had your third bowl of buffalo stew and admired your fourteenth charming little tapestry beer-mat, then there's not a lot to do."

That, Sheppard had to admit, was true. "I'm impressed," he said. "Should I say 'open sesame'?"

McKay flicked the controller on with a button press, and brandished it proudly. "If you must, but it won't help."

At the press of a second button, a series of lights switched on along the Jumper's flanks and there was an encouraging whirring from inside the vessel.

"Voilà!" cried McKay, just as alarmingly dark smoke started escaping from one of the starboard plasma vents.

Sheppard kept his voice as mild as possible. "That meant to be happening?"

McKay quickly pressed a series of switches on the controller. A curious stuttering, whining sound came from deep within the Jumper, and it looked for a minute as if the thing was trying to burrow back under the ice. Then there was an audible snap and the smoke belched more strongly. From within the ship came the sound of something electrical expiring and then the whole thing came to a shivering halt. Just as it looked as if the entire ship had been terminally affected, the rear door fell open with a clang.

"See?" said McKay. "It's all fine."

"You know how to reassure a guy," said Sheppard. He glanced up at the sky. His brow furrowed. There was no sign of a fresh storm. Yet.

"Let's get a move on," he said. "We don't know how long we've got."

Weir and Zelenka stood in the Operations Center, looking down at the Stargate. It was dormant, as it had been since Sheppard and the team had last passed through. Concerned faces looked up at Weir from the various consoles in the operations room; it was obvious that they all knew the risks.

"Right, people," said Weir. "Let's get that number dialed." Her heart was pumping strongly, but she retained her habitual cool demeanor. "Doctor Zelenka, ready with that databurst?"

"Got it." He was concentrating furiously on the screen in front in him. "We'll have a split-second, nothing more. When the aperture opens, it's going through."

Weir turned to the gate operator. "You heard him. Open the gate."

The operator keyed in the address and looked over at Zelenka before touching the final symbol. He nodded once, and the last glyph was entered.

Immediately, the Stargate fired up. The vacant surface filled with bubbling energy and an event horizon formed, bursting into life and shimmering with that strange, unnatural glow.

Almost immediately, the lack of power was apparent. The event horizon flickered and the lights around the edge of the Stargate dimmed. The vortex buckled, warped and finally sheered away. There was the faint sound of machinery winding down, and then nothing. The Stargate was as dead as it had been before.

Weir turned to Zelenka urgently. "Well?" The monitors were filling with data and Zelenka's eyes flicked across the rows of numbers and symbols. "We've lost the connection," he said.

"But did it *work*?" she asked. "Did the databurst get through?"

Zelenka looked up, concern etched into his face. "It was sent. Something went through the wormhole. Whether anyone was listening, that I don't know. We can hope."

Weir looked back at the now-silent gate, consumed with an impotent frustration. She had hoped at least for confirmation that the message had been delivered. Without that, the knowledge that they had sent potentially life-saving technology through the wormhole just added an extra layer of uncertainty.

"Yes, we will," she said, half to herself. "We'll just have to hope."

Ronon slipped his gun from his furs. The hunters had become uneasy, and the effect was contagious. The further they went, the darker it got. Surrounded by shadows, it was easy to start getting jumpy.

"What is it?" he hissed to Orand.

"The others sense something," he replied, keeping his voice low. "I can feel it too. It's like when..." He trailed off.

"Like when what?"

"Let's just keep going," said Orand, taking his *jar'hram* from his back and hefting it in his free hand.

They pressed on, heading ever downwards. The rock around them closed in, glazed with ice. Ronon couldn't sense anything. There was nothing but the distant, echoing cracks of the ice and the soft footfalls of the hunters.

Then he heard it.

"What's that?" he said, whirling round and pointing his gun into the darkness behind them.

"What?" said Orand, coming to his side. His eyes were wide with fear.

"Something back there. Like a... whisper."

"Ancestors preserve us..." breathed Orand. "We've got to move faster."

He hissed an order to the hunters, and they started traveling quicker. It wasn't easy — the dark was almost complete, and the rock corridor was uneven and twisting.

"Orand, you're gonna have to tell me what this is about," said Ronon, jogging to keep up.

"Maybe you don't have them on your world," said Orand, pushing the pace further. "They come at random, and you can't fight them. We've lost so many to them." He shot Ronon a worried glance. "They come to cull."

At that, Ronon felt a tremor pass through him. So the Wraith were here.

"*You* might not be able to fight them," he growled, looking about him eagerly, "but I can."

"I don't think—"

Orand was cut short. There was a cry of alarm from up ahead.

"They're here!" came a strangled shout from one of the hunters.

In the narrow confines of the tunnel, all became confusion. The hunters started to run, pushing past one another, stumbling against the rocks.

Ronon whirled round. The swishing sound was getting louder. He couldn't see a thing.

"Stand your ground!" he shouted to the others, but it was too late. Like a startled herd of animals, the hunters were running. They'd become the prey, darting down the tunnels like rabbits. Orand went after them, leaving Ronon alone at the rear.

He tried to make out what had got them so terrified. As their lights disappeared into the gloom it got even harder to make anything out. Keeping his gun raised, he followed them, scouring the dark to see what was going on.

The swishing got louder. He looked over his shoulder. There was something materializing behind him, emitting its own light. It was above him, hard against the roof of the tunnel. For a moment, he thought it was a figure transporting in, but the shape never solidified.

Ronon felt a rush of fear.

That was crazy. Even locked in the middle of a Hiveship, surrounded by his mortal enemies, he hadn't felt that kind of fear. What was getting into him? He flicked the gun setting to 'kill', and the white light flashed along its flank.

He forced himself to stop running and turned to face it. There was a face there, narrow and arrogant, distorted with anger. There were hands outstretched, fingers extended. It rushed toward him, arms grasping. Everything was insubstantial, hard to make out.

He fired off three rounds. The bolts of energy screamed

off, each perfectly aimed. They went straight through the apparition, shattering ice and rock beyond it. The ghost swept towards him.

"OK, *that's* no Wraith," he muttered, turning tail and running after the hunters. As he went, he could feel the apparition's presence coming up behind him. His heart started beating out of control, sweat breaking out across his forehead. He tried to fight it, but the fear built in his throat.

He sped onward, not risking turning. The tunnel continued to plunge down, taking him deeper and deeper into the planet's core. Soon he could see the lights of the hunters again. He spun round quickly and loosed another volley.

Same result. Nothing hit. But this time the apparition responded.

Crackling energy streaked from its ghostly fingers, aimed right for him.

Ronon sprang away from the blast, rolling as he hit the floor. The jagged rocks bit into his flesh, and he staggered as he found his feet again. Something hot had torn right past his shoulder.

He scrambled down the tunnel after the hunters, fear now thick in his throat. Orand was right. They couldn't fight this. Forgetting his training, forgetting his weapon, forgetting the mission, Ronon Dex ran for his life.

"I'm a genius!" cried McKay, enjoying the familiar warm glow of success. It was almost his favorite feeling. His absolute favorite involved Samantha Carter from SGC, and was not something he dwelt on very much these days.

Sheppard looked up wearily. He'd been dismantling, carrying, fixing and testing for what seemed like hours, and McKay even began to feel a little sorry for him.

"That's *great*, Rodney," Sheppard said. "Wanna tell me why?"

McKay favored him with his patent self-satisfied smirk. "Because, my good Colonel, I have restored power to the Jumper."

He picked up a small control panel and entered the command. Lights flickered on along the length of the rear bay. With a further press, the inner bulkhead doors slid open and the dark interior of the cockpit emerged. The windshield was covered with snow, but everything looked in working order.

"I gotta hand it to you," said Sheppard, looking relieved. "You sure know when to pull the rabbit out of the hat."

McKay knew Sheppard didn't usually enjoy paying compliments, but he could see the man was impressed.

McKay flicked a few more switches and a series of secondary systems began to power up. "It'll take a while for everything to get back up to speed," he said. "Some of the damage is irreparable and we'll be a little shaky for a while. I don't reckon we'll get more than a single flight, but we've got enough to get us home." Then a worried frown creased his forehead. "That is, of course, if we can get the Stargate to open. And of course we don't really know what went wrong last time, so we'd have to try and figure that out before making the jump to Atlantis. And if that's not possible, we might still be stuck here. Though of course, we can now get into orbit if we *really* have to, although how much that'll help when we're…"

Sheppard's cold stare silenced him. McKay stopped talking. Military types were never really interested in exploring all the possibilities. They wanted to be told which direction to move, and then allowed to get on with it. The very idea that there might be better alternatives, and that these might be worth considering in some detail, was anathema to them.

"Alright," said McKay. "There are still some things to

iron out. But we're making progress."

"I *love* it when you tell me that," said Sheppard. "Now fire up those sensors. Any sign of Teyla and Ronon?"

McKay frowned and adjusted some of the settings on the panel in front of him.

His euphoria gave way to worry. While absorbed in fixing the primary systems he could briefly forget the bigger picture. But the missing team members were never far from his mind and it had now been hours without word. That was too long. "I'm not getting anything at the moment," he said.

"What's the problem?"

"Power," replied McKay. "And only half the secondary systems are operating. Hang on—I'm getting something. Coming up now... But that can't be right. Can it? Oh, God."

Sheppard hovered at his shoulder. "What can't be right?"

McKay double-checked the readings. It was hard to make things out with any clarity, and the signal was weak. But he wasn't mistaken. "I'm getting some readings from the long-range scanners," he said. "Nothing precise enough to locate Teyla or Ronon, but enough to see what's coming. There are storms closing in on us from every side. Big ones."

Sheppard shrugged. "We *know* the place has storms, Rodney."

McKay adjusted the settings, back and forth, looking for some kind of error. "Yeah, but they were finite. These are joining up together. I don't like the look of them at all. The further you go out, there are no breaks at all." He looked up at John. He could feel the blood draining from his face. "We're in trouble," he said. "I don't think these clouds are going away. Something's happening here, and it's working fast."

Sheppard looked unconvinced, but Rodney could see he was troubled.

"Maybe you've missed something," he said.

McKay nodded, and got back to work. But the image of circling cloud formations, like the eternal storms of Jupiter, wouldn't leave him. He was sure he wasn't wrong. More data would just confirm his suspicions. Their time situation had just got much worse.

Once those fronts closed in, they were never going away.

Teyla and Miruva were standing on a balcony high in a rock wall. Unlike the sheer, polished surfaces in the Hall of Arrivals, this was living stone, uneven and mottled, as if carved that very day. If the Hall had seemed big, then this new chamber was gigantic.

They stood perhaps two-hundred feet up the near rock face on a wide ledge. On either side of them, the level surface continued as far as they could see, a shelf in the otherwise unadorned rock. The roof of the chamber was so far away it was hard to make out and there seemed to be wispy clouds drifting across its surface. But the real shock was how far the space extended before them. Teyla couldn't even see the far end. It was lost in a kind of mist. They were in a huge rectangular clearing in the heart of the earth, several miles wide at least. It looked as if thousands of people could shelter there comfortably and still have room for whatever they could desire.

Once again, she found herself wondering if Geran might actually be right. Who could possibly have manufactured such a vast space?

"Welcome to the underworld," said Geran, sounding a little proud of the theater of the whole thing. Presumably, he'd shown many new arrivals their new home. "This is where we live. And where you will spend the rest of your days."

On the distant floor below, Teyla could see a lush landscape. Fields stretched away for what looked like several miles, their crops green and healthy. Between the neat squares of cultivation, paved lanes ran, connecting small villages. Even from such a height, Teyla could see them bustling with life. Men and women hurried to and fro carrying baskets stuffed with produce. Children ran and laughed amidst the buildings. If this was the afterlife, it could have been a lot worse.

"This looks like… Athos," she breathed, thinking how like her homeworld of old the place seemed. The only difference was the vast rock walls enclosing them on all sides — and the fact there was no sky. Yet, there was light all around them. It was like a world in microcosm.

"Where does the light come from?" asked Miruva, echoing Teyla's thoughts. "I can see solid rock above us."

Geran shook his head. "We do not know," he said. "But every morning the light begins to grow, softly at first, until by noon it is as you see it. When the evening comes, it dims again. At night it is much the same as in the world we left, except there is no moon and there are no stars." He smiled. "And there is no ice, of course. The weather here is temperate. There are seasons, just as in the stories of old, but they are mild. Water wells up from beneath us, and there are many rivers. You probably can't see it from here, but the land becomes wilder as you head further from this place. None of us has explored all the regions of the underworld."

Teyla peered into the distance. It did seem indeed as if the land began to rise. There was the faint outline of forests, cliffs, and even hills.

"How far does it go on for?" she said, entranced by the vision before her.

"A man can walk it in for days," he said. "But eventu-

ally he will come to a barrier. As much as it may seem a
paradise here, eventually the rock encloses us completely.
Make no mistake, traveler. We are imprisoned here. Come,
follow me."

Geran withdrew from the edge of the rock balcony, and
led them along the narrow way to the left. Eventually, they
came across a spiral staircase cut from the rock. The steps
were wide and solid, and every so often there were places
to rest on the descent. Whoever built this place had clearly
kept their prisoners' comfort in mind. Soon they were at
ground level. There was a small gravel clearing in front of
them, before the land began to evolve into the farmland
they'd seen from the balcony. A wide road curved away,
leading to the villages.

"There is a house provided for all of you," said Geran,
matter-of-factly. "We are always building, knowing that new
arrivals will come from time to time. Now that you're here,
the work for the next group will commence."

They walked out into the countryside and as they went
they passed through inhabited villages. Their arrival seemed
to arouse very little curiosity. Presumably, for these people it was a regular occurrence. But then Miruva let slip a
cry of delight.

"Mother!" she shouted.

A women working in one of a fields straightened up and
shaded her eyes. When she caught sight of Miruva, she
dropped her tools and came hastening over. She was a tall
woman with raven hair, tanned and healthy-looking.

"Miruva!" she cried. "My child!"

The women embraced, clutching one another tenderly.
Miruva's face ran with tears. "I thought I'd never see you
again," she stammered. "The Banshees..."

"Hush," said her mother, brushing her hair back from her
brow. "I know. We never need to speak of them."

She pulled herself free from her daughter's arms, and looked at her proudly. "I had half-feared, half-longed-for this day," she said, tears shining in her own eyes. "Part of me wanted you to escape the clutches of the Banshees. The other wanted to see you again. How pretty you've grown!"

They embraced again and soon Miruva's body was shaking with sobs. Teyla looked on silently, uncertain how to react. Though the scene was touching, there was something very strange about all of this. The talk of an afterlife and an underworld was clearly nonsense, but now was probably not the time to press the point. She hung back, wondering what her next move would be.

Geran approached her. "So it is whenever someone new arrives," he said, softly. "They meet their lost family, their lost friends. It takes some of the bitterness away from being trapped here forever. But I suppose, being a 'traveler', you won't have that luxury, will you?"

Teyla looked back at him. The man was studying her suspiciously. This Geran was no fool.

"My friends will come for me," she said, firmly. "Even if I cannot, they will find a way to get us out of here. Have no fear of that."

"Do you really not understand?" asked Geran. "This is not a place that can be reached by normal means. This is the resting place of the Elect. We have fulfilled the demands of the Ancestors. In their wisdom, they pick those who most deserve to escape the endless cold. You cannot choose to come here, anymore than you can choose to leave. Unless, of course, you think you are wiser and stronger than the creators of this place."

Teyla knew she had to be wary here. There was much she didn't understand, and the conviction of Geran was genuine. If she moved too quickly to doubt him, things could get ugly.

"I do not doubt your beliefs," she said. "And I am certainly no wiser or stronger than any of you. But you have seen the terror of the Banshees. And even though you have been granted this place to live in, you cannot be reunited with your families and loved ones. That does not sound like paradise to me. So I for one will not give up on the chance of escape just yet."

Geran didn't look angry or perturbed, but she could see his suspicion remained.

"Like I said, many think such things when they arrive. They are always disappointed. In time they come to see that their life here, with all its blessings, is their true reward for a life well-lived. This is your home now, and no one can reach you."

"You do not know my friends."

Geran made to speak again, but Teyla turned away from him, not wanting to debate it any further. She walked towards Miruva to congratulate her and, as she did so, she wondered if she really believed her own words. Those rock walls looked very thick, and she had no idea how she'd got here. Only time would tell.

Another stream of energy seared past Ronon. He veered to the left, feeling the scorching heat of it as it crackled past his shoulder. It was getting closer, and he was out of ideas.

"This way!" Orand's voice came from the left turn of a fork in the tunnel. Without thinking, Ronon followed the sound. As he swung around the corner he fired off a couple of shots behind him. He knew it wasn't going to do any good, but it wasn't like there was anything else to try either.

Ahead of him, the hunters had stopped running and formed a barrier across the tunnel. They looked terrified, but were holding their ground. All of them carried their *jar'hrams*, as if that would have any effect against such a creature.

"Run!" barked Ronon as he careered towards them. "It ain't gonna stop!"

"We can't outrun it!" cried Orand, raising his spear. "If we die, we'll die like men!"

Ronon could hear the fear in the man's voice. He didn't look like he could stand up to a determined child, let alone a terror-inducing ghost that sent lightning from its fingers.

But he liked the sentiment. He reached the line of hunters and turned to face his enemy. It was only meters behind. As Ronon raised his gun to fire, it swooped down lower. Ronon saw that its outline had become even more indistinct. Its shape seemed to shudder, like a distorted video feed.

He aimed his particle gun right at the center of it, and fired again. The bolts slammed into it, tearing through the diaphanous form. Still it came, raising its fingers to let fly with a fresh lightning strike.

Ronon kept firing.

"This is it," he growled, then gritted his teeth for the impact.

It never came. With a sigh, the image broke up, shimmering out of existence. The fingers faded into shadow, and the swishing died away, echoing down the corridor.

For a moment, the hunters stood motionless, mouths open, waiting for some new trick. No one spoke, no one moved.

The party finally relaxed. Ronon lowered his gun. Only then did he notice how much his hands had been shaking.

"What *was* that thing?" he asked, trying to hide his fear.

Orand's face was pale and shiny with sweat.

"A Banshee," he said. "The curse of our people."

Ronon sank to the ground. All around him, the hunters were doing the same thing. He felt strung out. "You're gonna have to give me more than that."

"They come for us when the storms are bad. No one knows why, nor how to stop them. But I've never seen one down in the tunnels, and I've never seen one do that."

"The lightning act?"

"Yes. Normally, they just come, and then... some of us are gone. We never see how they do it." He looked up at the patch of shadow where the Banshee had been. "I've never seen one stop before. Not before it got what it wanted."

Ronon looked at his gun. Maybe the particle weapon had some effect. If the apparition had been some kind of shielded entity, then it was possible the bolts of energy had drained its power.

"No point sitting here talking about it," he muttered, getting back to his feet. "We gotta keep moving."

Orand nodded. All around them, the hunters did the same. "Agreed," he said. "I don't know what stopped it this time." He looked at Ronon, and his flesh remained pale. "But they'll keep coming until they get us, big man. They don't give up."

"Dammit!" hissed McKay, pulling his fingers back from a fizzing control unit. Things were going slowly. Too slowly. Why was he never given the time he needed?

"Got a fix on them?" asked Sheppard, hovering impatiently beside him.

McKay gave him a blunt stare. "What do you think?"

"Right. That's it. I'm outta here."

McKay thought about protesting, but then reconsidered. He *had* needed Sheppard during the early stages of Jumper reconstruction, but the point where he could help had passed. The scanners would eventually start functioning normally, but right now they were still a mess.

"So what are you going to do?" McKay asked. "Just set off on your own?"

Sheppard shrugged. "I've gotta do *something*," he protested. "I'll get help from the settlement. If you're right about those storms, we're running out of time."

"OK," McKay said, and slid some of the computer panels back into place. "I can manage the rest on my own. It'll probably be quicker in any case."

As Sheppard made to leave, McKay reached down behind a bulkhead and retrieved a bulky handheld instrument.

"Don't go without this," he said. "I've been powering up some of the portable kit. A lot of it was fried when we came through, but I've got this working. It's a proximity meter, like the ones we use on the city. Its range is nothing compared to the instruments here, but it'll give you a fighting chance of finding that needle."

Sheppard took the device. "A haystack scanner," he said. "Better than nothing, I guess."

McKay lowered the rear door. It descended smoothly, he was pleased to note. "Good luck."

"I'll send someone to collect you before sundown," said Sheppard, walking down the rear bay and out into the dazzling snowscape. "Keep your radio close. If you get this thing airborne, come find me."

McKay looked out beyond Sheppard's retreating back to where the icy wastes sat under the colorless sky. He could see the Stargate in the distance, a tiny speck against the otherwise flawless texture of the snow, the sun glinting against it.

Which was odd, since naquadah was not generally reflective.

Then, with a sudden lurch in his stomach, he realized what was happening. "The gate!" he yelled. But the glint had disappeared.

Sheppard looked at him quizzically. "What about it?"

McKay frowned. He could have sworn he'd seen an event horizon open. Granted, the thing was far away, but even so… "Er, maybe not," he said. "Perhaps just an optical illusion."

Sheppard looked at him with some concern. "I think we're all a little short on sleep, Rodney," he said. "Try to spend some quality time with your pillow when you can."

McKay was about to fire off a sarcastic comment when there was a sudden squawk from behind him.

"Oh God, not now…" he moaned, and turned back to the array of electronics in the rear of the bay. If a component was about to fail, he wouldn't be responsible for his actions. He quickly scanned the diagnostic read-outs. "I don't believe it…"

Sheppard ran back up the exit ramp. "What is it?"

"The gate was opened!" McKay looked down the list of data on the screen with mounting disbelief. "We've just had a communication from Atlantis."

Ronon felt his heartbeat return to normal. The fear was over, and the oppressive cold had returned. He kept his gun by his side. Imperfect as it was, it was still his only defense.

The low and winding tunnels were cramping his long limbs. They'd followed the course of the tunnel they'd been driven into by the Banshee, and it was just as long and circuitous as all the rest. Every so often the rock ceiling would rise a little, but it was never enough to allow him to stand at his full height, and the malevolent ice shimmered in the candlelight, mocking their attempts to escape the labyrinth.

Despite himself, he was beginning to lose hope. Dying here would be a bad way to go, locked in a freezing maze of narrow tunnels, far from the sunlight. How long would their bodies lay undisturbed in the ice, before the next band of foolish explorers stumbled across them? It was a ghoulish image.

In the dim candlelight, Orand looked worried. Sensing he was being watched, he glanced over at Ronon.

"I'm sorry, big man," he said. "This was meant to be a hunt like all the others. I've brought you into danger."

Ronon shook his head to dismiss the young man's concern. "I've been in worse places. Got outta them too."

Orand looked over his shoulder, back into the impenetrable darkness of the underground kingdom. "Perhaps we should have tried to ascend the crevasse you came down. I thought — "

"Orand!" The nervous cry came from up ahead, echoing down the narrow tunnel. Ronon raised his gun instinctively, even though it had proved useless against the Banshee earlier. "There's a light."

Ronon turned and saw a slight, almost imperceptible lightening up ahead. At last!

Pushing forward through the ranks of the other hunters, Ronon and Orand arrived at the front of the party. Lapraik was waiting for them.

"There's something up ahead," he said. His voice was a curious mixture of apprehension and relief.

"Let's take a look," said Orand. "Ronon?"

He answered only with a nod and together they walked on, stepping carefully over the treacherous ground. The ceiling was lifting slightly and with every step a faint bluish glow became stronger. After just a few yards, it was even possible to make out the surface of the walls around them without the aid of the candles.

"What's this?" whispered Ronon.

"No idea," Orand said. "Looks like sunlight filtered through ice, but we're a long way down."

They pressed on and the light continued to grow. The

tunnel snaked back on itself a couple of times, and then resolved into a smooth, straight course ahead. Ronon was able to stand up fully for the first time in hours. Despite his fatigue, the chance to stretch his muscles was a massive relief. He began to walk more easily, and the pain in his joints ebbed.

Ahead of them, the blue light had grown fierce. After so long in the perpetual gloom, Ronon's eyes watered as he looked at it. The tunnel plunged steeply toward it, the rock smooth and even — as if it had been worn by running water in the distant past.

"Guess that's where we're going," Ronon said.

Black ice underfoot made the sloping tunnel treacherous. Behind them, several hunters stumbled and slipped, and their muffled curses echoed against the rock and ice. Ronon missed his footing a couple of times, and at one point nearly fell; he was tired, they all were.

"It's a doorway," whispered Orand as they neared the light. Ronon came up alongside him and saw that Orand was right. There was a man-made object in front of them. The significance wasn't lost on the hunters.

Orand turned to Ronon, torn between relief and fear. "We've got to go on," he said. "One way or another, this is the end of our journey."

CHAPTER TWELVE

McKAY frowned as he read. Unbelievably, Atlantis had managed to send something through.

Sheppard stiffened. "Why'd they wait so long?"

There was a lot in the transmission and idiot questions weren't helpful. "Steady. Let me read it already."

McKay scanned a few more lines. This was Zelenka's work. He began to see what was going on. "OK, OK," he said to himself, feeling the pieces of the puzzle begin to slot into place. "Do you remember the big Wraith attack, the one where we thought we were all going to die?"

"Which one?" asked Sheppard.

McKay ignored him. "You'll remember that we didn't have enough power to send real objects through the intergalactic link," he said, his mind working rapidly. "That was purely a power issue: the network was fully intact. Zelenka's done something similar. A databurst. It's just coming across the screen now and the Jumper's storing it in memory."

"Good thing you got it working, then."

"Perfect timing, yes," said McKay. "More importantly, there's some data in here about our predicament. Radek thinks that our nasty little experience in the wormhole was an anomaly caused by a power outage. Apparently, this node within the gate network has some rather intriguing properties. The extreme power demands mean that we can't make it back with a standard Jumper. In fact, we never ought to have attempted it. The fact we got through was more dumb luck that anything else."

Sheppard looked awkward. "Dumb luck, eh?" he said. "Just *how* dumb?"

"Oh, sweet mother of molecules," said McKay. "And I

really hate this. According to Zelenka, the chamber we discovered was a laboratory for some new kind of power module. Without this in place, there's no hope for us getting back."

"Hey, you were gonna hold back on the bad news. Anything on the positive side?"

"Depends on how crazy you think Zelenka is."

"Try me."

"He reckons we can construct a suitable module from equipment on the Jumper. That's what the databurst is: a set of schematics. Apparently, he's managed to make one on Atlantis. Good for him. He'll no doubt want to boast about that when we get back. If there's anything — *anything* — I can't stand, it's arrogance."

"Yeah, I've always liked that about you."

"Anyway," McKay continued, "that potentially solves one of our problems. If we can construct the module, we can get back through the wormhole. In theory. That's the good news."

"There you go again with the *bad* news…"

"If I'm right," said McKay, "and I'm very seldom not, then Zelenka's little databurst will have finished off any residual power in the Stargate. Frankly, having seen it up close, I'm amazed there was anything left in the reserve at all. He must have gambled that we'd be able to make use of his information even without a working gate. I'm not ashamed to admit that I've absolutely no idea how to get enough juice to it again. We know that it can't draw power from the Atlantis end, and I'm guessing that buffalo oil won't quite do the trick."

Sheppard brightened up. "Yeah, but we're getting there, right?" he said. "I find the others, you get this thing working, and we'll be home and dry."

McKay felt a flare of deep-seated irritation. "Hardly,"

he snapped. "Radek couldn't have known this, but half the equipment he's used I already pulled out of their sockets on the way over. He's created this magical module in the Jumper bay with a team of support staff and a whole bank of diagnostic equipment. I'm going to have to do the whole thing with a few rolls of duct-tape and a hair-dryer."

"You brought a hair-dryer?"

"I'm speaking figuratively," said McKay, acidly. "The point is, this doesn't get us home. It doesn't even get us close to home. It just gives me a headache, and a whole lot more work."

As he finished speaking, there was a sudden cracking sound.

"Oh, God..." McKay said, and made for the rear door. Sheppard followed him. The cracking grew in volume, echoing across the ice. McKay scrambled out of the Jumper, Sheppard right behind him; the ground under their feet seemed pretty stable.

"Over there!" Sheppard cried, pointing towards the Stargate.

McKay's first emotion was relief—the Jumper wasn't likely to plunge into a chasm beneath them—but then he went cold.

"The Stargate..." he breathed. "Oh my God. Now we're *totally* screwed."

Sitting in the doorway of a small but immaculate hut, Teyla took a deep draught of the warm drink she had been given and felt its effects immediately. It had a tart fruity flavor and the more she had of it, the more she liked it. The food was similarly good. She had no idea how long she'd been out after the Banshee attack in the settlement, but she did know she had emerged very hungry and thirsty. The food and drink she'd been given had gone a long way to restoring her equilibrium.

The people of the Underworld — which, for want of a better name, Teyla had started to call the Taken — certainly had it good. The produce of the fields was bountiful, and the food the people produced was a welcome change from the endless pots of buffalo stew she had endured while in the settlement on Khost. The hot fruit-juice she had been given was a particular pleasure.

For all the horror engendered by the Banshees, the place to which they took their prey was much more comfortable than their old snow-bound home. Those Forgotten who had been taken seemed content, though somewhat withdrawn and taciturn. Teyla could understand part of their reaction — to be taken away from family and friends against their will was traumatic and, no matter how pleasant their surroundings, they were still at the capricious whim of the Banshees.

"Good morning, Teyla." She was roused from her introspection by Miruva. She had a line of flowers woven into her hair and was dressed in the simple fabric clothes of the others. "How are you feeling?"

Teyla smiled, pleased to see her looking so happy. "I am well," she said. "This is a beautiful place."

Miruva nodded, but looked briefly troubled. "It is," she said. "It is strange, though." She looked down. "My mother... I never thought to see her again. I feel somehow... Forgive me. I shouldn't speak of such things."

"There is nothing to forgive," said Teyla. Miruva's conflicting emotions were plain to see; only a day ago she had believed her mother dead, had grieved for her. "You have a big change to cope with. It will take time for you to adjust, but I am sure that you will feel better in time."

Miruva smiled her thanks. "I'm sure I shall. But you have had much to adjust to as well. How are you feeling?"

"Impatient," said Teyla. "I cannot just sit here and ponder the mystery of our journey here. There is a secret to this place, and even if the others are content to let it lie, I am not."

"What do you mean? For better or worse, we have been taken to the afterlife. We must resign ourselves to it."

Teyla gave her a sharp look. "Come, Miruva," she said. "You are an intelligent woman, you cannot believe that. These people are aging. The children grow older, just as they do on the surface. We are very much alive, but some force has transported us here. We need to find out how, and whether we can get back."

"Back?" Miruva stared. "To Khost? Why would you suggest such a thing? We were dying there, whatever my father may have thought. I don't know whether the Banshees are good or evil, but at least they've taken us away from that terrible place."

"What of your father?" Teyla asked, surprised. "And Orand? You cared for both of them. Do you not want them to join you here?"

"Of course. But the Banshees will bring them. This is our destiny. There is no point fighting against it."

There it was again, that fatalism so common in the Forgotten. Teyla couldn't help but feel disappointed. She had hoped for more from Miruva. "That may be good enough for you," she said, a little more strongly than she'd intended, "but it is not for me. We know nothing of the Banshees or their motives. We could have been brought here for all sorts of reasons, and they may not be good ones. In addition, my team is still out there. We cannot just rest and accept our fate. If there is a way back, I will find it."

Miruva looked a little ashamed. "Of course," she said, though without conviction. "Your destiny is not the same as ours. But where will you start? Some of these people have been here for several years. They've never found the way back."

"They didn't look hard enough," said Teyla. "They believe what they have been told. But there was a way in, so there has to be a way out. I am going, before I get too used to all this comfort. Are you coming with me?"

Miruva looked tortured. "You're going now? But we've only just arrived. It's a lot to ask..."

"I am going. I will wait for you if you need time to make up your mind, but not for long. I will leave before nightfall. You have the choice."

"Before nightfall," said Miruva, clearly locked in thought. She began to turn away. "I will think it over."

"You do that," said Teyla, watching her walk away. In truth, she knew that she didn't need Miruva's help to escape, but she hoped the young woman would come with her. It would show some spark of defiance, give a sign that the Forgotten didn't give into fate whenever they could.

Teyla sighed. Her hopes were not high. But she would wait all the same, just in case.

Sheppard and McKay broke into a run. The gate was some distance away and the snow made the going heavy. McKay felt his heart pounding, and not for the first time found himself wondering whether he should do some more to get in shape. It was getting a little tedious being left behind by grunts all the time. Right after that, he wondered whether running directly towards an ice sheet which was making cracking noises was such a great idea.

Thankfully, the noises abated as they arrived at their destination. The evidence of the tremor was easy to see. The Stargate was now standing at a pronounced angle, fresh cracks had opened up beneath its pedestal, and powder-fine snow was rapidly filling them. Sheppard looked at the off-center gate in dismay.

"This is bad," he said. "*Really* bad."

"Now who's heavy on the bad news?" said McKay, panting heavily. "But I do have to congratulate you on your powers of observation. The correct terminology, as I remarked earlier, is *totally screwed*."

"I dunno," said Sheppard. "I reckon I can squeeze a Jumper through there."

McKay squinted at the Stargate. "If it stays where it is, maybe," he said. "But we can't have any more movement. In fact, I think we ought to get away from it. Now."

The two of them gingerly retreated several meters from the leaning Stargate. Beneath them, the ice felt decidedly shaky.

"It was Radek," mumbled McKay. "If he hadn't sent that databurst through, the gate would still be standing."

"Yeah, and we'd still be stuck wondering how to get home," said Sheppard. "It's not as if it wasn't standing on Jell-O before." He ran his fingers through his hair. "Right, we've gotta use the time we have. I'm going back to the settlement — I've put off a search for Teyla too long."

McKay looked at Sheppard's determinedly hopeful expression and, for once, he bit his tongue. There was no point stating the obvious. But there was no point avoiding it either. The ice was cracking, and it was only a matter of time before the storms closed in for good. At some point they would have to try to escape. If that meant abandoning the Forgotten, or even their team-mates, then that was something they would have to come to terms with.

"OK," said McKay, failing to hide his doubt. "I'll be back at the Jumper when you need me."

The two men stalked off in different directions without saying anything else.

There was nothing else to say.

Artificial night had fallen in Sanctuary. Just as Geran had promised, the diffuse sunlight gradually faded into darkness, leaving a silvery sheen across the pastureland. The

Forgotten retired to their dwelling places, seemingly content with their lot. There were friendly calls across the village before the fires were extinguished. The whole place descended into a comfortable silence.

Teyla found herself strangely reluctant to move from the porch of her own dwelling. After the privations of life on the surface, it was hard to shift her muscles into action and contemplate moving away from Sanctuary. She had no idea how much time has passed since she'd awoken, nor whether the daylight patterns in Sanctuary matched those of Khost. In any case, she wasn't tired. She'd waited long enough. The time had come to get moving again.

Miruva had not come back. That was a disappointment. Teyla had hoped for more from her. Still, she couldn't wait forever. Uncurling her legs from under her, she stood up and began to walk out of the village.

No one was about. Starlight — or what passed for starlight — lit her way. Less than a mile ahead of her loomed the gigantic cliff she had been escorted down by Geran. There were no lights on it, no sign of life. Only the black hole of the balcony, two-hundred feet up, marred the dark surface.

Again, a dim sense of foreboding welled up within her. She admonished herself — such fear was unworthy, just as it had been with the Banshees. Clearly the architects of Sanctuary knew how to manipulate minds as well as matter. She pushed her fears down within her and concentrated on the task at hand.

Leaving the village behind, she began to walk back towards the cliff. The Hall of Arrivals was the obvious place to start looking for a way out. The size of it and its perpetual darkness, meant that any number of portals could be hidden within. She began to plan her journey, trying to remember the route she'd taken from the chamber in which she'd first found herself.

"Traveler."

The voice made her start, and she whirled round. Geran stood on the road. There were others behind him, cloaked as before.

"Geran," said Teyla. "I did not expect to see you here."

The man walked toward her. In the low light, his expression was hard to read.

"Nor I you," he said. "It is not... usual for us to venture out after dark."

Teyla kept her distance from him.

"Oh? Why not?"

"There are certain rules here. They are not onerous. Just designed to make sure that our peace is maintained."

"And who created these... rules?" asked Teyla. Geran came closer, and she began to back up.

"Does that matter? You know the importance of rules. You're a Forgotten, after all." Then a smile spread across Geran's face. It wasn't pleasant. "You *are* a Forgotten, aren't you?"

"I told you. I'm a traveler."

"Where from?"

Teyla stopped backing away. There were many of them, perhaps ten. They spread out, encircling her. A lot to take on, but not impossible. "I do not see what concern that is of yours. You have been very hospitable to me, but now I must go. My friends will be searching for me."

Geran shook his head. "I can't allow that."

"You have no power over me, Geran," warned Teyla. "If I choose to leave, you cannot stop me."

"We'll see about that," snapped Geran, motioning to his men. "Seize her."

But Teyla had already started moving. One man stretched out his hands to grab her. She ducked under them, evading his grasp. Another went for her waist. She grabbed his arm,

pulling it toward her, throwing him down to the ground.
Taken off-guard and off-balance, the man thumped into
the gravel hard.

The others tried to get a hand to her. Teyla weaved her
way through them, aiming precise punches and kicks to
disable without causing permanent injury. All she had to
do was break free of them and make a run for the Hall of
Arrivals. They wouldn't follow her up there.

A man came up towards her, fists balled. His blows
were clumsy, and she darted under his guard with ease.
One jab to the ribcage was all it took and he too was lying
in the dirt.

That gave her the opening she needed. Teyla sprang forward, running between the pursuing hands of two other
men. She twisted free, bursting out from the group and scat-
tering the Forgotten in her wake. She was out.

Almost. Something heavy hit her on the back of the head,
and she staggered. Stars cascaded before her eyes, and she
stumbled to the ground.

She tried to right herself, to maintain a defensive posture, but then she felt her arms clamped roughly behind
her back. Someone pushed her to the ground and she felt
the gravel against her own face.

"Keep her down." Geran's voice was angry. Teyla twisted
her head round, and saw him walking toward her. He had a
line of blood running from his lips. So she'd at least given
him something to think about. "Tie her up," he ordered his
men. "We'll bring her back to the village. There's something
about this one that needs further investigation."

Teyla struggled against her captors, but there were just
too many to shake off.

"You are making a mistake, Geran," she said, the frustration leaking into her voice. "If there is any hope for your
kind on Khost, you must let me go."

Geran squatted down beside her, feeling his jawline gingerly.

"Oh no," he said. "That's not how it's going to be. Don't you remember what I said when you first arrived?" He did his best to smile. "Once you come here, you *never* leave."

CHAPTER THIRTEEN

SHEPPARD stared at Aralen, trying to keep himself calm.
It wasn't easy.

"It's no good," said the old man, shaking his head. "Your
friend Teyla is gone. There's no point in searching."

"Just one guide. C'mon, Aralen — that's all I'm asking
for."

"You would be taking our guides into danger. And if the
storms close on you, you will perish on the ice. It is madness. You are a madman."

"Yeah, well I've been called a whole lot worse than that,"
growled Sheppard. "But I don't have a choice."

Aralen was unresponsive. He seemed to have been trau-
matized by Miruva's disappearance, and had a vacant look
in his eyes. Though Sheppard could sympathize with his
loss, time was short.

"Do you not think we've thought the same, many times?"
the old man said. "We have lost so many people. We have
never succeeded."

"Look, you don't have the gear I have," said Sheppard,
carefully keeping the frustration out of his voice. "I have
a... magic box. It's real good at finding people."

The leader of the Forgotten looked back at him with
mournful eyes. "You don't even know where to start looking."

That, Sheppard had to admit, was true. The only thing
anyone had been able to tell him about the Banshee abduc-
tions was that they never left a trace of their victims behind.
There were no trails, no marks, no clues. Just heading out
on to the ice wasn't much of a plan, but it was the best he'd
been able to come up with.

"Not *quite* true," Sheppard said, trying to make it sound as if he wasn't just making it up on the spot. "I'm gonna head where Ronon and Orand went. I should be able to detect them, even if they're holed up somewhere real inaccessible."

Aralen started to say something, but then shook his head resignedly. He didn't look like he had the energy for the argument.

"So be it," he said. "You will not listen to reason, but I cannot let you travel into the wastes on your own. You'll need a guide. Helmar will take you. I won't have your death on my conscience, too."

A young man came forward. He looked slight and unprepossessing, like most of the Forgotten, but he had a confident manner about him. He extended his hand to Sheppard.

"I am Helmar," he said. "We can leave whenever you wish."

Sheppard returned the handshake. That was all he'd wanted; taking along a local was always a good idea.

"Good to meet you, Helmar," he said. He turned back to Aralen. "I'll be back when I can. And you might wanna look in on Rodney while I'm gone — he can get a little cranky when he's left in sub-zero temperatures."

Aralen didn't smile. "We'll look after your friend," he said. "The laws of hospitality remain strong. While all around us changes, we'll keep a vigil here, tending the hearth until the Ancestors in their wisdom release us from calamity."

"Yeah, you do that," muttered Sheppard, turning away from the Foremost and heading from the chamber. He'd had just about enough of Aralen's passivity. "C'mon Helmar," he said. "We've got us some tracking to do."

"Why are you doing this, Geran?" asked Teyla.

They were alone in one of the dwellings. She was tied

to a chair near the middle of the room; he was standing at
the entrance. The rest of the men had left, some limping
or cradling sprained wrists. It hadn't been easy getting her
into confinement.

"Isn't it obvious? You are not one of us. You threaten the
peace of Sanctuary. This place is only for the Forgotten."

"Then let me go."

"I cannot. I must pray for guidance on what to do with
you. There is no escape from the land of the dead."

Teyla began to realize what this was about. Geran wanted
to believe the myths he had woven about Sanctuary. He
needed to trust that they were true. She was a threat to all
of that.

"Geran, I do not wish to challenge anything you hold dear.
But you have to understand that the people on Khost are
dying. My friends are there too. I *must* get back to them."

Geran drew a little closer. He had a strange expression
on his face. "Do not tell me what I must do here. This is
our realm. I will decide what to do with you in due course.
And *all* options remain open."

Teyla didn't like the sound of that at all. Geran didn't give
her a chance to respond, but turned on his heel and swept
out of the small room. From outside the hut there was the
sound of men standing to attention as he walked by.

Teyla tested her bonds carefully. No obvious weakness
in them. She felt frustration begin to rise up within her.
There was no time for this! She knew how precarious the
team's position was on Khost, and that every minute she
was held in captivity added another layer of difficulty to
the mission. She rocked the chair back and forth, trying to
find some weak link in the cords at her ankles and wrists.
It was pointless. They knew what they were doing.

Then, from outside, there was a thud. Teyla stopped, listening carefully. There was another heavy noise, and what

sounded like a groan.

Miruva slipped through the doorway, rubbing her knuckles. "That hurt more than I thought it would," she said, moving quickly to untie Teyla.

"Miruva! How did you…? I thought you'd told Geran…"

Miruva looked up from her work, a hurt expression on her face. "Geran's been watching you since you arrived, Teyla. I would have come to warn you, but he's had his men watching me too."

She finished loosening the cords and stood up. Teyla rubbed her wrists.

"I am sorry. I should have trusted you." She let slip a rueful smile. "I didn't know you could fight."

Miruva smiled back. "I couldn't. But I'm beginning to think there are lots of things women do just as well as men."

Teyla stood up, feeling the circulation return to her ankles. She had a nasty bump on the back of her head, but was otherwise in good shape. The game was back on.

"Then you'll come with me?" she asked.

Miruva grinned. "Just try and stop me."

Sheppard stole a glance at his young companion. Helmar looked full of beans. That was good. The two of them had been tracking out on the ice for well over an hour, and his eager expression hadn't changed. At least, Sheppard didn't think it had; the facemasks and furs made it hard to tell for sure.

The chat wasn't exactly flowing. Sheppard never sold himself as a conversationalist at the best of times. Breaking the ice — so to speak — with a hunter almost half his age wasn't going to be easy.

"So," he said eventually, searching for the right words. "You like hunting, Helmar?"

Helmar grinned, and nodded vociferously. "Oh, yes!" he beamed. "I'm an expert hunter, one of the best of my age. It'll only be two more winters and I'll be allowed to hunt the buffalo with Orand's team. They're the most honored."

"That's great," said Sheppard, doing his best to sound enthusiastic. "I've, er, done some hunting in my time, too. Mostly ducks, as it happens. A deer. Once. But mostly ducks."

He winced. Really not going well.

"We're not far from where Orand would have gone," continued Helmar, his enthusiasm undimmed by Sheppard's stumbling. "There are caches around here too. If they're holed-up, I'll find them."

"That's great, Helmar. Glad you came along."

He reached inside his deep pocket and retrieved the proximity meter he'd taken from the Jumper. It was a typical McKay hybrid model: Tauri technology grafted on to an Ancient core module. It was behaving a little strangely in the extreme cold, but was functioning well enough.

"Might give this thing a whirl again," he said. "You never know."

Sheppard adjusted the range, activated the locator, and turned a slow three-sixty.

Helmar, who regarded the instrument as a magic item of extreme potency, watched from a respectful distance. "Anything?" he said at length, sounding like he spoke more out of hope than expectation.

Sheppard frowned, trying to interpret the various patterns on the viewfinder. "I dunno," he said. "There's *something* out here, but I can't get the signal to hold."

He altered some of the control parameters and the display switched. Strange flecks danced across the screen. It looked as if the meter was picking up a whole cloud of indistinct shapes, something like human, but much fainter.

"Heap of junk," he muttered, giving up on improving the feed.

He looked northwest, the direction from which the readings were strongest.

"We'd better take a look that way," he said. "Call it a hunch."

Helmar swept his gaze across the flat horizon. His practiced hunter's eyes assessed their chances.

"The weather looks like it'll hold," he said, though not with huge conviction. "The wind can come down strongly here, and quickly. We need to be careful."

They continued for another half hour. The sun was low on the horizon by the time Sheppard called a halt.

"I reckon we should be about right," he said, flicking his hood up and looking around. No change, just endless flat ice-plains.

Helmar nodded and resumed his anxious scanning of the horizon. The few clouds seemed some distance off. Even with a stronger wind, they would take some time to arrive.

Sheppard pulled the meter out and activated it again.

"Here we go," he said to himself, adjusting the controls. "Gotta love these McKay specials."

The screen burst into life. Even before he'd had time to narrow the parameters, the display began to fill with data.

"Holy Moly," breathed Sheppard.

"What is it?" asked Helmar.

Sheppard looked at him, not bothering to hide his bafflement. "You know what?" he said, letting the proximity meter do its work. "I have no idea."

Teyla drew the fabric covering over the entrance to the hut. Two bodies lay beside it, both out cold. Apart from that, the village was silent and empty.

"Did you see any more of Geran's men?" she whispered to Miruva, who shook her head.

Together they crept through the huts and back on to the wide path leading back to the Hall of Arrivals. As they went, Miruva seemed to lose her earlier confidence.

"What if the Banshees discover us?" Miruva asked, sounding much more timid than she had done back on Khost.

"What harm can they do us?" said Teyla. "They have already done their worst by bringing us here."

"As far as you know," said Miruva. "Have you forgotten the terror?"

"We will have to take the risk, Miruva," she said.

Together they walked across the rolling plains and back towards the giant cliff-face. No one followed them out. For the time being at least, they were on their own.

Soon they were at the foot of the spiral staircase. The dark steps were lined by the soft silver starlight. Above them, the rock glistened. All was silent.

After a few steps, Miruva stopped. "I can't go on."

Teyla looked at her carefully. Her face was ashen and her hands trembled.

"Miruva, I am surprised at you," Teyla said. "When we spoke in the settlement, you seemed so full of strength. And now, at the first sign of — "

Teyla stopped herself. She felt the same thing. Even now, the anxiety began to return. It wasn't Miruva's fault.

Teyla took the young woman's shoulder. "Listen to me," she said. "There is some force at work here which affects your mind. I feel it too. You must try and resist it. You are braver than this — I know it. If you give in to the feeling now, you will never escape the Underworld."

Miruva looked back. The fields and crops stretched away under the benign starlight. "I know," she mumbled.

"But…"

"No more hesitation," snapped Teyla, losing patience. "Trust me. We passed through it before. We can pass through it again."

Miruva looked briefly as if she would relent and turn back the way they had come, but under Teyla's gaze a glow of resolve lit in her eyes. She took a deep breath and looked up at the forbidding cliff face. "I can do it," she said. "I must do it."

"*We* will do it," said Teyla, taking her by the hand.

"Is it broken?" asked Helmar, still prudently respectful of the device but keen to see what was going on.

Sheppard frowned and adjusted the settings. "Damn thing's telling me we've hit the bulls-eye."

"And, er, that isn't good?"

"Nope," he said. "According to this work of genius, we should be standing in the middle of several hundred people." He looked around at the empty icescape. "You see any?"

There was absolutely nothing — let alone people — for miles on end. Sheppard studied the display, trying to make sense of the readings. They were very odd-looking. Whereas a human would normally register on the scanner as a green blob of fairly consistent intensity, these readings flitted in and out of existence. Even when they were present, they were hazy and indeterminate.

Against his normal inclination, Sheppard found himself wishing McKay was there. At least the man would have a theory as to what was causing the anomaly. Was it instrumentation failure? Or was he picking something else up?

He tightened the search parameters, narrowing the set of phenomena picked up by the machine. The results remained stubbornly inconclusive.

"Rodney told me he'd *fixed* this," he said, frustration

rising. If his only means of detecting human life-signs was defective, then the whole rescue-mission was near-impossible. There weren't a whole lot of alternative strategies available.

Unwilling to concede defeat, Helmar kept going. "What range does the box have? Perhaps we can try and get closer?"

"Don't you get it, kid?" Sheppard snapped. "This box of junk is telling me we're right in the middle of a crowd of people! Unless they're invisible, or up in the air, or under the…"

As the words left his mouth, realization crashed in like a landslide. He looked at his feet. The snow and ice were as unmarked as ever, just another part of the featureless wastes.

"Gotcha."

Teyla looked over at her companion with satisfaction. Once the two of them had reached the wide rock shelf, Miruva had returned almost to normal. At the higher levels of the stairway the air was clearer, and even Teyla felt her spirits restored. Whatever phenomenon had clouded their judgment, it seemed to be at its strongest in the fields below.

"Do you have any idea what we're looking for?" said Miruva, peering through the entrance to the dark Hall of Arrivals.

"No," said Teyla. "But I am sure that there is something hidden in those shadows. We will just have to look carefully."

They walked into the gloomy chamber. At first it seemed entirely black. Gradually the dim red outline of the columns re-established themselves. If anything, the place looked even more grim and forbidding than the last time they'd been there.

"We know what lies straight ahead," said Teyla. "If there is anything to find, it will be in the shadows along either side. Now we have a choice. What do you think, Miruva? Left or right?"

Miruva, her face in shadow, peered into the gloom. "They're equally unattractive," she said. "But let's go left. For some reason, that feels correct."

Once they had moved away from the starlit outline of the entrance gate, the darkness grew ever more complete. They went slowly, placing their feet with care. Even though the floor was perfectly smooth, the shadow was so all-encompassing that it felt as if they might stride into a bottomless pit at any moment. Though the meager red glow allowed them to negotiate a path through the mighty columns in the dark, it was quickly swallowed by the endless shadows between them.

Several minutes passed. They were like a tiny, mobile island in an immense sea of shadow. Even after their eyes had adjusted, everything was obscured. Miruva fell silent, perhaps troubled by her doubts. Even Teyla felt her limbs stiffen. The effect of the dark was disorienting and she began to feel an odd sense of dislocation.

"This place goes on forever," whispered Miruva, her voice muffled and indistinct.

"It must end soon," said Teyla.

As she spoke, she saw a faint glint ahead. The reflection was weak, and only by moving her head back and forth could she be sure there was something really there. They came to a standstill. Ahead of them was a blank wall, as dark as every other surface in the hall.

Teyla ran her fingers carefully across its smooth cold surface. "We can go no further," she said. "That is something, at least."

Miruva stood alongside her, and pressed her face close

up against the flawless stone. "I can't see a thing," she said. "This is just a blank wall."

Teyla turned to her left and began to walk beside the sheer face, keeping her fingers lightly grazing the surface. "This wall continues for some distance," she said. "I think this may be what we are looking for. Let us follow it for a while."

The silence became ever more oppressive, the darkness ever more threatening. To their left, the dimly-lit columns passed in gloomy files, like an army of frozen giants.

Teyla began to lose heart. The hall was gigantic. If they tried to map out the entire area in the dark it would take them days. For all she knew, they had already passed several exits. It was almost impossible to make anything out.

She began to become despondent. "I think..." A sudden impact on her forehead sent her reeling backwards. She staggered.

"Are you alright?" cried Miruva, groping forward to find her in the dark.

"I am fine," said Teyla. Her forehead smarted, but it was nothing serious. She had walked into a wall, jutting out at right angles from the one she had been following. Easy enough to do in the circumstance, but still embarrassing.

Teyla peered at the obstacle. It was a buttress of some kind, set hard against the wall to her right. It was about five feet across and, for all she could tell, stretched up as far as the hidden ceiling far above them. She ran her fingers over it, testing for any indentation or marking. It was as smooth and featureless as everywhere else.

Just as she was about to give up, light blazed from its surface. The illumination was not severe, but after so long in the dark it brought tears to Teyla's eyes. She stepped back, shielding her face. The light dimmed and resolved into a shape. A symbol had sprung into life on the obsidian buttress, scored in lines of silver.

"By the Ancestors," breathed Miruva, looking at the emerging shape in wonder. "We've found it."

A dozen questions ran through Sheppard's mind at once. This was good. Very good. Probably.

"What d'you know about this place, Helmar?" he asked, seized by a sudden idea. "Anything special about it?"

Helmar shook his head. "We're out on the high plains," he said. "Nothing special that I know of."

Sheppard studied the proximity meter again. "You people live in caves, right?" he said, thinking out-loud. "Makes some sense — it's real cold. But maybe even when it *wasn't* you guys still did it." He started to talk more quickly, warming to the theme. "Maybe there are places down there you've forgotten even existed. Maybe…"

He looked down again, as if by concentrating hard enough he could penetrate the layers of ice and rock to see what lay beneath. If he was right, the signals were coming from a long way down. And if Ancient technology was having trouble penetrating that far, then that meant dense rock.

"You really don't know anything about this place?" he asked. "No scary stories of goblins living under the rock?"

Helmar shifted, uneasy. "I don't know much," he said. "No one pays much attention to stories. Aralen might be able to tell you."

Sheppard frowned; he couldn't imagine the Foremost liking what he had in mind. "Yeah, maybe he would," he said. "But one way or another, we're gonna have to get down there. You know how to mine, right?"

Helmar nodded enthusiastically. "Of course. Even our children know how to use a mallet and ice-axe."

"Just what I wanted to hear," said Sheppard, putting the

life signs detector away. "I like the way this conversation is going."

He glanced at the horizon. The clouds were still some distance off, but they looked like they were building. The window of opportunity was closing.

Helmar squinted at the clouds. "What are we going to do?"

"Get back to the settlement," Sheppard said. "We're gonna need every spare pair of hands you've got, and fast."

McKay placed his pliers down wearily and admired his handiwork. But as soon as he saw the pile of wiring in front if him, his heart sank. It looked ready to fall apart at any moment. Using crude tools on millennia-old Ancient technology was like trying to fix a computer with a flinthead axe. Not impossible, but you'd only want to try it if there was absolutely no alternative.

The module was almost complete. Zelenka's instructions had been frustratingly elliptical in places and the man had clearly not quite realized what conditions McKay would have to work in. It was one thing constructing a complex piece of equipment back on Atlantis, where there were whole banks of computers dedicated to running simulations and pinpointing structural weaknesses. Working in the rear bay of a semi-functional Jumper in the middle of a snowfield was somewhat different.

Still, it could have been worse. The life support was now more or less fully functional, making the environment in the Jumper pretty much as comfortable as it ever was. Fixing delicate control nodes to fragile input actuators was much easier when your fingers didn't feel like frozen sausages. Much of the power to the drive system was restored and it wouldn't be long before the Jumper could take off again.

As for the module itself, that was a complete mystery. It

was impossible to test before the Jumper actually attempted to break the event horizon. He looked across the jury-rigged equipment once again; its shoddy appearance didn't fully reassure him. However, as long as you were prepared to ignore the aesthetics, McKay couldn't see an obvious reason why it *wouldn't* work. It would just take some careful handling, a bit of faith, and a fair slice of luck.

McKay collected his essential equipment together, and shut down the experimental parts of the system. He powered up the long range scanners one last time, hoping against hope to see something different on them. It was just the same. No sign of Teyla or Ronon, just a wall of storm-cloud closing in on them from every direction. He adjusted the range, taking it out to its maximum setting. Mile upon mile of turbulence. It looked terrifying. He flicked off the viewscreen, pulled on his layers of furs again, and stood up stiffly. Hours of work had fused his joints together and he winced as he moved.

"Rodney? You there?" Sheppard's voice crackled over the radio.

McKay picked it up. "Just about. I hope you're enjoying yourself while I slave away here."

"Know what? I am. But we're heading back now."

"Any sign of Teyla or Ronon?"

"Maybe. I'll explain when I get back. How're you getting on?"

McKay didn't look at the pile of electronics again. He really had no faith in it at all. "Excellent," he said. "Well ahead of schedule."

"Good. We'll see you back at the settlement. Sheppard out."

McKay sighed. No 'thanks Rodney', or 'that's amazing Rodney — well done'. As ever, John seemed almost oblivious to how much work he'd had to do just to give them a fighting chance of getting home.

He flicked a switch and the rear door lowered. Immediately the biting air rushed in. McKay hurried outside and quickly sealed the Jumper. Turning his back on it, he began the trudge back to the Forgotten settlement.

CHAPTER FOURTEEN

RONON kept his eyes fixed on the light streaming through the doorway at the far end of the tunnel. It was low and almost perfectly round. Before Ronon could stop him, Orand ducked under the lintel and disappeared. Cursing beneath his breath, Ronon had no choice but to follow. He had to bend double to get under the lip of the rock, but after that he managed to squirm through easily enough. On the far side, surrounded by blue, he gasped with amazement.

They were standing on a shelf of rock about twenty feet wide. On either side of them, the ground fell away and, beyond the chasm, cliffs of unimaginable height reared up. They were at the edge of an abyss, a pit that delved into the very core of the planet.

"By the Ancestors…" breathed Orand, looking at the spectacle in wonder.

Sapphire light bathed the whole scene, spilling down from the distant roof of the vast chamber. Instead of the dark, soulless rock through which they had been creeping, the ceiling of the enormous space was entirely constructed of ice. Light filtered and winked from myriad facets, and massive icicles hung down like diamonds. Ronon was not normally given to flights of aesthetic fancy, but the sight was staggeringly beautiful.

The light was clearly sunlight, albeit filtered through many hundreds of feet of ice, but it was hard to gauge exactly how close to the surface they were — the ceiling itself was several hundred feet above them.

Ronon gingerly approached the edge of the rock shelf, and took a look over. The chasm stretched off into infinity, falling into darkness. There was no escape that way.

The remaining hunters came through the narrow opening, one after another. Soon there were a dozen of them standing on the narrow shelf, mouths open, gaping at the light show in front of them.

"Right," said Ronon, conscious of the need to keep things moving. "What are we going to do now?"

"I guess that's our only option," said Orand, pointing.

At the left hand side of the rock shelf, a thin pier of granite shot out into the void. The blue light caught its edges dimly, but otherwise it was nearly invisible against the bottomless shadow below. Ronon took a good look at it. It was maybe six feet wide, and looked dangerously fragile. It was clearly a bridge of some kind, though it was impossible to see where it led beyond the first few dozen feet. After that, the dim blue haze obscured everything.

"You think it takes us to the other side?" he said, looking toward the unseen far walls doubtfully.

"Where else could it go?" said Orand. Now that the Banshee had gone, some of his earlier lightness of spirit seemed to be returning. He was clearly excited at the prospect of crossing the chasm. "The entrance we saw back there was man-made. This whole place must be the work of our forefathers. I had no idea that we were once capable of things such as this. This was worth a trek under the ice."

Ronon studied him. Extreme tiredness could cause weakness of judgment, and Orand's eyes were dangerously bright. But perhaps the man was just exhilarated. He couldn't blame him for that; they had been through a bad time, and it finally looked like they might be getting somewhere. And it wasn't like they had much choice; they couldn't go back.

"I'll go first," he said by way of an answer.

Orand nodded. "I'll be right behind you."

Teyla looked at the glowing symbol carefully. It was vaguely familiar, though she couldn't remember from where. Miruva had no such trouble.

"That's the symbol you showed me," she said. "Do you remember? In the settlement, in the Hall of Artisans. You said it was of Ancestor design."

As soon as Miruva spoke, Teyla remembered. It did indeed bear the mark of Lantean technology, though she had no idea what it signified. It could be a warning, or an instruction, or maybe even a piece of decoration.

"Be careful," Teyla said, standing back from the shining symbol. It stood at about head height and was a foot or so across. She'd never seen anything similar and was momentarily at a loss for what to do. "We have to think."

"Don't worry," said Miruva, calmly. With the activation of the symbol, her demeanor had changed entirely. The last traces of uncertainty had left and she strode confidently towards the shimmering device. "I know what to do, Teyla. Don't ask me how, but I do. Thank you for bringing me here. This, I am sure, was the will of the Ancestors."

The Forgotten woman placed her hand on the device and it instantly responded. A hissing issued from the base of the buttress and the whole structure sighed, as if air was escaping from ancient valves. A thin line of light appeared at head height and then grew as a door slid smoothly open. There was a room on the far side, lit normally and lined with machinery. A faint hum was audible and lights flickered across consoles mounted in the wall.

"You have the gene," said Teyla, looking at Miruva with fresh eyes. "Of course. It was an activation device used by the Ancestors. Like Sheppard, you have the means to use it."

"So it seems," she said, staring with eagerness at the equipment in the room beyond. "Whatever the reason, I feel like I know how to use these things. It's as if I was born to them. We should go inside."

"Wait!" cried Teyla.

But it was too late. Miruva stepped over the threshold and the familiar swishing started immediately. The lights in the room flickered and a terrible feeling of dread surged through Teyla's body. It was all she could do not to run, heedless, back into the endless dark. She panicked, loathe to enter the chamber, but just as reluctant to leave Miruva on her own.

Then they came, sweeping down like vultures. Teyla caught a glimpse of one as it swooped: a haughty, severe face, fingers like talons. A high-pitched shriek echoed from the walls. Teyla backed-up frantically, her heart hammering with terror. How did they generate this sense of fear? She had no idea. All she knew was that they were in the room, and they were terrible. She tried to cover her face, but she could still see them between her fingers. They advanced without remorse and Teyla knew only despair.

They had broken the seal, they had tried to breach the Underworld. And the Banshees had come for them.

After his return, news of Sheppard's discovery spread quickly. Even as the long Khost day was drawing to a close, and the shadows on the ice were lengthening, many of the Forgotten clustered into the assembly hall to hear what he had to say. The whole settlement was roused. Extra fires were lit and their orange flames leapt high up the walls, throwing long barred shadows across the rough-cut rock.

Aralen and his advisors sat on a row of low chairs on a dais in front of the crowd. All of the ruling council were men, and all of them were old; Sheppard knew exactly what he'd be up against. He looked over his shoulder at the crowds. He saw McKay's face amongst them. That was a relief — at least he wasn't stuck in the Jumper. Rodney gave him an encouraging wave.

Then John turned back to the council.

"Colonel Sheppard." Aralen's voice dripped like melting ice from the dais. "You went looking for the missing members of your party, and yet you have come back alone. What is it you have to say?"

Sheppard cleared his throat before speaking. Diplomacy wasn't really his thing, but if he was going to do what needed to be done then he'd need the support of the ruling council.

"Look, I'm no politician like you guys," he said, "so I'll get straight to the point. Thing is, I did find the missing members of my team. In fact, I reckon I found more than that. You've lost hundreds of your people to these Banshees. But they're less than two hours' march away. They're underground, right here on Khost."

A murmur rippled across the crowd behind him, quickly silenced by a severe look from Aralen. The whispers died away.

"Impossible," Aralen objected. "There are caves all over our land. We know them all. None have ever been found there."

Sheppard held up the proximity meter. "Well, not according to this," he said, hoping that the obvious Ancient design would impress Aralen. "I used it to find where they were. It's absolutely foolproof."

"Actually, that's not *entirely* correct," came McKay's voice from the crowd. "Its harmonic spectrum is only about ninety-two per cent efficient, but that's probably due to imperfect connections with the viewfinder technology which we've grafted…"

"Rodney!" A poisonous look from Sheppard halted his explanation.

McKay shrunk back into his place. "But, er, to all intents and purposes it is very reliable. Yes, you can definitely rely on it. Absolutely."

Sheppard turned back to Aralen. "I used it to find my team," he explained. "If they were sheltering in one of those caches, the meter should've picked them up. It didn't. But there was something else. Aralen, your people are trapped underground. That's where they go. And we need to get them back."

A wave of shock rippled around the hall. It took a few moments for the elders to restore order.

"What madness is this?" hissed Aralen, his irritation turning to disbelief. "No one could survive that far under the ice. Even we need to surface to hunt for food and fuel. If we couldn't get out, we'd have died years ago. You must be mistaken."

"Hey, I know what it sounds like. But I know what I saw."

Aralen's face tightened "What is to say that you haven't simply uncovered the origin of the predators that haunt us?"

"Look, trust me, I don't want to disturb a nest of Banshees either. But we have to check this out."

Sheppard half-turned to face the crowd of people listening to the debate. Without exception they were concentrating on his words, their dark eyes glistening in the firelight. Many of them looked as tired as he did, exhausted by the increasingly hard pace of life. A glimmer of hope, however slight, was what they needed.

"Suppose we do walk into a bunch of Banshees? So what? They can come and get you here anyway. I was always told to take the fight to the enemy."

There were low mutters of assent from around the hall. Aralen clutched the arms of his chair, sensing he was losing the support of the assembled gathering. "This is dangerous talk!" he cried. "If the Ancestors had meant us to know of this hidden place, they would have shown us the way. If it is closed to us, what business have we there?"

"But it *isn't*," Sheppard insisted. "The one skill you people still have is excavation. Send a team of your best guys out on the ice and they'll find a way down. You can do it. You *must* do it."

Aralen smiled coldly. "Have you have moved from being our guest, Colonel Sheppard, to being our master? Do not forget that I am Foremost among the Forgotten."

Sheppard stopped in his tracks. This was dangerous. He needed to keep them on side. Before he could speak again, though, Helmar stood up.

"With respect, Foremost," he said, clearly nervous, "Colonel Sheppard is not asking the impossible. There are fissures in that area which some of us know. We've mined there before, looking for caches and future sites for new settlements. It won't be easy, but we might be able to extend some of those old tunnels. If we'd only known there were people there, we might have kept going before."

Aralen turned his hard stare on the young hunter. "And I suppose you now know more than your elders about such matters, do you?" He was getting angry. "Don't presume to tell me about the feasibility of this plan."

Helmar turned ashen, but stood his ground. "I will never have your knowledge and experience, Foremost," he said. "But things are changing. The planet is changing. If we don't look for new solutions to our problems, then we will surely die."

As Helmar spoke, Sheppard turned to look at the crowd in the chamber. Some of the younger members were excited at Helmar's words; some of the older ones were scandalized.

"Now that we know there are people alive under the ice," Helmar continued, his voice steady, "We have no choice but to investigate. If we are successful, and we discover how they're able to live so far below the rock, we may even find an answer to our own predicament. So I'm in favor of Colonel Sheppard's plan. It can be done."

Sheppard looked back at Aralen. The old man was staring in shock. Sheppard wondered whether any of the community had ever dared to defy him so openly. The hall remained as silent as a tomb. All eyes were fixed on Aralen. For a few moments, it looked as if no one would dare to speak. But then one of the other advisors of the Forgotten, an ancient-looking man with ivory hair and leathery skin, spoke up.

"For years we have dreamed of the return of the lost ones," he said, his voice shaking. "Now comes this news. We have prayed to the Ancestors for a sign. Is this what we have been waiting for?"

Aralen shot the man a startled look. "You too, Rogel?" he asked. "You believe in this plan?"

The advisor shrugged. "I no longer know what to believe. Visitors arrive amongst us after so many years of nothing. But can we afford to ignore this opportunity, Aralen? When we were young men, full of life, would we have done so? Have we really grown so old?"

That seemed to stop the Foremost dead. He briefly looked lost, as if trying to summon memories of some other life, long ago lost.

After a few moments, the old man collected himself, his features forming into something like resolution. "So be it," he said. "The torch passes from one generation to the next. They have had enough of my wisdom and we must hope that whoever comes after me will prove equal to the challenge."

Muffled whispers of consternation passed around the hall, broken only when Aralen lifted his voice. "Do what you need to prepare," he said, sharply. "I counsel against it: no good can come of tampering with the ways of the Ancestors. But your minds are clearly made up. Never shall it be said that I imposed my will against the wishes of the Forgotten."

Helmar looked at Sheppard, surprised that his defiance had worked. John smiled, then turned back to Aralen.

"Look, no one's changing anything round here," he said. "Least of all me. We just need to find out what's going on down there."

Aralen bowed his head in acknowledgement. "Very well," he said. "You may leave as soon as you can. And may the Ancestors be with you." He looked tired and anxious. "A storm is coming, though, Colonel Sheppard. I can feel it. Work quickly, if you must do this thing, for when it comes it will be terrible."

Teyla cowered against the wall. All she wanted to do was crawl away — escape, hide, flee. Deep down, she knew such an attitude was shameful, that she should stand up and fight, but the fear was overpowering. She pushed herself hard against the smooth steel wall, feeling the metal grate against her spine. There was nothing she could do, nowhere she could go.

The Banshees had found them.

Then, almost as soon as it had started, the dreadful fear evaporated. It was like a switch being flicked. Gingerly, she opened her eyes. A spectral figure hovered in front of her, but she wasn't afraid of it. The creature looked extremely strange: long, flowing translucent robes, long white hair, a thin face with mournful eyes. It stayed where it was, gazing at her impassively.

Teyla looked around for Miruva. The young woman was standing calmly, staring at the Banshee with an expression of benign interest. She didn't seem to have been affected at all.

"Miruva!" cried Teyla, still shaken. "What is happening? Why does it not attack?"

"Because it does as I command," Miruva said, as if it

were the most obvious thing in the world. "I don't think you fully understand my power, Teyla."

Teyla felt a sudden pang of anxiety in the pit of her stomach. There was something odd about Miruva. The diffident, sweet girl she had known in the settlement seemed to have been replaced by a cold, assured woman. Was she somehow in league with the Banshees? Was she being controlled by them?

Miruva laughed, and the fantasy was extinguished. Her smile was the same, her demeanor was the same. The effects of the Banshee attack had clearly confused Teyla's senses.

"I don't know how it happens," said Miruva, sounding delighted nonetheless. "It's as if they have a link to my mind. I tell them to do something, and they do it."

Teyla pulled herself to her feet, and tried to regain something of her dignity. Whatever was going on here was very strange.

"Can you make them depart?" she said, eyeing the hovering, silent Banshee.

Miruva frowned.

"I don't think so," she said. "It's not so much that I can *command* them, like you would a child, but more like they know what I want and act on it. They seem almost an extension of my thoughts. Like my thoughts made real. I can't really explain it."

Colonel Sheppard had once said similar things about flying Ancient vessels, as if the machinery became an extension of his mind. Slowly, the pieces of the puzzle began to fall into place.

"You have the means to the control the technology of the Ancestors," said Teyla. "We call this the ATA gene. Many of our number have it, though not all."

"Perhaps," she said. "I can hardly believe it. After so many years living in fear of these creatures, they seem like nothing more than nightmares that have faded with the morning."

Teyla frowned. "The fear was real," she said. "I do not normally run from battle, but I had no choice. How was this effect created?" She looked at the flickering shape intently. The Banshee's eyes followed her, but it made no move towards her. "Miruva, can you instruct it to talk?"

Miruva's face became a mask of concentration. After a few moments, the halo of energy surrounding the Banshee flickered and became brighter. It looked down at Teyla, still expressionless, and its mouth began to move.

"Full-power protocol established," came a tinny voice from the ethereal presence. "Thirty-seven minutes remaining until power-down."

"I do not understand."

"The Banshee has been saving its energy," said Miruva. "It's terrified of losing power. In my head I can hear it saying the same thing over and over again: 'Must maintain power'."

"Miruva," said Teyla. "How can you know of these things? Your people work with simple tools: fire, rock and fur. You are talking as if you understand how this device works. If I did not know better, I would even say that you sound like Doctor McKay."

"I *do* understand," said Miruva. "Somehow, I can *feel* what this thing needs, what it wants. I have the words for it — or at least some of them. It's as if I was born for this."

Teyla felt completely out of her depth. Ancient technology was not her specialty, but in the absence of Doctor McKay she would just have to do her best to unravel things, one step at a time. She looked back at the Banshee.

"Who are you?" she said, in as commanding a voice as she could muster.

The Banshee looked over at Miruva, who nodded to give her assent.

"I am EX-567, an avatar of my creator, Telion," came the thin, rasping voice. "We are the guardians of the Sanctuary. We carry out the great work."

"Why are you persecuting the Forgotten?"

"We carry out the great work. There is no power. The protocols are minimal."

"I'm not sure I understand this," said Teyla, looking to Miruva for support.

"There's something there," Miruva said, frowning. "It's as if I can see inside the mind of this thing. Its thoughts are arranged like sheaves of grass in the drying chambers."

"You have the gene. Perhaps you can see more clearly than any others what is going on here. Can you do anything to access those... sheaves?"

Miruva closed her eyes. "I'm inside its mind... It's so strange. It's as if 'I' and 'it' are one person. But I still retain myself. I've never experienced anything like this before."

Teyla stepped back, unwilling to interfere with the process. She was as content as she ever would be that Miruva was safe and knew what she was doing. There had to be way of getting at the answers and if anything was capable of transporting them back to where they'd come from, it was the Banshee.

"I've got something," said Miruva, her eyes still closed. "There is a key, just like the sign we used to get in here. I think it's some kind of sequence. Shall I access it?"

"Yes, please do," said Teyla. This sounded promising.

A few moments passed and nothing happened. Miruva opened her eyes and came to stand by Teyla.

"I've asked it to speak to us," she said, calmly. "We must listen. I think this will give us the answers we're looking for."

Sheppard was pleased. About as pleased as he had been since arriving on Khost. The day was waning, but there was still time. Now he had a target, something to aim for, he could get stuck in. It was the waiting around that killed him.

Helmar had rounded up about fifty young men. They were keen, most looked pretty competent, too. Within moments of getting agreement to go, they had rounded up a fearsome array of mining equipment. Axes, hammers, twine-wound rope, material for making fire, it was all there. Helmar's words had kindled their enthusiasm; they had listened to the cautionary words of their leaders for too long. Now their time had come.

They had assembled in one the large chambers near the settlement's entrance, together with McKay. All of them looked at Sheppard expectantly.

"OK, guys," he said. "We're gonna have to work fast. The site isn't far away — we can get there quickly. But there's a storm coming, and it's a beast. We've only got one chance at this, so let's get it right."

He paused for a moment, thinking of Teyla. He didn't like to imagine her trapped so far under the ice. He hoped to God things weren't too desperate down there.

"You've all got family who've been taken by these critters," he continued. "One of my team was taken too. It's time to take them back. I'm relying on you. All of you. Let's get this done."

Helmar began to stomp his feet on the rock floor. The others followed suit. Clearly, that was how they showed appreciation round here. The men started to tramp off toward the front gate of the settlement.

"And what exactly do you want me to do while you're off on this expedition?" said McKay to Sheppard. His face looked sour — he was getting fed up with being left behind.

"How close are you to fixing the Jumper?"

"It's not a simple operation…"

"How *close*, Rodney?"

McKay gave an exasperated sigh. "Three, maybe four hours."

"Well, that's just perfect," said Sheppard. "We'll be there and back before you know it."

"Why do I find it so hard to believe you when you say that?"

Sheppard shrugged. "You should learn to be more trusting."

He gave McKay a reassuring cuff on the shoulder, then joined the hunters. They'd started singing. The words were barely comprehensible, but it was clear they were keyed up for the task ahead.

Sheppard liked the men's spirit. He hoped they could keep it up. If they were going to recover Teyla and the others in time, they'd need every ounce of it.

CHAPTER FIFTEEN

THE BANSHEE looked briefly at both Teyla and Miruva, then promptly disappeared. The lights in the room dimmed and a holographic representation of a solar system swirled into view in the space before them. A voice, full and warm, emanated from the air around them.

"If you are listening to this message," it said, "then you have accessed the databanks of my Avatar. I cannot know how many years have passed, nor the status of our experiment on Caliost, but it gives me comfort to believe that one day these words will be heard by another."

Miruva listened, her eyes shining with wonder; the voice of the Ancestors. Teyla was transfixed as well, the recording was at least 10,000 years old and, as ever where the ways of the Ancients were concerned, she felt a quiver of awe.

"The days grow dark," continued the voice. "Though it saddens my soul, we have to leave. The Wraith are despoiling everything and all resources are being pulled back to the City. The only small victory we have achieved is keeping Caliost safe from their predations. My hope is that the planet is so far away, and that the Stargate node is so remote, that they will never find it. The thought of those monsters being let loose on the Inhabitants is too horrendous to contemplate."

"I guess that means you," said Teyla to Miruva. "Or your ancestors, at least."

"The dreams of founding a refuge for my people are over," said the voice. "There is not the time to perfect the drive technology, nor to establish the defenses here. We must place our hope in the City, and trust that it will prove strong enough. If it does not, then this place may well endure when all else has been destroyed. As you have demonstrated your kinship with us through the use of the gene, you must know more of what we intended here."

"Here it comes," said Miruva, listening intently.

"My dream was two-fold," the voice went on. "First, to extend the range of our Stargate-capable vessels so that we could travel further than ever before. In this I hoped to find a way to escape the Wraith while leaving a route back should we recover our strength. Second, I wished to make Caliost a hidden bastion against their expansion. The planet has everything we could need: it is temperate, benign and abundant. The huge variety of plants and animals here would have been an excellent study for our scientists, as well as providing for our people. The Inhabitants would have lived alongside us, and we would have instructed them in the ways of our technology. In time, we would have existed as equals together, not as gods and servants. My dream was to make this a reality."

The solar system graphic began to speed up. Planets whirled around an orange sun faster and faster. Streams of data in a language Teyla couldn't understand flickered past her eyes.

"None of that will now come to pass," said the voice. "All has been overtaken by the war. We must leave at once, and do what we can to safeguard the lives of those we leave behind. The time has been too short. We have done what we could. A Sanctuary has been established deep within the planet's core, close to the Stargate and the temporary shelters. When the time is right, the Inhabitants will be evacuated there, where they may lead their lives free from the fear of the Wraith. All my knowledge has been placed there. When they are mature enough, they can tap this store and learn how to use the machines we have left behind. These are devices of enormous power, capable of molding and reshaping the continents themselves. As their power is so great, they may only be operated by one wielding the power of the gene. Even then, the Inhabitants will have to learn how to use them slowly."

The solar system graphic continued to speed up. Gradually, the color of some of the planets changed, and the sun became paler.

"Why is this necessary?" said the voice. "Let me tell you. Our predictions show that Caliost will enter a giant dust cloud some nine-thousand years hence. Over the course of the following centuries, it will become slowly uninhabitable. The surface will be choked by ice and the rays of the sun will cease to penetrate the endless storms. Hence the need for the Sanctuary. The hidden place is powered from the core of the planet and will remain perfect for as long as any of us can foresee. Safe from both the ice and the Wraith, the Inhabitants can live out their lives in peace, until the day when they know enough of our technology to break free to the surface once more and escape the solar system altogether."

Miruva looked at Teyla. "So it's all been planned."

"And this really is Sanctuary," Teyla said. "None of which explains the Banshees, however."

The solar system graphic flicked off, to be replaced by a revolving schematic of the underground chambers. Teyla recognized the Hall of Arrivals and the various antechambers. Fully revealed, the size and complexity were astonishing. "Sadly, we could not complete the work in the time that remained to us," continued the voice in its mournful way. "We have to leave now, or all will be lost. I have set the machines to run in my absence, overseen by the Avatars. It will take many thousands of years to seed the underground chambers properly and to make them perfect. When they are complete, the dust will come. Then will my Avatars summon the Inhabitants from their settlements on the planet surface and lead them to safety. This will be their great work."

The graphic was filled with visions of forests and streams within the massive chambers. Over time, tiny people appeared among them. It was a vision of plenty, just like its real-life counterpart in the chambers below them.

"I can only hope that you who are listening to this are safely in the Sanctuary, and that the evidence of the great work is all around you. Though I will be long departed by the time you hear this, I wish you well."

The graphic shuddered and sheered away. The lights in the room rose again, and the Banshee flickered back into life. It hung as silently and eerily as before.

For a moment, neither of them said anything. Then Teyla looked at Miruva.

"The great work," she said. "And we are in it."

"Okay, this is it." Sheppard shoved the proximity meter back inside his furs. "Time to start digging, guys."

He stamped his feet. Once he stopped walking, his body temperature dropped alarmingly. The sun was sinking fast towards the horizon, and what little strength remained in its rays had gone. It was a risk, starting the dig this late in the day, but time was short.

Helmar looked hard at the ice. There wasn't much shelter, and nowhere obvious to begin work, but the young man looked untroubled.

"If the weather holds," he said, "we can make a start." Helmar grinned under his mask, creasing the leather. "Get ready to be impressed, Colonel Sheppard. You haven't seen how the Forgotten work yet."

He called out the others. Instantly, they began to unpack their equipment. Some unstrapped huge shovels from their backs. Under Helmar's direction, they began to clear the top layers of snow. They were followed by a second team, heavily built by Forgotten standards, who hauled the broken ice and slush away. Others began to secure the growing hole in the ground with heavy mats of woven twine. Within moments, a gash in the ice appeared, and began to grow. The miners worked at it like ants around a honeypot.

Helmar gave Sheppard a satisfied look. "They go quickly, once they're roused."

"Yeah. I can see."

Sheppard gazed out at the horizon. The clouds on the horizon had drawn no closer, but he trusted Rodney's prediction. The storm would come. "How much time do they need?"

"We need to hit a crevasse," replied Helmar. "If we have to delve through solid rock, it'll take days, maybe weeks. But if we find a tunnel, we'll be down to your friend in no time."

"Liking the sound of that," said Sheppard. "But it's not just my friend down there."

"I haven't forgotten," said Helmar, reaching for a spare ice-ax. "We could do with another pair of hands. Have you ever used one of these?"

Sheppard looked at the implement. It was heavy, the shaft wooden and the blade bone. He ran his finger along the edge. It was sharp, and more sturdy than he would have thought possible. These buffalos were amazing things.

"Nope," he said, hefting the blade in his hand and looking over the growing mine-head. "So why don't you show me how it's done?"

Miruva looked up at the form hovering above her. "So these Banshees are the Avatars," she said, looking up at EX-567 with a renewed appreciation. "They are the work of the Ancestors."

"So it seems," said Teyla. "But why do they have such an aura of fear? If the Ancestors intended them to lead you to safety here, why do they sweep through the settlement and abduct you?"

Miruva frowned and let her mind link with that of the Avatar again. "I do not fully understand," said Miruva slowly, clearly working hard to decipher what the Avatar was telling her. "But one thing keeps being repeated — there is no power. The Avatars are frustrated. They wish to bring all of the Inhabitants to Sanctuary, but there's not enough energy. Something has gone wrong."

Teyla pursed her lips, pondering the implications. "It is clear that the Banshees are malfunctioning. Their programming has been corrupted by a lack of power and their functions are distorted. Presumably, if it were otherwise, they could have explained Telion's great work to your people and you would have come willingly to Sanctuary."

"Yes," she said, thoughtfully. "It's a strange idea — our mortal enemies being our one means for salvation. Should we get out of here, I'll have trouble making anyone believe it."

The Banshee hung before them, as implacable as ever. It seemed perfectly oblivious to their discussion.

"Can you instruct the Banshee to teleport us back to the surface?" said Teyla. "While it's good to know that Sanctuary exists for your people, I am not one of them. I need to get back to my team."

Miruva shook her head. "I am sorry," she said. "The Banshee won't do it. It uses up all their power and they're worried about where more will come from."

Teyla felt her heart sink. "That is unwelcome news. Is there no way back to the surface?"

Miruva sank back into her trance-like state.

"There were access tunnels to the surface once," she said

at length. "Perhaps the Avatars waited too long to begin their mission, and the tunnels were filled with ice. That would explain why they have to teleport our people in small groups. There is no power for anything more."

"That sounds plausible, but it does not help find a way out."

Miruva's brow furrowed as she interrogated the mind of the Avatar again. "There may be exits still in operation," she said. "I can see the plan of this place in the Banshee's mind. We are in a control room near the perimeter of the cave complex. There is a passage leading back towards the settlement and the Stargate. It must have been used in the past by the Ancestors. It is long, and the Avatar tells me it is no longer complete. But we could try it."

She opened her eyes, and looked at Teyla. The Athosian could see that the young woman was only half willing to go; now that she had discovered the true nature of Sanctuary, it was clear that some part of her wished to head back down to the fertile plains and forget about Khost's troubles.

"You do not need to come with me," said Teyla. "Your destiny lies here, in discovering how to use the machinery of the Ancestors."

But Miruva smiled. "Of course I'm coming with you," she said. "We need to get you back to the surface, and find a way to bring the rest of my people down here."

"Very well," she said. "We must go quickly. If what the Avatar has told us is correct, then the situation on the surface will only get worse."

Miruva gave a significant look to the Avatar, and it winked out of existence.

"Even being present drains their power," she explained. "I believe I can summon it at will now. Once the link has been established, it remains with me."

Teyla pulled her furs closely around her, guessing the

journey ahead would be a cold one.

"I am glad to hear it," she said. "We may have need of it later."

"Not too close," Ronon warned as he carefully stepped on to the rock bridge. Testing his weight on it he felt the solidity of the stone beneath him. He stamped a little harder, and the echoes of the muffled blows rang across the yawning gap. The bridge felt solid.

Ronon pulled his furs close around him and began to walk. He could hear Orand follow him a few yards behind, but concentrated solely on what he was doing. The bridge continued, perfectly straight and rigid, until it dissolved into the gloom and haze ahead. It was like walking along a road in the mist with the horizon just out of view. Except that, in this case, stepping off the trail would result in a long, long fall.

He paused and turned to look behind him. The hunting party had made their way on to the pier, one by one, a few yards apart. Each shuffled forward carefully, knowing the price of a slip. Thankfully, the stone surface was smooth and well-made. The surface was shiny with ancient ice, but the thick leather of the Forgotten boots did much to maintain a secure footing.

Ronon turned back and inched further along the narrow way. His heart thumped powerfully; the need to concentrate was paramount, and he kept his eyes securely fixed on the hazy passage before him. If a Banshee came now... He didn't want to think about that.

Time was hard to measure. Gradually, the cliff-edge behind him shrank back into shadow and it felt like they were marooned on a tiny rock of stability within a void. For a terrifying second, Ronon was consumed by the urge to leap out into the darkness, to fall into its seductive embrace. He shook his head, angry with himself. Such flights of fancy, even in his tired state, were unworthy of him. He took a breath and his concentration returned.

After what may have been just a few minutes, or maybe much longer, Ronon began to see something solidify from the haze in front of him. He crept forward, his eyes flicking back and forth between the bridge and whatever he was approaching. The darkness gave way, hardening into another vast wall of rock — they had reached the other side.

As before, the towering cliffs extended incredibly far both upwards and down into the abyss. There was a stone shelf with a circular doorway carved into the rock-face.

Taking care not to slip at the last minute, Ronon negotiated the last few yards of the bridge. With enormous relief he stepped on to the shelf at the other side. Despite the endless chill of the subterranean passage, he felt his palms slick with sweat.

He turned and watched the rest of the party carefully file from the bridge and on to the safety of the cliff-face.

"I don't want to do that again," said Orand, looking shaky. "Ever." His earlier ebullience had clearly deserted him.

"Know what you mean," said Ronon, turning to the circular doorway before them. It was as black as ink, but it was the only way they could go. "We'll need candles."

Ronon ducked under the narrow gap. Orand didn't object to him taking the lead. His eyes took a moment to get used to the gloomy candle flame again and he waited, watching the little column of tallow as it glowed softly in his hand. It was nearly burned through. If they were going to get out, they had better do so quickly.

Gradually, the dim outline of the tunnel began to resolve itself and he pushed on. From behind, he could hear the uncertain progress of the others as they followed him. Some of the candles must have failed and there were muttered curses as the hunters stumbled in the dark.

The journey continued much as it had done before. After a few minutes, Ronon began to wonder if the bridge over the chasm was some kind of cruel joke. For all he knew, the passages could lead on like this for miles. Once the candles went out, they would be entirely in the dark and then the game would be up. His earlier morbid thoughts about death underground came back. With a low growl of frustration, he shook them off.

As he recovered himself, he heard the first swishing noise.

"Hear that?" he hissed, stopping in his tracks and crouching low.

"Hear what?" said Orand, close behind him. Then something swished past them again and his face went white. "Oh, by the Ancestors…"

Suddenly, the entire tunnel was bathed in light. It blazed from all sides, and the swishing noise became a roar.

Dazzled, Ronon scrambled backwards, shielding his eyes. He was blind and disorientated. Behind him he heard shouting and the sound of running feet.

"Banshees!" cried a voice which might have been Orand's.

His eyes streaming from the light, Ronon forced himself to look up. Towering over him was an insubstantial shape, flickering like a flame. There were long, flowing robes, and pale flesh. A lean alien face looked down at him. The expression was haughty and cruel.

Then there were others, sweeping through the corridor like ghosts. There was no escape. With a howl, the Banshees were upon them. Ronon felt a brief surge of resistance, but then it was banished. Despite all his training, all his experience, he felt a rising tide of horror. There was nowhere to run. There were too many to evade. The hunters fell on their faces.

Ronon reached for his weapon, but his hands were cold and clumsy. He didn't even get a shot away. The Banshee came for him, and all hope fled.

Sheppard hacked at the rock. Despite the cold, he had worked up a sweat and he could feel rivulets of it running down his back. It was hard work, exhausting and dangerous. The ice shattered easily enough under the blows of the axes, but the rock was a different matter. He didn't even attempt to break that up. Forgotten miners stepped up for that job, wheeling massive hammers to crack the heavy boulders in their way. Metal pins — which must have been extremely rare on Khost — were hammered into the stone to weaken it, and the hammer-blows did the rest. Sheppard was amazed at their strength and skill. He wouldn't have been so confident that Earth miners, no matter how tough, could have worked the rock so fast.

After an hour of solid, back-breaking work, they had succeeded in delving beneath the ice shelf. Night was fast approaching, and torches had been lit across the workings. Now the task was to bolster the walls of ice around them so they weren't buried as they descended. There wasn't much wood to spare, so most of the structure was self-supporting. Helmar and his colleagues had done enough excavation to know what to leave and what to attack. Sheppard just did as he was told.

"How're doing?" asked Helmar, coming to stand at his shoulder.

Sheppard turned awkwardly in the cramped space. "Feel like I've been wrestling a grizzly," he panted. "Otherwise fine. What's our progress?"

Helmar smiled. "We're in luck," he said. "Larem has broken into a fissure. They're all over the place here. Come."

Helmar pushed his way past other miners, all working hard. Sheppard followed him, grateful for the break. A couple of meters further down, the miners had opened up a narrow cleft and were busy widening it. The stone seemed laced with lodes of ice, weakening the structure, and every so often a huge chunk would break from the sides and come crashing down. Sheppard watched the work intently. It looked perilous. "You've done this before, right?"

"Of course," said Helmar. "A thousand times. They know what they're doing."

Sheppard peered into the open chasm, trying to see how far it went. "What do you think?"

"This is good," Helmar said. "I reckon this runs a long way down. We'll secure the breach above us and then follow it. No doubt we'll have more digging to do, but this makes our task much easier."

Sheppard looked at the gaping fissure warily. In the gloom it looked treacherous. "Guess you're right," he said. "I can't tell you how far down we need to go."

Helmar laughed. "You sound worried, Colonel," he said. "That's not like you. Trust me. Some of these tunnels run for miles. However far we need to go, we will get you there. We are at home under the ground. It is our way of life."

Sheppard tried to look reassured. "Let's keep going," he said. "The sooner we get to the bottom, the happier I'll be."

Teyla and Miruva went quickly. They passed rooms full of equipment displaying various diagnostic readings from Sanctuary. Some looked like the medical read-outs in Dr Beckett's infirmary. There were rooms lined with computers arranged in galley format, and others full of gently humming machinery. One was dominated by a circular machine, dark and monolithic. Lights flickered uncertainly up and down its flanks and the symbol of the Ancients had been etched into its surface.

"That is where the Banshees come from," said Miruva, looking at the machine with fascination. "To think that the object of our fear is generated by such a thing."

They pressed on. Smooth metal surfaces gave way to hurriedly-worked rock-faces. On the fringes of the Sanctuary, the Ancestors' haste to leave was readily apparent. The meager heat levels began to plummet, and the deathly chill of Khost reasserted itself. After working their way through the dark of the Ancient tunnels, a red light grew ahead of them until there was a clear opening in the rock face. It looked like a pool of fire against the rock.

Teyla ducked through it and found herself on a narrow ledge on a sheer cliff-face. It resembled the precipice at the entrance to the living areas of Sanctuary, only this time dark and throbbing with noise. If the peaceful chambers they had left resembled paradise, then this place looked like hell.

Garish red flares illuminated the chiseled rock faces, which were black as pitch. The reason for their charred appearance lay below. Dimly, Teyla could make out vast machinery operating in the depths of the chasm. Massive power couplings shone weakly in the in the deep, huge pistons revolving with magisterial slowness. The size of it all was phenomenal. Clearly, such technology was required to keep the ecosystem behind them in full working order.

"So this is what Telion wanted you to learn how to use," said Teyla. "He expected much."

"It will take us lifetimes," Miruva said, the daunting scale of the task dawning on her.

"At least you have the gene," said Teyla, trying to reassure. "That gives you many advantages."

They walked along the ledge, keeping their fingers against the stone wall on their right. Eventually they came to the far

side of the chamber and passed once more into chill dark
of the narrow tunnels. It was now clear that they had left
the main areas of the Sanctuary. Everything was haphazard
and makeshift, and corridor looked like it had been blasted
out in a hurry. The way became difficult, and Teyla lost her
footing a number of times. Ice lay in the cracks and inden
tations of the stone, making the going treacherous. The red
light ebbed almost to nothing and darkness enveloped them
pierced only by the narrow beam of Teyla's flashlight.

As they went, the noise of the machinery grew weaker and
the deathly silence of the underworld returned. Teyla started
to speak to Miruva — anything to break the unearthly qui
et — but was interrupted by muffled cries of distress from
far ahead.

She looked at Miruva, startled. It sounded like human
voices raised in anger and fear.

"I hear it too," said Miruva.

They started to run. Teyla held the flashlight low as
she went, trying as best she could to pick out the perilous
shards of rock barring their way. Her heart began to race
Who could be down here, so far from the habitable areas
Was it Sheppard? If so, that meant there was a route to the
surface...

The tunnel took a sharp bend to the right. Miruva and
Teyla tore round it, and stumbled into a scene of bedlam
There were fur-clad figures cowering against the stone. Some
had covered their faces; others were trying to scramble back
the way they had come. The reason for their panic was obvi
ous. Banshees were hovering, staring at the humans with
their baleful eyes. Despite knowing what she did about the
Avatars, Teyla felt the fear rise in her too.

"Enough!" Miruva made a dismissive gesture with her
hands and, almost instantly, the Banshees rippled out of
existence. The chamber sunk back into darkness, lit only

by Teyla's flashlight and the stubs of a few candles.

"They were confused," said Miruva to Teyla, almost by way of apology. "Their programming is corrupted. They can't help it."

Teyla nodded, still feeling the after-effects of her receding fear. Whatever the bug was, it really needed to be ironed-out.

Shakily, the men in the room began to get to their feet. One of them came forward, his face pasty and haggard.

"Orand!" cried Miruva, and threw herself at him, embracing him fervently.

"Miruva!" Orand exclaimed. "What are you doing here? You should be at the settlement."

"It is a long story," said Teyla.

A huge shadowy figure loomed over Orand's shoulder. Teyla flicked the torch up, illuminating Ronon's shaggy face. She burst into a smile.

"Ronon!" she cried. "I am *very* glad to see you."

The Satedan looked too weary to smile back. "Me too," he said, gruffly. "How d'you get rid of those things?"

"I'll fill you in when there's time," said Miruva. "Right now, we need to know how you got down here. We need a route back to the surface."

Orand's face fell. "This isn't the way out? There's no exit back there. Just tunnels. Miles of them."

Teyla felt the relief at meeting the hunters begin to fade. If the tunnel led to a dead end, then her hopes of reaching Sheppard were close to disappearing.

"There must be," she insisted. "We should press on. Perhaps there is an exit that you missed in the dark."

Miruva put her hand on Teyla's arm. "Teyla, these men are exhausted. We don't have the supplies for a long trek under the ice."

Teyla felt a stab of frustration. The longer they delayed,

the less likely it was any of them would ever leave Khost. Frantically, she searched for a reason to keep going.

Deep down, though, she knew that Miruva was right. The hunters needed to rest, and Sanctuary was the best place for them. For the time being, they would have to withdraw. The escape attempt would have to wait until they had gathered their strength.

"Very well," she said. "We will go back to the inhabited areas."

She looked back at Ronon. "There is much that has been hidden here," she said. "And you will not believe what we have found."

Sheppard looked down at the newly-exposed tunnel. He had to suppress a whoop of triumph. Helmar had been as good as his word, and the miners had smashed their way further than he would have thought possible.

Breathing heavily from his exertions, he joined the others as they scrambled down the loose stone. He had little idea how far they'd gone, but it must have been many meters. The light from the aperture above was now almost useless, and the miners lit fresh torches.

"That it?" he asked, looking at the bare rock below him.

"It is," said Helmar, looking proud. "There's a hollow space under us, or I'm a buffalo's *hrnmar*."

"Oh, I wouldn't say that," said Sheppard. "Whatever 'that' is."

"How are your arms? Have you got strength for more work?"

Sheppard felt his biceps ache as he flexed them. He hadn't been this strung out for a long, long time. "You *promise* we're nearly there?"

Helmar grinned. "I wouldn't lie to you, Sheppard."

"Glad to hear it," said Sheppard. "Then let's go. Final push."

Together with the hunters around him, he began to hack at the stone. The sound of rock chipping and ice shattering filled the narrow space. The axes hammered down again and again, aimed with precision. The Forgotten knew what they were doing. First one crack appeared, then another. They widened, attacked relentlessly by the miners.

"Back!" cried Helmar suddenly. The nearest miners sprung away from the crumbling rock floor. There was the sound of falling debris under them.

Helmar turned to Sheppard, his eyes alive with triumph.

"It's giving way!" he said. "We're breaking through!"

The hunting party gathered itself together and the group limped back through the tunnels towards Sanctuary. As they passed the massive chamber of machinery, it was all the hunters could do not to stumble into the chasm. None of them seemed much interested in the machines below; they were on their last legs.

They picked up the pace slightly as the light increased. In the distance, Teyla could see the bright lights of the Banshee's control room and suddenly realized how weary she was herself. A rest, some warmth, and some food would do all of them good. Only then would they be in any state to reconsider how they were going to get out.

Suddenly, there was the sound of grinding rock above them. Teyla stopped walking, her senses alert. "What's that?" she hissed. "Banshees?"

The sound got louder, a terrible renting and grinding. "There are no Banshees activated," said Miruva, looking at the rock roof with alarm. "Must be a tremor. Run!"

She broke into a jog. Behind her, the hunters staggered

forward; it was all they could do to stay on their feet. Lines of rock-dust began to stream down from the ceiling. The sound of breaking rock grew until the entire corridor echoed with it.

"Keep going!" yelled Teyla, pushing the fatigued hunters onwards, letting herself slip to the rear of the group. "The tunnel is collapsing!"

The noise reached a painful crescendo. The very stone was being tortured, and now rocks the size of fists were falling from the roof. Teyla pushed the last of the hunters in front of her and the man stumbled into a staggering run. From further down the tunnel, the thump of falling earth echoed. It was as if the world was being reshaped around her.

Teyla sprung forward, seeing the light of the Banshee control room entrance tantalizingly close. Her shoulders were showered with debris, and the sound of scraping, breaking rock hammered in her ears.

She was just a few dozen feet away when the stone hit her. She crumpled to the ground. Her hand shakily touched her forehead, and hot blood ran over her fingers. She looked up, seeing the ceiling above her crack and splinter.

"Must keep going…" she murmured, but knew she was losing consciousness.

The world lurched. It felt as if she was spinning into the void. Teyla pulled herself up to her elbows with difficulty, but then the rocks began falling in earnest. A shard shattered across her neck, and she fell back down to earth. The corridor tilted on its axis. The flashlight beam guttered and went out. Somewhere, dimly, she heard someone calling her name. But a glut of nausea was rising in her throat, her vision closing in, and then she knew no more.

CHAPTER SIXTEEN

WITH a final shiver of defeat, the rock floor caved in. A huge plume of dust and debris flew up into the cramped workings, and Sheppard had to turn his face away.

After it subsided, the miners began to drop into the gap. Their torches unveiled a deep well carved into the stone. On either side of the well, there were two gaping holes, only partly choked by the rubble. They'd broken into some kind of tunnel. Even in the flickering light Sheppard could see that it was man-made.

Relief flooded over him. They'd made it.

He took out the proximity meter. It was going crazy. There were signals all around him, and not just those of Helmar and his men.

"C'mon!" he cried. "They'll be down here somewhere."

He started to clamber down into the gap. As he went, the torches threw long, snaking shadows across the cracked rock. The floor of the tunnel was becoming visible. There was more light, bleeding up from somewhere deeper down, and he began to make sense of the chaos around him.

Sheppard froze. He felt his heart beating powerfully in his chest. Beneath him, where the newly opened tunnel snaked downwards, there was a body lying in the rubble on the floor. It looked horribly familiar.

"Helmar!" he cried, hurrying towards it. "I'm gonna need some help here."

Within seconds, other miners bearing torches had scrambled over to his position. They were still calling to one another with triumph as they came. All Sheppard could feel was the sick sensation in his stomach. As the miners caught sight of the body, they fell quiet.

Teyla lay slumped across a collapsed section of stone. She was out cold, and there was an ugly cut on her forehead.

He crouched down, feeling for a pulse. It was there, thank God. Not strong, but she was alive. Helmar dropped down beside him.

"Will she be well?" he asked, his voice full of concern. Sheppard wished he had Dr Beckett around to answer that. Teyla looked like she'd taken a battering when the miners had broken through. "You got any healers with you?"

"We'll do what we can."

"Quickly!"

Helmar disappeared. Working carefully, the other miners began to clear the stone from around her. They took care not to move her. Sheppard stayed crouched by her side.

He felt impotent, and angry. All of a sudden he regretted his desire for a speedy resolution to the mission. The gathering storm on the surface had unsettled him. McKay clearly thought his plan was crazy. The fact that the miners had managed to break through the layers of rock to the hidden tunnels beneath should have been Sheppard's vindication. As it was, looking down at Teyla lying prone on the rock floor, he wondered if the price for his daring had been far too high.

A surge of warmth moved through McKay's body, bathing him in pleasure. Of course, he wasn't *actually* warm. He hadn't been anything other than freezing ever since they'd landed on Khost. The heat was metaphorical: the glow of success, the sustaining balm of genius. He had done it.

At last, the Jumper was good to go. It almost looked normal, though a genuine pilot would have balked at the bolted-together equipment lining the walls of the rear bay. Zelenka's gadget had finally been constructed, more or less as intended. There were a few modifications, of course. Some were due to there not being enough parts in the Jumper; some were enhancements supplied by McKay's own ingenuity. Rodney found himself looking forward to explaining the weaknesses in the Zelenka's schematics in person. Now that the Jumper could fly again, the chances of him being able to do that had significantly increased.

The Stargate had been something else. Working in the cold, on his own, in the failing light and without access to any routine diagnostic instruments had nearly killed him. There had been moments out on the ice with the wind biting hard and his fingers frozen to the bone when he'd almost given up. No matter what he tried, there was no way of coaxing enough power to kick it into life. All he needed was enough to hold open the gate for a centisecond or two, but even that was far beyond him. Once within the wormhole, Zelenka's machine would kick in and the experimental Ancient tech would do the rest. The waiting was too frustrating for words.

Of course, even if the power could be found, getting home relied on an entirely unproven hypotheses about wormhole physics — and a good degree of faith that his makeshift power array would stand up to the strain. Not to mention an absolute conviction that Sheppard would be able to pilot the vessel at the optimum speed, at the correct angle, and would switch to the Zelenka-inspired grid at just the right moment.

But that was all fine. Hardly a day went by on Atlantis without some kind of impossible odds to conquer, and at least they were back in the game now. The important thing was that he *believed* it was going to work. Though the source eluded him for the moment, he was sure something could be done about the power shortfall. When it came to technology, that was really all that was important. He never got it wrong.

Or at least, he seldom did. Which was almost as good. But now it was well into the night, and there was nothing more he could do. With a shudder, he looked over at the rear bay doors. It would be a cold walk back to the settlement.

The tunnel was gradually cleared of rubble and the breach in the roof secured. As they had done throughout, the miners worked tirelessly and skillfully. More torches were brought down and placed against the walls of the corridor.

Sheppard hardly took any of it in. He'd remained by Teyla's side. He barely noticed Helmar return.

"We've sent some men down into the complex beyond," the hunter said. "It's just as you thought. There's room there for everyone. There are others further down. I've sent for a healer."

Sheppard looked up, hearing what the man said but barely taking it in.

"Who's down there?" he asked

"Miruva, and she's explained what's going on," he said. "There's power, and light, and air. All those taken by the Banshees are here. Orand is too. And your friend, the big man."

As Helmar finished speaking, Ronon emerged from behind him. The huge Satedan looked haggard and unsteady on his feet.

"You made it then, Sheppard," the Runner said, gruffly. He was staring at Teyla. "How bad?"

Sheppard shook his head. "Dammit, I need a *doctor*!"

His voice broke at that point, despite all his hours on active duty. They had all been pushed to the limit by Khost's hostile environment. This was a step too far.

"Do not worry, Colonel Sheppard," came Teyla's voice, weakly from her bruised lips. "It would take more than a few stones to finish me off."

Her eyes flickered open. She smiled a grim smile, then winced immediately from the pain.

"Teyla!" cried Sheppard, resisting the urge to grab her by the shoulders with joy. "How bad are you hurt? Can you feel your legs?"

Teyla nodded gingerly. She seemed to be coming round more fully and the grogginess left her eyes.

"I can feel them," she said. "And I can see you quite plainly. Give me a moment, and I will be back on my feet."

"The hell you won't," said Sheppard, firmly. "You're staying right where you are."

Teyla let her eyes close. Ronon sank down on his haunches next to her.

"Quite an entrance," he said to Sheppard. "How d'you know we were down here?"

"Proximity meter," Sheppard replied. "These guys did most of the work — they know what they're doing. This place's riddled with tunnels."

"You're telling me," said Ronon, with feeling. "So, what's the plan now?"

"You want a *plan*? Sheesh." Sheppard took a deep breath. "Well, we've got an entrance to this 'Sanctuary' sorted. So long as the weather holds, all of the Forgotten will be able to get down here. As for how *we* get out, that's in Rodney's hands. He's working on feeding power from the Jumper to the Stargate. Though I've gotta say, he didn't look real confident about it."

"Rodney not confident?" said Ronon. "Don't like that." Dr McKay was generally confident about anything involving his technological prowess. When he looked worried, everyone else did too.

"Yeah, I hear you," said Sheppard. "Want more great news? We've got a storm coming. I told you about the one that nearly sunk the city back on Atlantis, right? Imagine that, but worse. And forever."

Ronon gave a low whistle. "That's bad. But not much we can do about it."

"Sure we can," said Sheppard. "We gotta persuade Aralen to get his people down here double quick. He misses this chance, he won't get another."

Ronon paused, taking in the implications of that.

"You know we should just get the hell outta here, right?" he said.

Sheppard nodded. "Yeah, I know. And *you* know that ain't gonna happen; we can't just leave these people in the deep freeze, not when there's a chance to save them."

"So I guess you're going back to talk to Aralen?"

"Guess I am." He stood up gingerly, feeling his battered body protest. "Anyway, how the hell are you down here too? I'm beginning to get my head round this Banshee thing, but I thought you were out hunting cows."

Ronon gave him a sour look. "We took a wrong turn. I'll fill you in later."

"Can't wait."

"You'd better go. Don't worry about Teyla — I've got her back. And we'll get the breach secure while you're gone."

"Right," said Sheppard. "Don't let her get up too soon. And where's Miruva? I hear she's in charge around here."

"I am here, Colonel Sheppard," came a voice from further down the tunnel. Miruva came forward hesitantly, loathe to look at Teyla's prone body.

"Will she...?" she started, and then looked at Sheppard directly.

"Oh, she's made of strong stuff," he said, with more conviction than he felt. "Just like you guys. But you know, if you don't all get down here — "

"I've seen the future of this planet too, Colonel Sheppard," said Miruva. "I'll come with you. The ice is treacherous at night, and you'll never convince my father by yourself — he's too stubborn and set in his ways."

Sheppard looked doubtful. "You sure about that? It's blowing pretty hard up there."

"You would do no less for your father," she said. "Nor your people. I will come with you, and that is an end to it. We can go now."

Sheppard made to leave, then paused. A thought had just occurred. "Hey, you've been in the Ancestor control rooms?"

"Yes."

"Then we'll take a little detour down there first," said Sheppard. "We can't leave without presents, and I'm guessing there'll be something down there that'll make Rodney's day."

CHAPTER SEVENTEEN

McKAY had woken up with a sore head. He always woke up with a sore head, but this morning it was particularly bad. He'd slept badly, plagued by the sound of tremors under the settlement and troubled by dreams of Ancient crystal circuitry. After a whole, long day working on the Jumper schematics, he hadn't been able to switch off. With a weary sigh, he realized he'd got a whole lot more work ahead of him. There wasn't even anyone to yell at. For a minute, he found himself missing Zelenka.

He shook his head. What was getting *into* him? He dressed hurriedly, tried to make himself look not entirely uncivilized, and headed straight for one of the refectories. There was no one about outside his chamber. It was no different as he neared the eating areas. The settlement was entirely empty and silent.

McKay frowned. An absence of food right now, after all the work he'd done, was a bitter blow. It wasn't that he actually looked forward to another bowl of gently congealed buffalo fat, but it was food of a kind, and his stomach was growling with all the bad-tempered expectation of a feral grizzly.

He headed back into the main network of corridors. Had the Banshees come back and stripped the whole place of life? That would really limit the culinary possibilities. Picking up his pace, he headed for the assembly rooms. Reassuringly, as he neared them, the low buzz of voices drifted up the corridor. Many voices. It sounded like the entire population had gathered there. Either they'd got there early, or he'd overslept. Badly.

The central hall was full of people. McKay shuffled over

to a quiet spot near the back of the hall and made himself as comfortable as possible against the uneven rock wall. A debate was going on, and it sounded pretty impassioned.

The reason for the disturbance quickly became apparent. Sheppard was back. He was standing before Aralen and the council as he had done before. The old man looked torn between annoyance and profound relief. The reason for the latter was obvious; his daughter stood next to Sheppard, relaxed and unharmed.

McKay shook his head. He had to hand it to John, when there was a pretty girl to be rescued he had a Kirk-like knack for pulling it off. No Teyla or Ronon, though. McKay almost blurted out a demand to know where they were, but managed to keep a lid on his burning curiosity. Sheppard looked like he'd come back to deliver a sitrep, and the crowd were rapt with attention. Perhaps now they'd start getting some answers to all their questions.

Aralen stood up, face clearly marked by his conflicting emotions.

"Colonel Sheppard," he said, voice shaking, "no one could be more grateful than I. You've brought my daughter back from the clutches of the Banshees. My reason for living has been restored to me." He looked at Miruva and there was real fear in his eyes. "But it is for this very reason that I don't understand why you're advocating this plan. Now that we know how to retrieve our people from the clutches of these monsters, why would we willingly go back to their imprisonment?"

Sheppard sighed. "Look, I dunno what more I can tell you," he said. "Believe me, I've seen prisons, and this ain't it. It's a paradise, Aralen."

Aralen shook his head. "I can't believe it," he said. "All our records tell us that our place is here. The Ancestors will provide — they have promised."

"The Ancestors *have* provided!" cried Sheppard, his frustration getting the better of him. "What are you gonna do? This place is dying. You know it's happening, and you know you're almost outta time."

Aralen glared at Sheppard. A lifetime of faith in the ways of the Ancestors was being shaken. It was painful to watch.

"Colonel Sheppard speaks the truth, Father," said Miruva. "I've seen this place. We could want for nothing there. Those who have been taken by the Banshees live in peace. There is food, water, and warmth. In time, we will come to understand the Ancestors' plan. We won't be there forever. Once we have mastered their powerful machines, we can break free and become like them ourselves."

Aralen's face sharpened into anger. "That is heresy!" he hissed. "We could never become like the Ancestors. They guide, and we follow. Who knows what plans of theirs we have ruined by blundering into their secret realm? And you haven't explained one thing; if the Ancestors truly intended us to make our way to this Sanctuary, why did they hide it so well? And why do their servants, the Banshees, attack us? They are creatures of terror!"

Sheppard looked a little uncomfortable. "Hey, we don't know everything," he said. "There's been a problem somewhere, that's for sure. But you gotta trust me on this. I've been there."

Aralen shook his head. "If the Ancestors had created this Sanctuary for us," he said, "it would be perfect. If it was their creation, it would not be inhabited by Banshees. It would not lack power or—"

"Of course!" cried McKay, standing up.

All eyes turned to him, and he realized he'd spoken when he had meant to think. He coughed awkwardly and looked apologetically at Sheppard. "Sorry. Didn't mean to interrupt," he said. "But what you're saying makes a lot of sense. The Ancients wouldn't have left an experiment of theirs without making some provision for the future. They were clever like that. And the Banshees — they must be some kind of projected avatar of their creators. If there was something wrong with the holographic projection system — and it's very hard to keep all the bugs out over 10,000 years — they would appear like ghosts."

Miruva turned to him and gave an amused smile. "Dr McKay," she said. "I wish we'd had you in Sanctuary with us. And you're right: the Banshees called themselves Avatars."

"Let me guess," continued McKay, enjoying Miruva's approval. "They have really catchy names. Like GH7X, or something. Right?"

"Something like that," she said.

McKay turned to Aralen. "Look, I don't want to butt-in," he said. "I'm generally happier sorting out the tech than getting involved in politics. But Sheppard's right, this whole planet is screwed. You'd have to be insane not to get into this 'Sanctuary' — demonstrably suicidal, in fact. Power problems can be sorted. We have them all the time on Atl — back home. And projecting AI avatars across large distances can be a big energy drain. Just because the Banshees flicker on and off doesn't mean the whole system's shot."

Aralen looked at the scientist with skepticism. "So why do they cause such fear?" he said.

Miruva and Sheppard looked at McKay. Clearly, neither of them had any idea either.

"Well, er," he started, hoping his complete lack of actual knowledge about Banshees wasn't entirely obvious, "that's probably down to the psychic techniques the Ancients use. In ways we don't understand, they can tap directly into our minds." It was entirely conjecture, but he hoped the

Forgotten wouldn't know that. "That's how we're able to use their technology. They create a neural link — a way to respond to the thoughts and emotions of the user. In this case, it's likely that the Banshees' neural manipulation has been distorted by the power drain. They appear as terrifying ghouls, when actually they're just trying to do their job. If what Colonel Sheppard says is true, then I don't think you have anything to worry about from them. In fact, you should probably stop calling them 'banshees'. The origin of the term in fact comes from…"

Aralen's scowl stopped him in his tracks. The etymological explanation could probably wait.

"What you say sounds convincing, Dr McKay," he said. "If I were a less careful man, I would happily do what you suggest. But I have kept our people safe against all threats for longer than you have been alive. If I'd given-in to every theory and idea that had come my way, we would have been lost long ago. This thing needs study. We cannot risk—"

"There's no time!" cried Sheppard. He took a deep breath. "With respect, Aralen, you're not gonna *survive* another storm here."

Aralen's face went red with anger and he stood up. "How dare you speak to me that way," he said, icily. "You are our guests, and now you lecture us like children."

Sheppard opened his mouth to reply, but Miruva interjected.

"Enough," she said. She turned to Aralen. "I hadn't wanted to do this, Father. But if it's proof you need, it's proof you'll get."

Aralen stared at her, startled. The young woman threw him a defiant look, and then gazed up to the symbol carved on the roof of the chamber. She closed her eyes and extended her hand towards it. Immediately, the symbol glowed and a beam of energy passed between them. The familiar swishing sound filled the hall and a wave of panic washed over the crowd.

"Stay where you are!" shouted Sheppard. "You've nothing to fear."

Despite himself, McKay was impressed by Miruva's mastery of the technology — she must have been a quick study.

The figure that materialized before her was clearly an AI avatar, albeit slightly rusty around the edges. For some reason, McKay felt a sudden and overwhelming sense of terror. He shrank back, and it was all he could do not to run. "Ignore your feelings," Miruva urged the crowd. "I can control it. The Banshees are our servants, they cannot hurt you."

The apparition hovered motionless before Miruva. The people in the chamber gaped at it in horror, but none of them moved. Moment by moment the air of menace emanating from the Avatar dissipated until McKay found he could breathe again and could observe the device quite dispassionately. Clearly, the emotional response it generated was linked to the emotions of the observer. Clever, really.

"Announce yourself," Miruva commanded.

"I am TF-34," replied the Banshee in a scratchy voice. "My function is to provide teleported transportation to Sanctuary. This is the great work. Minimal power readings. I cannot remain instantiated. Shutting-down link."

The vision guttered and faded out.

"They have been charged with bringing us to the Sanctuary created for us by the Ancestors," said Miruva. "Their failing power supply has necessitated the transportation without explanation. But now we can access the caves directly, and you've seen the way I can control them. Surely you will relent, Father?"

Aralen gazed at her in wonder. "You can control them…"

"Yeah, it's a gift," Sheppard said. "All the best people have it."

Aralen looked up at the symbol, and then back over the gathered crowd in the chamber. An unbroken hush had descended over the hall as the Forgotten awaited his verdict. McKay had an urge to say something, but bit his tongue.

The wait seemed interminable, but finally Aralen took a deep breath. "If you can summon the Banshees at will, how can I fail to take note of what you say? Everything I have clung on to has been turned to ashes." He looked at Miruva, and his eyes shone with emotion. "My daughter, you have returned to us when we thought you lost. It is time for you to lead our people and fulfill the will of the Ancestors. Lead us to our Sanctuary."

An expression of profound relief passed between Miruva and Sheppard as the crowd dissolved into excited chatter. The decision had been made, and it was the right one.

McKay elbowed his way through the press of people towards Sheppard. "Glad to have you back," he called over the hubbub. "But what about Teyla? Ronon? Did you find them?"

"Yeah, my hunch paid out," replied Sheppard. "They're in Sanctuary right now. They've had a rough ride — I figured they needed the rest."

"Thank God. When you came back without them, I started to imagine the worst. Not that I'm getting into irrational fears, or anything. But, well, it's been a bit lonely out on the ice."

Sheppard raised an eyebrow. "I'll remember you said that," he said. "Where are we with the Jumper?"

McKay looked troubled. "I can get us airborne," he said. "Not for long, and probably only for a single flight. But the gate is a dead as stone. And that's a problem."

Sheppard smiled, and produced a large tubular item from

his furs. "Oh, really?"

McKay let his mouth drop open. It shut again, then fell back.

"My God!" he cried. "A ZPM! Where the hell… Of course. Sanctuary."

"There was more than one and Miruva says they can spare it — but I don't think it has much juice left. You can use it, right?"

"Yes. I can. You've just brought me our ticket home, Colonel."

"Glad to be of service," said Sheppard. "As soon as we've got these people to safety there we can — "

"Wait." Rodney was appalled. "We're not leaving now? You do know there's a storm of utterly monumental proportions coming our way? In fact, *the* storm of utterly monumental proportions."

"Yeah, and that's why we've got to get these people underground *before* we lose the chance."

McKay looked exasperated. "Is that our job?" he asked. "Did we come here to escort a bunch of primitives into the ground? No. We thought there'd be tech here we could use. There isn't, and we're in a lot of trouble. Weir would say the same thing, John, and you know it. We've got to get out. Pronto. Let them sort out their own mess."

"Hey," Sheppard growled. "Even by your standards, Rodney, that's a pretty low shot. Maybe we shouldn't have come here, but we did, and now we gotta help out. We've got one shot. We're gonna get these folks safely underground, and *then* we'll power-up the Jumper. That's it. No debate."

McKay glared at him for a moment. He didn't like it, but he'd seen Sheppard in these moods before. They didn't have the time to fight it out, and he didn't have the strength. "How long do you need?"

"Same as before. You'll hardly miss us."

"A matter of hours?" said Rodney. "A lot can happen in that time. You've seen the gate. You know what the ice is doing round here. My God, this is crazy."

Sheppard drew the proximity meter from his furs and handed it to Rodney.

"Take this," he said. "It's got the coordinates of Sanctuary in it. If you can't get the Jumper started, or something happens to the gate, you'll know where we've headed."

McKay took the device and looked at it miserably. "That doesn't make me feel a lot better," he said. "When that storm hits, all bets are off."

"You got it," said Sheppard. "And you know the drill. If we're not back when you need to get out, don't wait. That Jumper's going back to Atlantis, whether we're on it or not."

Even after so long on Khost, the cold was astonishing. It seeped into every pore, probed under every flap of fur and leather. Once in the bones, it stayed there.

Sheppard shuddered, pulled his furs more tightly around him, and looked over his shoulder. The entire population of the settlement stretched out behind him, huddling under glowering skies. Once Aralen had given the order, the Forgotten had acted quickly. Many of them had been waiting all their lives for this day. None had been left behind. Years of living in such an unpredictable environment had made them quick to respect the destructive power of the storms, and they followed Aralen's orders without question.

Sheppard pulled his arms tight around his chest and checked to see if there were any stragglers. The column of people stretched back a long way. He was reminded of the aftermath of combat he'd seen before in the Gulf: lines of refugees leaving their homes, fleeing the destruction of their lives. The situation was not so different. The planet itself was at war with them. What they were doing was the only possible solution.

A gust of wind snagged against his hood and Sheppard shook himself out of his thoughts. He set off again and it took him a few moments to realize that Miruva was walking alongside.

"You OK?" he asked, his voice muffled against the leather facemask.

"They are all here," she replied. "All that is left of us. You have done a great thing for our people. If you had not arrived when you did…"

"Oh, you'd have found a way outta there in the end," he said, but not with conviction. The truth was that things were far too tight for comfort. The storm was on their shoulder already. He wondered if it would have been better to have waited it out. But then, according to McKay, there wouldn't *be* another chance. This was it. They had to leave before surface travel became impossible.

A sudden gust buffeted him, and Sheppard staggered forward. He almost lost his footing. "I'm getting the hint," he said. "This place really doesn't like us,"

Black clouds crouched above them and, in the far distance, flickers of lightning scored the horizon. The wind was growing stronger and the incessant moan of the highlands was being replaced by a higher-pitched whine.

Miruva scanned the sky with practiced eyes. "It's coming up quickly," she said. "I've not seen one come so fast. I thought we had time to get everyone in before it hit. But these winds…"

She tailed off, looking at the piled clouds with concern.

"We'll make it," said Sheppard. "You people are pretty tough."

"Maybe," she said. "But we need to pick up the pace. A lot."

Sheppard looked along the column of trudging figures and winced. Some were children, many were old.

"I hear you," he said. "But some of those guys are struggling. I'll go back and help out."

Miruva nodded. "Take care," she said, and struggled onwards.

Ahead of them, the wind screamed. Behind, the darkness deepened, and thunder growled in the distance. The end would not be long in coming.

McKay wrapped his arms around his chest and stamped hard. The Jumper's life support was now within operational limits, but it was still damned cold. He plugged the proximity meter into the console in the cockpit. The Ancient computer picked up Sheppard's encoded instructions and the coordinates of Sanctuary flashed up on the screen. A stream of figures, most of them incomprehensible, ran down the HUD.

"Well, that's a lot of use to me," he muttered, and turned his attention to the long-range scanners.

Nothing had changed. In every direction, the weather was closing in. It was the same on every monitor. The few patches of open sky were disappearing, almost as he watched. It had a strange attraction, a macabre beauty. But it didn't improve his mood. It wasn't much fun watching a planet die.

He shivered, and flicked the display to the rear, back toward the Stargate. Getting the ailing ZPM hooked up had been one the worst experiences of his life. But it was ready. The gate would open, if only for a millisecond. He didn't expect much more than that, but once the wormhole had formed, the Zelenka module should do the rest. In theory.

"John?" he said into the radio, hoping he'd still get a signal. There was nothing but static from the other end. Just as he'd expected. These weren't ordinary storms.

The visual feed was almost as bad. Snow was everywhere and the light was failing fast. It was still early, but the weak light of the sun was already being blotted by the clouds.

"At least it's still intact," said McKay, before realizing he was talking to himself again. "Dammit. This isn't healthy. They've got to stop leaving me on my own like this."

The image rocked as the Jumper was buffeted by a heavy gust. McKay studied the screen intently. Had the Stargate moved? Surely not. It couldn't have. That would be just *unfair*.

It moved. Gently, almost imperceptibly, it shifted down into the ice.

"No!" growled McKay, leaping out of his seat. "Not again. It was looking so much *better*."

He fumbled for the rear door release mechanism, knowing that opening the Jumper up now would hurt. But the gate was their only route out and if it was going down, he needed to know about it.

The rear door swung upwards, and the wind tore into the cabin. Gritting his teeth, McKay staggered into the rear bay and out into the howling gale. The short journey to the Stargate was agonizing. Every step was like dipping his feet into liquid nitrogen. The weather was worse than it had ever been. The horizon was black on three sides, and the light from up ahead was running out fast. He swore under his breath.

"If we've missed our window to get off this God-forsaken rock," he growled, "then I'll kill him. Sanctuary or not."

Sheppard grimaced. Behind him, the long snake of Forgotten refugees — men, women and children — toiled in the snow.

From the lowlands of the settlement area, they had passed

quickly up on to the high plateau where the White Buffalo roamed. The wind continued to pick up. It became difficult to walk against it, and Sheppard found himself leaning hard into the gale. The powdery snow was churned-up from the surface in writhing curls and flew through the air in thick, cold gouts. It felt like night was falling, even though dusk was hours away.

Infants had to be carried. A group of young hunters formed a cordon around the older members of the community, trying to shield them from the full force of the growing wind. Many had to be helped along. Even after a lifetime of living in the deep freeze, some of the Forgotten looked perilously cold. Sheppard worked his way back down the column, looking for any individuals in trouble. Most were coping better than him, but for some the trek looked like a nightmare. One man was almost bent double against the searing wind. Sheppard went up to him, and put an arm under his.

"How're you doing?" he said, as cheerily as he could.

The old man looked up sourly. With a grim inevitability, Sheppard recognized Aralen.

"Not as well as I'd like," he said, his voice choked by the snow. His facemask had slipped slightly, revealing some of his ice-blasted face. He looked in pretty bad shape.

Sheppard propped him up as best he could, anxious that the old man should keep moving. Conditions would only get worse.

"You still think this is a mistake?" said Sheppard, raising his voice against the growing volume of the wind.

"What does it matter what I think?" he said, his voice sour. "Everything I thought was right has been turned on its head. Everything I counseled has been undermined. Even my own daughter has turned against me. There'd be no role for me in Sanctuary, even if we could get there."

He looked up at Sheppard, and his expression was savage. "But we can't get there, can we? We're going to die out here. Is this what you came to do? To destroy us all?"

Sheppard was taken aback by the old man's ferocity. He began to speak, but the wind snatched his words away. Looking into Aralen's eyes, he began to doubt his decision. Rodney had given him the same look. And Ronon. He should have left. He should have allowed the Forgotten to make their own way to Sanctuary, on their own terms.

Above, the last patches of open sky faded. The maelstrom had closed. With it went his hopes. Without speaking further to Aralen, Sheppard slogged his way further up the line. He'd made a call, and right now it looked pretty bad. Unless they reached Sanctuary soon, they would pay for it with their lives.

Teyla awoke. Her head throbbed and she could feel pain all down her side. For a moment, she had no idea where she was. But then the memories came rushing back. She was in Sanctuary. The rock fall, Sheppard, Ronon. The sequence of events was confused and she felt a surge of anxiety. Where were the others?

Teyla raised her head, ignoring the pain. She was lying in her hut, down in the fertile plain. All around was tranquil and quiet. The light from outside was warm and soft. Inside the darkness of the small chamber, a single figure sat, waiting for her to recover.

"Miruva?" said Teyla.

"No," came a man's voice. "She has gone out to the surface to bring the others back. More of your friends are here. They are restoring the tunnel to the outside."

The voice was familiar. Teyla felt a sudden tremor of alarm. "Geran?" she said. "Why are you here? My friends..."

"The one you call Ronon is securing the breach. The others have left for the settlement." Geran's voice was subdued. The certainty he'd displayed in the past had disappeared.

Teyla pushed herself upright. She had no idea how much time had passed, but she'd seen the holographic weather projection in the control room. If they weren't off the planet soon, then they might never escape. "How long have I been asleep?"

Geran shrugged. "Hours. You were taken here when Miruva left."

"Then I ask you again," she said, her voice hard. "Why are *you* here?"

Geran had the decency to look ashamed. "To make amends," he said. "I was wrong. Even I cannot believe the stories about the Underworld now. I wanted to come and say that to you as soon as I could. I am sorry."

Teyla didn't find the words of much comfort. "You *should* be sorry, Geran," she said. "Your actions delayed me. I do not yet know what that has cost." She started to get up. Her head throbbed and her vision was cloudy, but she could keep her feet.

"You must rest! Ronon asked me make sure you were cared for."

"Ironic, that he chose you," she said. "My friends will need me. You have no idea what is happening."

"There is no hurry," protested Geran.

"Maybe not for you." Teyla pushed past him, still woozy, out of the hut and into the artificial light of Sanctuary. "You can muse on your mistakes later," she said. "I am going to find Ronon. Much as I might envy your life in this place, I do not wish to share it."

Sheppard shielded his eyes against the worst of the driving snowfall. In the distance, far down the long column of trudging people, he could half hear the cries of children. It was hard to make out anything beyond a few dozen meters. His fingers were numb, and his eyebrows were already crusted with ice.

One of the Forgotten loomed towards him out of the swirling haze. It was Miruva.

"This is pretty bad!" yelled Sheppard, his words snatched away by the tearing wind. "We should be there by now."

Miruva shook her head. Covered with furs as she was, the movement was slightly comical.

"We must be close!" she shouted back. "Some of the old folk are nearly frozen. We must find a way to pick up the pace."

Sheppard winced. His legs already felt as heavy and unresponsive as iron. The trek to the settlement and back had taken it out of him. The way was short, but the environment was murderous. What was worse, he knew that he had a third journey ahead once the Forgotten were safely stowed in Sanctuary. He felt like he had been criss-crossing the surface of Khost for days.

"OK!" he shouted, and began to move down the column, exhorting a final push from the struggling lines of people.

Miruva passed in the other direction, towards the vanguard, making sure that none got separated in the whiteout and that the column retained as much cohesion as possible.

The wind remained fierce. The snow piled up around them in thick swathes, and it soon became impossible to have any idea about footing. Many of the Forgotten stumbled. Sheppard and the other able-bodied members of the exodus were soon employed full-time in keeping the stragglers on their feet, keeping them moving, preventing the seductive collapse into the inviting banks of powder snow. Despite their long exposure to Khost's harsh environment, some of the older folk were beginning to show the first signs of hypothermia, and Sheppard had become very worried about the smallest of the children. When not being carried by their exhausted parents, some of them had to wade at nearly waist-height through the snow to make any progress at all.

Then, suddenly, the breach became visible. Looming out of the driving snowfall, dark shapes became gradually apparent. A perimeter had been constructed around the opening. Some of it had collapsed in the howling wind, but enough remained to prevent them blundering blindly down into the workings.

"Bingo!" shouted Sheppard, trying to keep everyone's spirits up. "Keep going! The worst is over."

As if angered by their imminent escape, the storm threw one last desperate flurry at them. Sheppard felt the blast barrel into him as he turned to lift a child from the snow, and he stumbled badly. The heavy furs hindered him, and he sprawled face-down on the ground. The heavy snow cushioned his fall, but the wind was momentarily knocked from him. He staggered back to his feet, vision swimming. There were others staggering in the gale. They had reached the Sanctuary only just in time.

As they began to descend into the breach, fur-wrapped figures from below emerged to help them down the shaky ladders and into safety. Sheppard found himself yearning for the warmth of the tunnels, and would have given almost anything to get out of the frigid wind, but there were those weaker than him who still needed help. As he staggered over to a huddled group of older people, shuffling along painfully in the howling maelstrom, several tall figures surrounded him.

"How's it going, Colonel?" came a cheerful voice. It was Orand.

Sheppard's smile was more of a grimace. "I've had better days."

McKay pushed against the Stargate; it was a futile gesture. There was nothing he could do to right it again. It had sunk over a meter into the cracked ice, and leaned at a sharp angle. The ZPM was still connected, but only just. Rodney stood back, squinting up at the curve of the ring. Could they get the Jumper through it? Maybe. But it'd be close. Very close.

But where were Sheppard and the others? If John had been right about how close this Sanctuary was, then he should have been back by now.

McKay had a sudden bad feeling. He should be at the Jumper controls. If they'd sent a message, he'd have missed it.

Breaking into a halting run, he began to hurry back to the Jumper. He was making poor decisions. He was tired, cold, and worried. The best thing he could do now was stay in the Jumper and wait. The Stargate would have to look after itself.

As he went, he heard a familiar cracking noise behind him. He speeded up, working his legs as fast as they'd go, plunging through the snow. Ending up in a crevasse would make a bad situation even worse.

The cracking stopped and McKay risked a glance over his shoulder. The gate was still there, but it looked like the top of the circle was swaying in the wind. Fresh lines of broken ice radiated from the buried base.

"C'mon, John!" McKay hissed to himself. "Get back here."

"Did you secure the breach?" asked Sheppard, brushing the snow from his furs. He limped down the tunnel beside Orand.

"As well as we could," Orand replied. "We'll get these folk down as soon as we can. Some of them are in a bad way. Talking of which, you'd better get down below too. What have you been doing, swimming in snow?"

Sheppard let slip a rueful smile. "Yeah, kinda."

Above them, the column filed down into the opening in an orderly fashion, herded by Orand's team. As he watched them, Sheppard felt an overwhelming relief. Against all the odds, they had done it. The Forgotten would be safe. Whatever else happened to them on this mission, at least they'd done that; they'd saved a whole people.

Seeing that the hunters had everything in hand, he turned with some relief to the descent into Sanctuary. The steep way had been made easier with ladders and handrails and even the frailest of the Forgotten ought to be able to make the journey with help. Taking his place in the line, Sheppard joined the mass of bodies waiting to get into the warmth of the lower levels. As he went further down into the sheltering rock, the wind above gave a last, defiant howl, then guttered out.

Teyla limped across the Hall of Arrivals. It was not as dark as it had been, for the Forgotten had been busy placing braziers along the route up from the valley and into the control chambers. In time, the whole place would be illuminated. Though it would be a marvelous sight when completed, she heartily hoped she would not be there to witness it.

As she went, she saw reunited Forgotten celebrating. Some had already found there way down to the valley below, others lingered in the tunnels, helping newcomers down from the ice storm above. Not everyone celebrated. Some of the Forgotten in Sanctuary had discovered their loved ones had died on the surface, perhaps years ago. For every happy reunion, there were also isolated figures who lingered sadly in the shadows. Teyla's heart went out to them; to suffer grief when all around were rejoicing was a hard burden to bear. And there was much adjusting to be done, on both sides. Many of the Forgotten in Sanctuary had honestly believed they were condemned to a twilight existence in the Underworld. To discover that they had been safely on Khost all the time, and that the route back to the surface had been opened again, required a profound shift in their beliefs. It would take time to become reconciled to the changes. Geran was proof of that; he had not come with her. He was one of those who needed time to adjust.

Teyla approached the control chambers where she and Miruva had discovered the Avatar and saw people coming and going without fear. It was quite a change. She was watching the celebrating Forgotten so intently that she hardly noticed the approach of the others. But then they were at her side, Sheppard and Ronon, looking as ragged around the edges as she felt herself.

"Hey, what are you doin' up here?" said Sheppard, failing to disguise his concern. "We were coming to find you, and there were doctor's orders."

Teyla smiled. John's anxiety was touching, but after several hours sleep in the warmth of the valley she thought she was probably in better shape than they were. Both men looked exhausted.

"I am much better," she said, ignoring her persistent headache. "This place is good for healing. The Forgotten will find it so as well."

"Well I'm glad to hear it. Right now, I need to take five."

Sheppard slumped down on the floor against the wall, Teyla and Ronon either side of him. Around them, the Forgotten continued to come and go, all but oblivious to them. Cries of delight echoed down the corridors as long-sundered friends were reunited.

"Tell me what has happened," said Teyla.

"It's a real heartwarming story," said Sheppard. "We've got the perfect storm up there, but these guys are safe."

Ronon grunted. "Not looking forward to going back out there."

"You and me both, but we don't have a whole heap of options." Sheppard closed his eyes, head back against the wall. He looked exhausted. "Besides, Rodney's on his own and you know how much he enjoys that."

Teyla's brow furrowed with concern. Amid all the excitement at getting the Forgotten into Sanctuary, she had forgotten about Dr McKay. "He is not with you? The surface is no place to be on his own. Someone should have stayed with him."

"Hey, *he'll* be fine. The Jumper's back up to full power. Anyhow, someone had to keep an eye on the Stargate. Let's just say the ice beneath it isn't entirely... reliable."

"Sounds bad," said Ronon.

"It is."

"And we could've headed back hours ago..."

"Trust me, I heard it all from McKay." Sheppard sighed. "Sometimes it sucks being the good guys."

"You said it."

"What is done is done," Teyla said sharply. "Is the storm still blowing? Can we afford to wait it out?"

Sheppard shook his head. "Not unless you want to wait about nine thousand years."

Before she could answer, Miruva and Orand approached, walking hand in hand. Beside them, Aralen hobbled, too proud to use a stick despite the arduous journey. His long-mourned wife supported him, and they leaned on one another closely. Sheppard, Ronon and Teyla rose to meet them.

"Teyla, you are well," said Miruva. "That makes this day

perfect. We cannot thank you enough. We would never have discovered it without you."

"Oh, I dunno," said Sheppard, putting a brave face on their own problems. "You'd have probably figured it out in time. We just gave you a little push."

"But without that push we would all be dead," Aralan said. All trace of bitterness had gone from his voice. "I see now that this is our future — and that it is clearly the will of the Ancestors." He looked at his wife in affection and wonder. "We have all gained more than we could have hoped. I was wrong to judge you, Colonel Sheppard."

"Aw, forget it," said Sheppard, waving his hand dismissively. "If I'd been in your position, I'd have done the same. Can't be a leader and let yourself get pushed around by a bunch of scruffy-looking travelers."

Aralen smiled, though the expression was tinged with sadness. "A leader no more," he said. "All things change."

Without asking, Teyla knew who to address. "Congratulations," she said to Miruva, clasping her hand. "You will be a fine Foremost of your people."

Miruva looked at Orand, and they both grinned. "Not just me," she said, pride evident in her voice. "There is much for us to do, and all skills will be needed. When the route to the surface has been made safe, then we must start the work of exploring this place. Even with the gene, it will take us many years to uncover its mysteries."

"What'll you do about the tunnels?" said Ronon.

"We will preserve them," said Orand. "We cannot allow ourselves to become trapped. We will explore them for new resources and one day, when the planet is restored, we will use them to return to the surface."

"Good," said Ronon. "Hate to think all that wandering around was for nothing. Gotta admit, I didn't think we'd ever get out."

"Do not even think of that," said Miruva. "You were all preserved, and that is enough. But what will you do now?"

"We gotta go," said Sheppard. "Much as it looks nice around here."

"Dr McKay is with our vessel," said Teyla. "He thinks that we can still use the Stargate to return home."

Aralen frowned. "You mean to return to the ice? The storm will still be fierce."

"We have no choice," said Teyla. "If the portal fails us, we will be stranded here — it is our only route home."

"I wish you could stay," said Miruva. "There is still much to learn about this place."

Sheppard gave a grim smile. "Rodney would've liked to see it," he said. "He'll be mad as hell when we tell him what's down here."

"I'll come with you," said Orand. "You'll need help on the ice."

"No way," said Ronon.

Sheppard nodded. "No dice, I'm afraid. You can't help us out there."

Miruva embraced Teyla. There were tears in her eyes, and Teyla felt her own throat tighten. "We will remember you always," Miruva said. "The Ancestors will be with you."

Ronon cast Sheppard a dark look. "They'd better be."

CHAPTER EIGHTEEN

MCKAY was getting angry. Mostly because he was scared. And the fact that he was scared was making him angrier.

The constant cracks and moans from the ice beneath the Jumper tore his nerves to shreds. The scanner told him the Stargate was still there, but any moment he expected to see the blip disappear. And that would be the end of it.

He'd looked over the flight controls a hundred times. Should he try and take off? Sheppard had shown him how to fly the thing once, but in this weather? And even if he'd been confident about flying the Jumper, he wasn't sure there was enough juice in the tank for more than one short burst of atmospheric flight. If he tried to take off and seek higher ground, he might ruin their chances of escaping the planet entirely. And with the blizzard still howling around the Jumper with terrifying force, leaving the vessel was no longer an option. He'd never make it back to the empty settlement alone.

The choices were looking pretty bad.

He looked over the Jumper's instrumentation one last time. The power configuration was set for optimal delivery at the right times, and the improvised Zelenka module (he'd have to think of a better name for that) was sending out a steady stream of helpful diagnostic readings to the central computer. Everything was ready to go. All, that was, except for the crew.

McKay flicked open the dividing doors between the rear bay and the cockpit, and took a look at the external viewfinders. Nothing. The screens were white with occasional flecks of gray. The snow was tearing around the ship at frightening speeds and even inside the heavily shielded frame, the sheer noise of the maelstrom was terrifying.

He sat down in the co-pilot's chair and began to bite his nails. It had been hours since he'd heard from Sheppard and the others. And he couldn't shake the image of them lost, in the heart of the storm, their meager furs flapping around their freezing bodies, their limbs ravaged by frostbite. Despite all they had endured since arriving on Khost, this maelstrom was something else. The planet had begun the process of inexorably scrubbing all life from its frozen surface.

Unable to settle, McKay got up from the chair and started pacing backwards and forwards. He had to make a decision, do *something*. If he'd been Sheppard, he might have been able to think of a cunning intervention to resolve things. McKay was proud enough of his brain, but even he would admit that it was better at some things than others. Fixing Ancient technology against hopeless odds with terrible equipment was something he could do; making split-second choices in the absence of any helpful information at all was something he couldn't.

He started to run down the options again. Outside, the dark of the storm was gathering. According to the plan, they should have been back by now. According to the plan, they should have made radio contact hours ago. According to the plan, they should have been long-gone through the Stargate and home again, sitting around a table drinking a cool beer and vowing never to try out experimental gate devices again.

Enough of the plan; what was he going to *do*? He could sit tight, and hope that the team had merely been delayed. If the radios were still affected by the storm, they might turn up at any moment, dusted with a light layer of ice and eager to get going through the wormhole. On the other hand, they might be horribly lost, or lying under a snowdrift, or stuck down a crevasse. Should he try to take off to find them?

The vessel's built-in proximity sensors would work better at short range, even in such hellish conditions. But then he risked draining the fragile power cells, dooming them all. And he couldn't fly the Jumper. No one but Sheppard could fly it with such a storm blowing.

McKay sat down again in the cockpit. He glanced at the controls in the pilot's seat. They looked intimidating and dangerous. He hated flying. Most of all, he hated flying in Jumpers. They had a habit of crashing, or pitching you into the sea, or getting stuck half-way through a Stargate. Really, flying them was best left to the professionals.

His thoughts were suddenly broken by a massive crack right beneath him. McKay sat bolt upright, heart thumping. That was a huge one. The Jumper groaned and shifted to one side. For a moment, nothing happened. There was the faint sound of snow tumbling against the outer walls, just audible over the scream of the wind.

McKay found that he had frozen. He tried to lift his hand, and it obeyed him only reluctantly. For all its robust design, it was clear that the hull of the Jumper was being put under some strain. The ice was moving. Things were getting very, very difficult.

There was another crack, and then a rolling, booming groan. The Jumper dropped a few inches, coming to a rest with a harsh snap. McKay leapt from his seat in panic. Was the ice completely collapsing? Or was it just a mild resettling?

Another crack — the Jumper began to slide. McKay raced to the controls in the cockpit and glanced at the external monitors. Three of them were black. He was slipping. The Jumper was tumbling into the abyss.

"We are not going to last much longer in this, Colonel!" shouted Teyla.

She was a proud woman and hated showing any weakness, but the situation was becoming desperate. She had been hurt in the rock fall, and the extreme cold had caused her right leg to seize up. Limping through the knee-deep snow was almost impossible.

Ronon came up on her left shoulder. He was badly hunched himself, and draped with layers of clinging ice, but he put his arm under her shoulders and helped to prop her up against the biting wind.

"Keep going," he urged. "We stop, we're dead."

"Hate to admit it," Sheppard shouted, "but he's right!"

Teyla grimaced. Her leg was agonizing and her headache pounding, but for as long as there was a shred of power in her muscles she would keep going.

They toiled onwards. Ronon stayed at her side, a powerful buttress against the tearing gale. Visibility was down to a few meters and they could only walk in halting, difficult steps. With every passing minute, more snow piled up around them. What had originally reached their calves now rose above their knees. Soon it would be impassable.

She clenched her teeth, taking some comfort from Ronon's massive presence. But the cold was terrifying, she could feel its bitter fingers clenching around her heart, and she realized that the most terrifying thing on Khost was not the Banshees, but the planet itself.

Khost was their enemy now, and like some malevolent intelligence it seemed bent on their destruction.

His stomach doing acrobatics, McKay leapt into the pilot's seat and stared at the controls. His fingers raced across the panel and a series of lights flashed on the display. With a brief flicker, the HUD sprang up, and power surged into the drive systems.

There were more resounding cracks beneath him and the

Jumper slid forward. Even without the use of the monitors, he could sense the acceleration. He was being pitched headlong into the ice. His mind racing, McKay tried to recall the procedure for a reverse take-off.

"What's the command, dammit?" he cried out loud. "Concentrate!"

He grabbed more controls, willing his mind to make the connection. He'd done it before. He could do it again. It was just a matter of making the connection.

The Jumper continued to slide. There were more creaks from the structure. Snow cascaded across the viewscreen.

"Come on!" he cried, panic rising in his throat. "Fly, damn you!"

He screwed his eyes up, grabbed the control panel and bent his whole mind towards the link nodes on the Jumper system. It had to work!

Nothing. The slide into oblivion accelerated. He could sense the ice closing around him. So this was death. This was the end. He had failed. It was over. There was no point fighting.

His mind relaxed.

And with a stuttering blast, the engines kicked-in. The dampeners were still only semi-operational and McKay was thrown forward as the Jumper burst out from the ice. He had a vague impression of a heavy slew of snow being shed from the front of the vessel, then some of the monitors cleared and data began to pour across the HUD. He was airborne. He was moving. He couldn't see a thing.

"Not dead…" he breathed, his heart hammering. "Really not dead. That's a start. Now, what the hell am I doing?"

Leaning forward in the chair, he tried to get his bearings. He needed to get everything on a level for long enough to figure out where he was going and what he wanted to do. The fact that he hadn't flown straight into a mountainside was a minor relief. Avoiding plunging into the ground was something he'd have to work on.

He ran his fingers over the display before him and the HUD finally began to give him some useful information. The Jumper had stabilized at low altitude and was cruising roughly north-west. That was lucky. Gingerly, McKay tried to adjust the course. The craft skidded wildly off-center and he was thrown over to his left. Fighting against the controls, he brought things back to equilibrium. The wind didn't make it easy, nor did the almost total lack of visibility. His palms were sweaty, blood pounding in his ears. Between snatched breaths, he briefly had time to wonder if this was the most terrified he had ever been.

It was at that point that things began to improve.

"C'mon," he snapped out-loud. "Would you want Carter to see you like this? Get a grip, man. You've made the link. Use it!"

Very slowly, the readings on the HUD started to make sense. The short-range sensors were clearly operating, and a pseudo-map of the terrain was scrolling across the display. Just like using a flight simulator, he found he could navigate pretty well using that. Looking out of the windshield was a dead loss; there was nothing but flying snow hurling itself against the screen.

"Right, now where are we going?" he said. "Concentrate! Sheppard left the coordinates. We just need to retrieve them."

Keeping one eye firmly on the motion control readings, he scanned across the computer panels in front of him. The options were pretty complicated, but after a moment's scrabbling around he managed to pull the coordinates out of the system.

"Good," he said. "You're doing well. She'd be proud of you. Now, how do you get this thing to follow them?"

That took a bit more doing. Applying the coordinates Sheppard had left in the central computer turned out to be no easy matter, especially while trying to keep the Jumper airborne in the middle of the perfect storm. In the end, the best he could do was to superimpose the destination point over the HUD's contoured terrain map and fly toward it. There was none of the easy control that Sheppard enjoyed; he was trying to make a connection across badly faulty equipment. McKay tentatively maneuvered in what he hoped was the right direction, and the Jumper slewed across the sky like a drunkard. Despite its robust self-righting design, it was buffeted by the wind and hammered by the heavily falling sleet.

"Come *on*!" yelled McKay, battling against the controls with mounting frustration. Now that the imminent danger of death has passed, his irritation at not being able to control the craft had assumed priority.

"That's better," he growled, as the Jumper started to head along roughly the right course. The landscape scrolled across the HUD increasingly smoothly and McKay found that he was getting the hang of things. With a slight qualm, he fed more power to the drive systems and felt the vessel respond. He was now traveling at cruising speed. But it was pretty bumpy.

"Right, we should be nearly there," mumbled McKay, staring at the readings in front of him. "They were walking in heavy snow and this thing can travel very, very fast. So, they should be anywhere from here onwards. Keep your eyes peeled."

There was no way of gauging distance, no way of telling where they were. All that was real was the pain and the cold. Only mechanical instinct kept Teyla moving, but as her body slowly froze even that began to give out. The last shreds of energy faded away.

"I am weakening, Ronon," she gasped. There was no point in keeping the truth from him.

The Satedan pulled her forward, plunging into the snow. "Keep moving." His voice betrayed him. His strength was near its end too, and if Ronon failed...

Ahead of them, Sheppard fell. He was little more than a shadow in the snow, but the cord that bound them together tugged, pitching Teyla forward. In a heap, all three of them tumbled together. The snow enveloped them, blocking some of the wind.

It was a blessing to stop moving, to stop fighting.

"Get up!" Ronon growled, floundering in the snow. But he didn't make it to his feet.

The pain was too much. The cold was too much.

"I'm sorry," said Sheppard, his voice little more than a hoarse croak. "Guess I got this one wrong, guys."

And above them the storm howled a mocking cry of victory.

"So where the hell *are* they?" muttered McKay as he slowed and the Jumper and tried to bring it around in a loop. According to the HUD, he was over the designated coordinates, but the monitor he'd assigned to display life-sign readings remained stubbornly blank.

A new, chilling thought occurred to him. What if Sheppard's plan had failed? What if Sanctuary had turned out to be some awful trap after all, or they had fallen into a crevasse on the way over?

A warning light blinked on; the power supply had dropped again. In desperation, he started to calculate the odds of following Sheppard's last order and getting through the Stargate on his own. He couldn't be sure the others were even alive and, if they were, he couldn't be expected to find them in such conditions. And the power was going down. And...

He shook his head, disgusted with himself. While there was a milliamp of power left in the Jumper, he would use it to find the team. They would do the same for him. No one gets left behind. Isn't that what they always said?

With a slight tremor in his hands, McKay nudged the Jumper downwards. Maybe if he got closer to the surface he'd pick up their life signs. Watching the altimeter readings like a hawk, he gently eased the Jumper into a lower flight pattern. The ice rushed up to meet him terrifyingly fast and through the occasional tears in the storm clouds, he saw blank sheets of white streaking beneath him. McKay's palms were sweaty, his heart beating fast. He began to wonder how much longer he could keep this up without having some kind of coronary episode.

Then he saw it. Just a flicker, almost a ghost of a reading. He'd passed it, and as soon as it appeared it vanished again. McKay immediately pulled the Jumper around for another pass. It responded erratically, and almost fell into a tumble. Grappling with the controls, he gradually got it back on the level. No more sudden moves. That was best left to the experts.

More carefully, he coaxed the Jumper back around. Despite all his scientific training, he found himself willing the equipment to help him out. He flew as low as he dared, scouring the HUD for anything at all. There was nothing. Maybe the readings had been an anomaly? His euphoria began to dissolve. Then he saw them again — three signals, barely moving, just beneath him.

"Yes!" He punched the air. "Yes!"

But his exuberance lost him control of the Jumper, and it pitched to one side. "Damn!" He tried to pull up, but the Jumper's inertial compensators were far from perfect and it jerked into a too-steep climb and almost stalled. Auxiliary thrusters whined into action, but it wasn't enough. The

Jumper flipped onto its side, and started to plummet earthwards.

"What's that?" cried Ronon, roused from his deathly stupor by a shadow in the sky.

He shook his head, flinging snow in every direction. Focus. Painfully, he hauled himself to his feet. "There's something out there."

Teyla rolled over in the snow, looking as content as a child in her bed. Her limbs were floppy, and the snow was beginning to mass against her. Sheppard was little better. The cords between them had come loose.

"C'mon!" cried Ronon, shaking Teyla. He dragged her to her knees.

She looked up at him blearily. "Let me sleep…"

The words were fatal. Ronon felt the drag on his fatigued limbs like they did. He could hear the siren voice within him, urging him to give in, end the pain, collapse into the snow.

"No!" he growled. "There's something out there! Get up!"

He yanked her roughly to her feet. For a moment, she looked furious. Then something seemed to kindle inside her and the old Teyla returned. "What did you see?"

"Dunno," he said, reaching for Sheppard's slumped figure. "Help me get him up. We gotta move."

"Where?" yelled Teyla. Even as she finished speaking, there was a roar from above them. Something big, black against the skirling grey of the sky, hurtled earthwards. It flew low over their heads and was lost in the white-out ahead.

"There!" said Ronon. He started to run.

McKay acted instinctively. He punched the panel, gave a flurry of mental commands, shouted out orders. When that failed, he resorted to the final tool in his repertoire — letting go of the controls and cradling his head in his hands.

With a crunch, the Jumper hit the ground. McKay was thrown forward hard in his seat as it skidded across the ice. The world whirled around him for a minute, then everything slowed.

The Jumper came to a standstill. Gingerly, McKay opened his eyes and peered at the control panel. All systems were still active. Thank God. Hands shaking, he returned to the life-sign signals. They were still there, even fainter than before, maybe a hundred meters away from where the Jumper had come down.

Clambering into the rear bay he scrambled into his fur clothing again. There was no guarantee that the others had seen his descent in such weather, and if they had missed him and kept walking then all would have been for nothing.

Quickly, clumsily, McKay pulled the hides over his standard fatigues. They smelled even worse than the last time he'd worn them. Once fully clad, he took a deep breath, and prepared to lower the rear door. His hand hesitated as he took a look at the sensor readings again. The wind was blowing at ridiculous speeds, visibility was close to zero, and the temperature wasn't even worth thinking about. Opening the door was very silly, as silly as anything he'd ever done in the Pegasus galaxy.

McKay sighed, and pressed the a button on the improvised door release mechanism. When he finally found the others, he thought to himself, they had better be grateful.

The rear door juddered open, and immediately a storm of snow shot into the narrow space. Within a second, every surface was covered in a layer of white. The wind was mind-blowing, and once inside it began to rock the Jumper like a toy. McKay grabbed a bulkhead for support and staggered forward. He couldn't see a thing beyond the entrance to the vessel. His heart quailed and he hesitated, clinging to the fragile hull. He couldn't go out. He just couldn't.

"About damn time!" came a muffled shout from the void.

Three gray figures emerged from the white-out, staggering against the force of the wind.

"Ronon!" cried McKay, rushing forward. Sheppard, Teyla and Ronon stumbled into the rear bay, barely visible beneath the snow that clung to their clothing. Once inside the rear bay, they collapsed.

"Close the door!" yelled Ronon.

McKay hurried to comply, struggling to find the closing mechanism in the swirling confusion. Eventually, his fingers located the control panel and he activated the switch. The door slammed upwards, locking out the maelstrom. The noise was reduced to a booming rumble.

"All right, that was *too* close," Sheppard's voice was alarmingly slurred. "Anyone else feel their fingers?"

McKay frowned. "We're not out of this yet," he said. "I don't want to hurry you, but most of the readings here are somewhere close to critical and I don't even want to think about what's happening to the Stargate in our absence."

"Just gimme a minute, will ya?" The Colonel looked horribly fatigued. McKay could only imagine what a few hours in that storm must have been like. But there was no time to rest. He looked at Ronon, who made to speak, but then the Jumper was rocked by a massive gust. It tipped to one side. McKay had difficulty keeping his feet, then fell back heavily as a series of amber lights flickered across the HUD display.

"Minute up," Sheppard groaned, climbing painfully to his feet, beginning to strip off his sodden furs. "Just don't expect first-class service here."

Weir walked into the Operations Center, just as she had done every couple of hours since the databurst had been sent. It had become a ritual, increasingly devoid of hope. But it had to be done.

"Anything?" she asked Zelenka.

Just as always, Radek shook his head. Each time, he looked a little wearier, a little less full of life.

"Nothing," he said. Weir looked at the empty Stargate below. It gazed back up at her, vacant and hollow. Every time she looked at it, she imagined the addresses whirling around the rim, the sudden burst of a new event horizon. Staring at it too long played tricks on you. She let her gaze return to Zelenka.

"How long do you think they could last in that climate?" she asked. "Have we run any models?"

Zelenka shook his head. "Not enough data. We have the readings from the MALP, but I don't know what good it would do to speculate. We can't reach them. We must wait."

"Keep running the sensor tests," she said. "We're not giving up yet. Let me know if you get anything. I don't care how small."

Zelenka nodded.

"Will do," he said, but his voice was empty.

The team clambered into the cockpit, taking their usual places and strapping in. McKay sat back against the hard seat-back with some pleasure. Sheppard brought up the controls quickly.

"So what happened out there?" said McKay. "Did it go to plan?"

"Another time, Rodney," said Sheppard wearily. "Just sit back and enjoy the flight."

With a sudden surge, the Jumper powered smoothly into the air once more. Unlike Rodney's chaotic ascent, this time it traced a straight line into the storm-driven sky, the power increasing steadily as Sheppard deftly managed the power fluctuations. The Jumper turned in a wide arc and headed back towards the Stargate.

"Coming up on the Stargate now," said Sheppard. "Anything I should know about, Rodney?"

"Aside from the fact that it might already be at the bottom of a crevasse?"

"Right. Anything *useful*?"

"Just keep us near to the ice. At best, it will have sunk further since we were last there. The closer you can hug the ground, the easier our passage will be."

Sheppard shook his head and dipped the Jumper further towards the planet's surface. "Sure, piece of cake," he said.

McKay didn't reply, but the Jumper noticeably slowed and the altitude continued to fall. In the rare gaps between the driving snow, McKay saw flashes of the ice speeding below them. It was happening. This was the important moment. And there was so much to get right.

"Remember what I told you about the module!" McKay said, aware that getting into the Stargate was only part of their task. "You'll need to activate it straightaway. A second too late, and we'll be threading through the anomaly again."

"Don't need to remind me," said Sheppard. "Dialing the gate now. Hold tight folks. We're going in — see you on the other side."

McKay screwed his eyes shut, then opened them again. It was hard to decide which way was worse.

The Jumper dropped sharply. They were racing along. Sheppard remained silent, looking at the figures on the HUD intently. Teyla seemed barely conscious and Ronon said nothing.

And then, as if Khost wanted to give them a view to remember it by, the cloud cover broke. They were in the open, hurtling earthwards. The Stargate was directly in front of them, only partly obscured by the tearing flurries of snow and ice, and its surface boiled with the massive contained energies of the event horizon. The ZPM had kicked in. The wormhole was open.

But the power unleashed was doing dangerous things to the ice around it; there were jagged cracks all around the base. The gate itself was still above ground, but only just. As they plunged towards it, dark lines were radiating out across the plain. The Stargate was going down.

"Faster!" McKay yelled. Sheppard didn't need to be told. As the Stargate tottered on the brink, he poured on the power and the Jumper hurled itself forward. McKay was thrown back in his seat, his heart pounding. Cracks opened, fissures yawned, and the ice floe collapsed.

The Stargate plunged into the abyss.

"We've got something!"

Zelenka's voice cracked with excitement. Around him, scientists scrambled to get at a monitor. Down in the gate room, the landing bay was flooded with light. The event horizon had formed.

"Try to feed power to the link!" cried Zelenka. "I don't care what readings you're getting, we need to keep it open!"

The Atlantis squads swung into action. The medical team was already on its way to the gate room. Marines snapped to combat alertness, just in case. But they all knew what was coming through. Or, more accurately, they all knew what they *wanted* to come through.

Weir arrived, out of breath. "What is it?" she demanded. "Do you have them?"

"Don't know yet," said Zelenka. "But the wormhole is from Dead End, or I'm a Slovak!"

Elizabeth raced over to the balcony and Zelenka turned

back to the screen. The numbers were all over the place; this was definitely no normal transit. For a moment it looked as if they would lose the signal. Then it came back. Then it dimmed again.

"Come on, Rodney," he breathed, gripped by the fluctuating readings. "Come *on*."

The top of the Jumper screamed as they hit the falling gate, metal scraping away. It was enough. Though battered and listing, they were inside the event horizon.

"Now!" screamed McKay. "Route the power!"

For a moment, the Jumper viewscreen was filled with a confused pool of energy. It looked horribly like the tunnel of plasma they had seen before.

McKay felt the contents of his stomach rise.

"I'm losing power, Rodney!" shouted Sheppard.

McKay leapt from his seat. "This should be *working*!" he wailed. "Did you trip the Zelenka module?"

The Jumper swung round hard. Something up ahead was forming. The plasma conduit. Not again.

"What d'you think?" yelled Sheppard. "We can't survive another trip into that."

"I know!"

McKay ran his fingers over the module. It was working. Power was being routed. But not enough. Why? It wasn't *fair*.

"Here it comes!" warned Sheppard. "We're gonna hit it…"

"I've got it!" cried Rodney. "There it is!"

One of the nodes on the Zelenka module had worked loose. Probably knocked when the Jumper had hit the ice. Rodney slammed it back into place. Immediately, the power feed doubled. "Hit it!"

The plasma tore away. A shimmering curtain of light

formed in front of them and they were out. McKay looked nervously out of the front windshield. He didn't quite know what to expect. Part of him wouldn't have been surprised to see a wall of ice, another part of him still expected to see the anomaly in all its horrifying glory.

The reality was much more comforting. They were in the gate room on Atlantis. With shaking hands, Sheppard brought the vessel smoothly down on to the solid floor. Once stationary, he turned to the rest of the team. His face was white.

"*Hit it?*" he asked. "What the hell was that?"

"It just seemed, you know, the right thing to say," said Rodney.

He looked around the cockpit for support. Teyla was out cold and even Ronon wasn't moving. The full enormity of what they'd just done hit home. He felt queasy.

"Oh, God," he said, and promptly passed out.

CHAPTER NINETEEN

"I'LL SEE you."

Sheppard felt confident. Real confident. Rodney was a terrible bluffer. He had trouble hiding his emotions at the best of times, but when there was money at stake his composure left him entirely.

"Are you sure you want to do that?" said McKay, looking a little uncomfortable. "You don't want to raise the bet just a little?"

Teyla rolled her eyes. She was looking a lot healthier, Sheppard thought. Since the team had returned from Khost, she'd been kept in the infirmary longest. She'd been lucky — the injuries from the rock collapse had been relatively minor. Then again, they'd all been lucky. A few more minutes in the that storm, and it could all have been over. Not something he really wanted to think about.

"Rodney, that will hardly encourage him to raise his stake," she said. "I am not sure you fully appreciate the subtleties of this game."

McKay scowled.

"Subtleties?" he muttered. "It's all a matter of probability, that's what it is. And that's where I score *very highly*. So here's what I've got."

He slapped his hand on to the table. Two queens. Not bad. But not worth the pile of bills stacked in the middle of the table.

"Hell, yeah!" cried Sheppard in triumph. "My first haul of the night."

He threw his own hand down, revealing a full house. Rodney rolled his eyes.

"This is the stupidest game I've ever played," he

moaned. "I mean, where's the skill? Where's the technique?"

"It's all in your attitude to risk, my friend," said Sheppard, moving to gather his winnings.

"Not so fast," interrupted Ronon. All eyes turned to the Runner, who'd been characteristically quiet the whole round.

"You're *kidding* me," Sheppard groaned. "What have you got?"

Four jacks. The other three players looked disgusted.

"Even I am truly amazed," said Teyla. Though she hid it better than Rodney, everyone knew she hated losing. Ronon was now sitting on a substantial pile of cash. He grinned and pulled the wad of bills towards him.

"Like the man said, it's all about risk," he said. "You'll learn."

"Yeah, once I'm bankrupt," Rodney sighed. "This is too rich for my blood. I'm out, guys."

"Glad to hear it," came a new voice. Weir was standing in the doorway to the card room. She looked amused. "I don't want any of my people getting into trouble over this. You've caused enough worry recently."

The gentle dig was well-intentioned, but it brought an awkward silence around the table. Though the physical wounds from Khost had all healed, there'd been some soul-searching in the post-mission briefing.

Sheppard felt it keenly. To have gone so far and encountered so much danger for so little reward was still something that bothered him.

"Hey, it wasn't a wasted journey," protested McKay. "We learned something about Jumper propulsion we didn't know before. And we got an insight into what the Ancients were up to before they left the city."

"And the wonders of Sanctuary were truly worth

seeing," said Teyla. "Their technology is still so far in advance of anything we can achieve."

"Well, that's not quite fair," muttered McKay. "And if you'd *told* me there were atmospheric generators and underground terraforming equipment, I might have liked to have taken a look myself. Could have proved pretty useful for us in the future."

Weir leaned against the doorway, an amused expression on her face. "You can talk about the technology all you want. That's not what made this mission a justified risk."

"An entire people was saved from destruction," said Teyla. "That is something to be celebrated, whatever the danger."

"We *are* good at that," agreed McKay.

"Kinda wish we could check up on them, all the same," mused Sheppard. "I mean, it *was* a little cold…"

"Sure you can check up on them," said Weir. "Just call by in another few thousand years."

Teyla smiled. "By then, they will be masters of a city every bit as powerful as this one."

"If they can figure out how to use it," said McKay. "In any case, it's given me an idea." His face took on the eager expression that warned he'd been working on something. "We've seen what the Ancients were trying to do with the Jumpers to try and extend their range. Let's *not* do that again: it's far too gribbly."

"*Gribbly?*" said Sheppard.

"Technical term. Anyway, they had the right idea. Except that we could do it much more simply."

"Oh yeah?"

McKay gave Sheppard a mysterious look. "Oh yes. I've already started working on the plans. It's time we stopped just taking the gate network as we find it, and started shifting Stargates around. By stringing them together, we could do what the Ancients never dreamed of." He shot Teyla a significant look. "It's all on the drawing board, but I'm thinking of christening it the McKay Intergalactic Gate Avenue."

"Might need to work on that title," said Sheppard.

"Really? Just what *is* it with you and names?"

Weir raised an eyebrow. "Well, I'm sure we'll hear all about it when it's ready, Rodney," she said. "For now, I want you all to make the most of your down-time while it lasts. We ran that one a little *too* close."

Teyla and Ronon looked like they were about to protest — they were already itching to report fit for the next mission — but Sheppard gave them a warning look. Too soon. Far too soon.

"Deal you in, Elizabeth?" he said, changing the subject. Weir laughed, and shook her head.

"Not while Ronon's playing," she said. "I'm guessing you wish you'd never taught him to play."

Ronon looked smug, but Sheppard snorted.

"Nah. He's just got lucky. Now whiskey, *that's* another matter."

"He can put it away?"

"Oh yeah. Doesn't even take ice."

Weir smiled. They all did. After so many days of worry, it felt good.

"After what you've been through," she said, "I can't say I blame him."

ABOUT THE AUTHOR

CHRIS WRAIGHT is a freelance author with a wide and growing portfolio of published work. His main interest is science fiction and fantasy, and since 2007 he has published four novels based in the Warhammer game setting (the latest being *Sword of Justice*, due for release in July 2010). He is a long-time fan of the Stargate franchise, dating back to the original 1994 movie, and *Dead End* is his first novel set in the Stargate Atlantis universe. He is 34, and lives in the south west of England. You can catch up with news of his latest work at http://chriswraight.wordpress.com.

SNEAK PREVIEW

STARGATE ATLANTIS: DEATH GAME

by Jo Graham

LT. COLONEL John Sheppard was sure he'd had better days. That he couldn't remember any of them right now was just one disturbing thing. Another one was the great big crack in the puddle jumper's front window. He was pretty sure that shouldn't be there. He was almost sure that the view out the window shouldn't be mostly dirt, with what looked like the trunks of several big trees in it. Also, the board of instruments under his chest shouldn't be sputtering and smoking.

The latter seemed like a really bad thing, so he cautiously pulled himself off the panel and sat back in his seat. Moving hurt, but not as much as it would have if he'd broken ribs, which was something, but there was a long wet smear of blood across the docking indicators and the tactical controls, which couldn't be good. Several droplets splashed against the board as he watched, and he put his hand to his head. It came away drenched in blood. Great. Holding his left hand to the general vicinity as tightly as possible, John looked around the jumper. What was he doing? Who was with him? He remembered the jumper descending into the gate room, the bright blue fire of the gate kindling. And after that… Nothing.

He took a deep breath and made himself let it out slowly. Some short term memory loss was normal with a head wound. He knew who he was and what he was doing, Lt. Colonel John Sheppard, with a gate team mission to M32-3R1 to check out an anomalous energy reading. He had punched the gate and...

John heard a moan behind him and scrambled backward out of the pilot's seat as quickly as possible. "Teyla?"

She seemed to have been thrown clear of the co-pilot's seat, lying crumpled between the pair of rear seats, her left arm twisted at an odd angle that couldn't possibly be right. He heard the swift hiss of her breath as she moved, her fingers opening and closing against the floor.

"Hang on," John said, kneeling beside her. "Careful." When he bent over, blood ran down into his eyes and he dashed it away.

Teyla pushed herself up with her right arm, half rolling into a sitting position, her left arm clutched tight against her side. When she saw him her eyes widened. "John? You are bleeding badly."

"I know," he said. "I think I hit my head on the board." He took his hand away. Yeah, it was bleeding hard.

Teyla reached up to get a look at it, wincing as she moved. Not good.

"Can you move your fingers?" he asked, reaching across to her left arm. She was wearing a jacket, and he couldn't tell if the shape of her arm looked right or not.

"Yes," she said, wiggling them. "But I cannot move my arm as it should or put any weight on it." She leaned back against one of the rear seats, fumbling in her pants pockets with her right hand and producing a dressing. "But you are bleeding. Here, now."

"Got it," John said, unrolling it and putting it to his head holding it in place as tightly as he could stand. Not good. There was a world of not good here. Teyla's shoulder was probably broken or at least dislocated, and his head was bleeding hard — in addition to not being able to remember anything since he'd dialed the gate... A thought struck him and he glanced wildly around the jumper. "Where are Rodney and Ronon and Zelenka?"

"What do you mean, where are they?" Teyla looked at him with concern. "We dropped them off. Do you not remember?"

"No, actually." He'd dialed the gate and watched it open, said something to Rodney, and then... Nothing. Everything after that was a blank until he'd picked himself up from the board in the crashed jumper.

"We left Rodney at the gate to try to figure out what had been done to the DHD because it was tampered with in a way he had never seen before," Teyla said. "And we dropped off Radek and Ronon on the island with the Ancient ruins to investigate the energy readings because Rodney said it was a waste of time. You do not remember?" Her voice was concerned, and the two small lines between her brows deepened.

John shook his head slowly. Good to know no one else from his team was lying bleeding around here, but... "What happened?"

"We had just lifted off from the island when we spotted a Wraith cruiser. It was at low altitude and we did not see it at first, not before it got off a number of shots that disabled the cloaking mechanism. You ran hard at extremely low altitude, trying to put some distance between us, but without the cloak there wasn't any way to hide, especially over open sea. We took fire and crossed the coast, and you said we were going down." Teyla's eyes were apprehensive. "Do you truly not remember any of this?"

"No." A cruiser. That was very, very bad, much worse than a few Wraith Darts.

Teyla pushed herself up, using the seat to get to her feet.

"John, we have to get out of here. The cruiser is still out there undamaged, and it will be able to find our wreckage. We have to get as far away from it as we can before the Wraith arrive. We are in no shape to face them."

"I have to agree with that," John said, dragging himself upright. There were backpacks in the rear compartment with survival gear, and they needed ammunition and preferably the P90s, not just the sidearms they carried in the field. He tied the dressing on and grabbed for supplies, aware that Teyla was doing the same beside him, stuffing her pockets with various things as she usually did. He felt like he was missing something, but annoyingly couldn't remember what. Something he'd lost along with what sounded like the better part of a couple of hours.

Dressings. The first aid kit. They were going to need that. Flares? Not so much so. A drill? He hoped not.

"We need to go," he said, reaching for the emergency release for the back hatch. Even if he'd eluded the cruiser in the last moments of their flight, the wreckage of the jumper would be obvious from the air.

"Understood," Teyla said, making a last awkward lunge for something.

The air that poured in the back was hot and dry, bright sunlight dazzling him. John blinked, his eyes watering as he refocused on blindingly blue sky and the tall palm trees that surrounded the jumper. It had come down in a grove of trees, the right drive pod sheared off entirely by the cruiser's fire. Ok. That was pretty impressive looking if he did say so himself. The crippled jumper should have dropped like a rock instead of landing upright and more or less level, a long scar through the trees marking their passage. He must have used the trees to bleed off airspeed and soften the crash. Nice, but even more easily spotted from above. He might as well have drawn a big arrow across the landscape pointing to them.

Teyla dragged at his arm with her good hand. "Come on, John. We must go."

The trees seemed thicker in one direction, and so they set off toward the heavier cover, though there was very little undergrowth. Taller palm trees shaded shorter, but the sky was always visible, lambent and bright through the trees above. It was also hot. That was going to get old fast. But it wasn't humid. Not a jungle. An oasis. Beyond the edges of the trees were the stark lines of desert, sand and ridges of stone showing gold and white under the glaring sun.

John stopped and swore. That limited their options a lot. He knew all too well that two people trekking across the desert were very, very vulnerable, not to mention that it would be incredibly stupid to set off across it without any idea where they were going. He must have seen from the air. They'd flown this way, dodging the cruiser. He must have seen how the course lay, how far they were from the sea and the island where they'd left Zelenka and Ronon, from more hospitable areas. But he couldn't remember.

"Did we see anything when we came over?" he asked Teyla. "Towns or anything? Any idea how far it is to the coast?"

She shook her head, shading her eyes with her good hand. "I do not know," she said. "It happened very quickly and I do not know how fast we were moving. I am certain there were settlements that we passed over, and some areas that looked farmed, but I do not know how far. Forty miles? Seventy miles?"

John winced. Whether forty or seventy miles of desert, neither was good news in this heat. And in broad daylight they'd be an easy target. "Settlements?"

"Yes," she said. "I am sure we are not far from some. I thought I saw a village not long before we crashed. Though I know nothing of the people of this world."

There were voices behind them, human voices raised in

shouts, the sounds of running feet.

Slinging the P90 around, John turned toward the sound. "I think we're about to," he said.

DUE OUT SEPTEMBER 2010

Original novels based on the hit TV shows STARGATE SG-1, STARGATE ATLANTIS and STARGATE UNIVERSE

AVAILABLE NOW

For more information, visit
www.stargatenovels.com

STARGATE UNIVERSE: AIR

by James Swallow
Price: £6.99 UK | $7.95 US
ISBN-13: 978-1-905586-46-2
Publication date: November 2009

Without food, supplies, or a way home, Colonel Everett Young finds himself in charge of a mission that has gone wrong before it has even begun. Stranded and alone on the far side of the universe, the mismatched team of scientists, technicians, and military personnel have only one objective: staying alive.

As personalities clash and desperation takes hold, salvation lies in the hands of Dr. Nicholas Rush, the man responsible for their plight, a man with an agenda of his own…

Stargate Universe is the gritty new spin-off of the hit TV shows Stargate SG-1 and Stargate Atlantis. Working from the original screenplay, award-winning author James Swallow has combined the three pilot episodes into this thrilling full-length novel which includes deleted scenes and dialog, making it a must-read for all Stargate fans.

STARGATE ATLANTIS: HUNT AND RUN

by Aaron Rosenberg
Price: £6.99 UK | $7.95 US
ISBN-10: 1-905586-44-2
ISBN-13: 978-1-905586-44-8
Publication date: June 2010

Ronon Dex is a mystery. His past is a closed book and he likes it that way. But when the Atlantis team trigger a trap that leaves them stranded on a hostile world, only Ronon's past can save them – if it doesn't kill them first.

As the gripping tale unfolds, we return to Ronon's earliest days as a Runner and meet the charismatic leader who transformed him into a hunter of Wraith. But grief and rage can change the best of men and it soon becomes clear that those Ronon once considered brothers-in-arms are now on the hunt – and that the Atlantis team are their prey.

Unless Ronon can out hunt the hunters, Colonel Sheppard's team will fall victim to the vengeance of the *V'rdai*.